The Bequest

Mike Farris

ISBN 978-0-9888777-8-8

STAIRWAY≡PRESS

The Armchair Adventurer

An Armchair Adventurer book
STAIRWAY PRESS—SEATTLE

Cover Design by Denise Lipiansky
www.stairwaypress.com
1500A East College Way #554
Mount Vernon, WA 98273

To Susan—thank you for always believing in me.

PART ONE:

THE BEQUEST

CHAPTER 1

TONIGHT WAS AS good a night to die as any.

The thought kept floating through Leland Crowell's mind as his older model Buick Regal rounded a curve along the Big Sur coastline near Ragged Point, just fifteen miles north of Randolph Hearst's famous mansion at San Simeon, California. To the east, forests darkened the mountainside; to the west, sheer cliffs, hundreds of feet high, dropped to the hellish maelstrom of waves crashing on rock below, creating a foam swirl of white that gleamed in the moonlight. At the late hour, no other vehicles traveled this dangerous track of the Pacific Coast Highway that stretched between Los Angeles and San Francisco.

A flick of the wrist, a turn of the steering wheel, and it would all be over. No one would be the wiser. Just another tragic accident.

But that wasn't the plan. It was a carefully laid plan, one that required attention to detail. Everything had to be done just right.

He pulled the Regal to a stop on the wrong side of the road, almost touching the guardrail. The driver's side window was down, and the roar from below filled the interior of the car. After thirty seconds, the driver's door opened and Leland stepped out. Thin, in the way drug addicts often appear, his long scraggly hair swirled around his face in the brisk wind. In one hand, he held a sheaf of papers, bound by brass fasteners. He stood between the car and the guardrail for a moment, the papers clutched tightly.

Slowly, deliberately, he first put one leg over the guardrail, then another. He stood for a moment on the precipice, scant inches from the drop-off. He teetered for a moment as a particularly strong gust of wind slammed against his frail frame. He peered down. All that was visible in the darkness was the swirling foam hundreds of feet below.

He glanced at the bound pages in his hand. The words spoke to him as they had when he had first written them. A tear trickled down one cheek.

Without looking back, he tossed the pages into the car through the driver's side window. He held his arms at his side, almost as if standing at attention. He had to carry out the plan.

He stepped out into the blackness.

CHAPTER 2

TERI SQUIRE SAT on the couch in her den, eyes glued to the newspaper. A soft breeze, with the faint odor of creosote, wafted in from the open sliding doors to her right that afforded a spectacular view of the Santa Monica Mountains from her Beverly Hills home in the hills north of Sunset Boulevard. Not a conventional beauty, Teri's skin bore signs of wear beyond her 36 years, as if she'd had some exposure to sun in her early days. Auburn hair hung to her shoulders, pulled casually back to emphasize piercing green eyes. Dressed in faded jeans and a denim workshirt, she had a fresh-scrubbed, girl-next-door aura about her. Based upon her surroundings—a luxurious stucco home that sprawled across nearly an acre of hillside, lavishly furnished with all the latest in home décor, topped off by twin golden statues on the mantle above the fireplace—one might assume that all was right in the two-time Oscar winner's world.

But the expression on her face as she read the *Los Angeles Times* told a different story. "Latest Flop for Squire" screamed the headline over an article that described, almost with glee, that Teri now had four consecutive box office bombs to her credit. The latest, a period drama about the first female FBI agent, had arrived with all kinds of promise. A screenplay by a three-time Oscar-winning screenwriter based on a *New York Times* bestselling book, a four-time nominee director, and produced by last year's winner for best picture—the project bore all the earmarks of success.

Top it off with the two-time Oscar winner Teri Squire playing the lead, and how could it go wrong?

But it had. The critics had panned the advance screenings, though no one put much stock in that. What did critics know? But the test audiences hadn't thought too much of it, either. A few scenes had been re-shot, a few new ones added, a re-edit, then it was unveiled in over 3,000 theaters over the past weekend—and the crowds stayed away in droves. Now the trades were attributing the bomb to Teri, not the script, not the directing, not the cast in general. "Box office poison" was what they called Teri. After all, this made four in a row, with a total loss threatened that could approach half a billion dollars when all was said and done. The producers deserved more for the twenty million a picture they paid her, the trades said. They certainly should rethink her price. Maybe she ought to pay to be in the next film, one smartass suggested.

Teri slammed the paper down on the coffee table just as her phone rang, the theme from *Magnum, P.I.* filling the air. She snatched it and checked the printout to identify the caller, then answered.

"Hi, Mama," she said in a distinctly Texas drawl.

"Hi, Baby," Mary Tucker said. "I'm sorry I missed your call. Is everything okay?"

Teri shifted sideways on the couch so as not to be mocked by the headline. "Yeah, everything's fine. It's not always bad news when I call."

"I know. It's just that—"

"It seems like it?"

Mary laughed, a forced sound that seemed to catch in her throat.

"Sometimes I just need to hear a familiar voice," Teri said.

"That's what mothers are for."

Teri felt tears well in her eyes, but she quickly blinked them away. She made an effort to suppress the self-pity she knew would permeate her tone if she allowed it, resulting in an ever more pronounced drawl.

"Where were you when I called?"

"Your daddy and I were down at the barn. Bingo's having a tough time. Chad's out there now and—"

Teri's pulse quickened at Bingo's name. "Is she all right?"

"She's just getting old, that's all. Sooner or later we've got to start thinking about—" Her mother's voice halted, interrupted by a male voice in the background. Teri couldn't hear the words, but she knew her father's tone. The same tone he always used with her, at least during the last few years when she had been at home. Whatever he was saying, it wasn't good.

Mary came back on the line. "Listen, Baby, I've got to go."

"Was that Daddy?"

"Yes."

"Tell him—"

The words choked off in her throat and the tears returned. This time blinking failed, and a stray rolled down her cheek.

"Tell him what, Baby?"

That was a good question. Tell him what, indeed. I'm sorry? She'd said that enough times already. But it didn't matter. It never did. I miss you? That wouldn't work either. I love you? Just to give him a chance to not say it in return? No, she'd pass on that, too.

"Nothing, Mama. You take care of Bingo, now, you hear?"

"I will. Bye-bye, Baby."

Teri held the phone to her ear long after her mother hung up, as if something still lingered in the wireless ether. Some little part of home that now seemed so long ago and so very far away.

Mary Tucker hung up the phone and turned to her husband Tom washing his hands in the kitchen sink. It was easy to see where

Teri got her looks. Even sun-washed and wearing no make-up, lined with sixty-three years of age, Mary's beauty shone through. It was not enough, though, to cover the sadness that darkened her countenance.

"Who was that?" Tom asked.

"No one," Mary said.

Tom was a big man in his mid-60s, well over six feet tall and a fit two hundred plus pounds. He grabbed a dishtowel from beside his sweat-stained cowboy hat that lay on the counter next to the sink and dried his hands and face. Where Mary's face was sun-washed, his was sun-weathered, lines etched deep around his eyes and mouth. Where Mary's countenance was perpetually sad, his was perpetually angry. His was a face that had seen too many rodeos and taken too many hard falls. His shoulders slumped under the weight of too many chips.

He wadded the towel and tossed it on the counter. He put his hat on, wiped his not-totally-dry hands on his jeans, and eyed Mary through a squint. She knew that he knew exactly who it was, the name that dare not be spoken lest it dredge up dark memories and break hearts all over again.

"Chad says to keep a close eye on her," Tom said.

Mary nodded.

"We ought to put her down," he added.

Mary knew Tom was talking about Bingo, but there was something about the way he said it, something in his tone, that made her uneasy—as if he were talking about someone else.

"We can't," she said.

"We damn sure can."

"No, Tom," she said evenly and firmly. "We can't."

"Then you keep an eye on her. Ain't my job no more. Ain't been for a long time."

Again, Mary got the sense he had someone else in mind when he spoke the words.

Tom abruptly turned, walked out the door, and trudged across the yard toward the barn. Beyond him, the beautiful Texas Hill Country beckoned, but its beauty belied the ugliness that lived in this house.

Her heart heavy, Mary went to the refrigerator to take out the makings for supper. She froze when her hand gripped the handle. The picture that was stuck to the door with a magnet tugged at her heart. Her daughter at sixteen-years-old, astride a black horse, rifle in one hand, a trophy in the other. Tom stood beside Bingo, reins in his hands, pride in his heart, his smile as big as all Texas. Mary tried to recall the last time she had seen Tom smile that way.

For the life of her, she couldn't remember.

Teri put the phone on the coffee table then picked up the offending paper again. The headline seemed bigger and bolder than mere moments before.

"You can't put any stock in that," a voice said from behind her. She looked over her shoulder at Mike Capalletti standing behind the couch, adjusting the Windsor knot in his dark blue tie. His tailored suit clung to his thin frame, screaming "European" and "expensive" all in one breath. Five years Teri's junior, with his slicked-back hair and swarthy complexion, he looked more Mafioso than he did high-powered Hollywood agent, something he had used to his advantage in more than one negotiation.

"You put stock in it when the news is good," Teri said.

"That's different."

"How is it different?"

"It just is."

"Tell me how it's different, Mike," she said. "Tell me why I'm supposed to believe all of the good stuff and not believe the bad."

"Because you know as well as I do that it's easier for a critic to criticize than it is to praise. They're called critics for a reason. Slamming someone doesn't require any thought. But they'd rather slit their wrists than say something good, so when they do praise your work, it's gotta mean something."

Teri focused on a paragraph midway through the article and read aloud. "'Teri Squire has long since given up any hope of a third Oscar. Now it's all about the money for her, but if she doesn't start turning in better performances, she might as well give up that hope, too. She sleepwalks through her latest disaster as if embarrassed to be associated with it, which is hard to do when her name is so prominently affixed to it as a producer and its star.'"

She dropped the paper on the coffee table again. "Sounds like he put some thought into that one."

Mike came around the couch and sat next to Teri. He took her hand in his and kissed the palm. "It was bad material."

"I picked the script."

"We just gotta find a better one."

"What if we can't find one?"

"There are a million scripts floating around out there. The law of averages says that at least some of them have to be good. And to be honest, the one we pick doesn't have to be great. It just has to be better than the others. It's all relative."

"I could always go back to Texas."

"Guitars and Cadillacs and Bob Wills music, huh?"

"It's home."

He kissed her on the cheek. "*Was* home, not *is* home. Now home is here, and Texas is just a bad memory."

He stood and adjusted his tie. "How do I look?"

But Teri was staring out the window and not looking at him. "It's gonna be bad, isn't it?"

"Don't worry about it. I'll just work my magic and everything'll be okay."

Without looking back, he went to the door and then he was gone.

CHAPTER 3

THE PACIFIC COAST Highway was awash in red and blue lights as half a dozen law enforcement vehicles sat on the edge of the drop-off, with the old Regal sticking out like a sore thumb in their midst. In front of the Regal, paramedics waited by the open back door of their vehicle. Behind it, a construction crane had been set up, its cable lowered down the cliffside. Every now and then, a car slowed as it passed by, its occupants transfixed by the flashing lights but unable to see or even speculate what lay below.

A two-year-old Chevy Tahoe pulled up next to the Regal and came to a halt. A blue light flashed on its dashboard as the occupants got out. California Highway Patrol detective Howie Stillman slid from the driver's side, his partner Jeff Nichols from the other. Both men were young in appearance, with neatly-trimmed mustaches and sideburns, as if they were the uniform of the day. The casual observer might even have thought the two were brothers, both roughly the same mid-30s in age and both with thick brown hair. But Stillman topped out at five feet nine inches, with the thick build of a linebacker, while Nichols rose at least six inches taller, his lanky frame more suited for basketball.

Nichols came around the car and stood by Stillman's side as they peered over the railing. The body basket was still a good hundred feet below, the crane's chain working slowly. A paramedic rode up with the body. Far below the basket, waves crashed aggressively against jagged black rocks. The drop was sheer, the sides of the cliff bare.

"Not much to break a fall," Nichols said.

"I think that's the point. If you're going to do it, do it right."

Nichols glanced at the back seat of the Tahoe. In the glare on the window glass, he could barely make out the outline of the lone occupant. "You sure bringing her was a good idea?"

"It's a little late to second guess. Besides, you were there, and I didn't see you trying to stop her from coming along."

"She scares me a little," Nichols said.

"Ain't it the truth."

Stillman approached the car and opened the rear driver's side door. "You want to step out, ma'am?"

Annemarie Crowell slid her legs out, then stood. She was nearly as tall as Nichols, nearly as lanky, but the most striking thing about her appearance was a thick cake of white make-up, face pale, eyes highlighted in black, and lips a garish red, that almost made her resemble a circus clown. All she lacked was a big red nose and floppy shoes to complete the look. Her face was frozen in place, though whether by the make-up or simply by lack of emotion, neither detective was sure. She approached the guardrail, her steps shaky in high-heeled shoes. She stood beside the detectives and looked down at the basket, which was nearing the lip of the precipice.

"You sure you want to do this, ma'am?" Stillman asked.

"That's my son," Annemarie said.

"We don't know that for a fact, ma'am. Like I told you before, we just know that's his car."

"He never lets anyone drive it. If Leland's car is here, then that's my Leland down there."

Stillman cut Nichols a look. At a glance, he could see that his partner was as taken by the lifeless tone as he was. And that's when Stillman saw it. He couldn't be sure at first, but a second look confirmed it. Tears had amassed along Annemarie's eyelids.

They looked out of place against the backdrop of her frozen features. What he couldn't tell, though, was whether they were real or simply had been summoned up because she deemed them appropriate for the moment.

It seemed to take minutes but was really only seconds before the basket reached the top. The paramedic jumped off onto solid ground, relief on his face. The detectives and Annemarie approached slowly.

"Unzip it," Nichols said.

"He's a mess, Detective. Face first on a rock."

All three men looked at Annemarie, who remained stoic.

"Unzip it," Nichols said again.

The paramedic slowly drew the zipper downward about a foot, then spread open the plastic to reveal a pulpy mass of red and gray, mixed with the white of skull fragments. Stillman recoiled. It wasn't recognizable as a face even though they all knew it was. Stillman could tell from the proportions where there should be a nose, where the mouth and eyes should be, but for all he knew, this man never had a face.

Annemarie remained emotionless. The tears remained frozen on her lids, unwilling or unable to fall. "He had a tattoo," she said. "On his right forearm. A blue star in a football helmet."

The paramedic pulled the zipper down farther then extricated the corpse's right arm. He rolled up the sleeve and, sure enough, there was a blue star in a football helmet.

"How 'bout them Cowboys," Annemarie said in a deep monotone.

Stillman and Nichols exchanged looks. What a perfectly bizarre thing to say.

"Is that him, ma'am?" Stillman asked.

"Deserted his mother again."

Yet another perfectly bizarre thing to say.

"Take me home," she said.

Stillman took Annemarie by the arm and turned her to the car. "Get the thing," he said to Nichols.

As Stillman put Annemarie in the car, Nichols approached the Regal, reached in through the open window, and grabbed the bound pages that Leland had tossed inside before jumping. He carried it back to the Tahoe and handed it to Annemarie. She looked at the cover—"THE PRECIPICE, a Screenplay by Leland Crowell"—and put it on her lap without opening it.

"Ahh, yes, the masterpiece," she said.

Then she pulled her door shut.

CHAPTER 4

TERI CARRIED A tray with ice, diet soft drinks, and two glasses onto the deck. In the distance, a smoky haze hung over the hills, testifying to yet another wildfire out of control. This one had raged for nearly a week now, but news reports had firefighters finally turning the tide.

She set the tray on a table. Mona Hirsch, her partner in SH Productions, curled her legs under herself on the padded loveseat as she poured a drink into one of the glasses. Mona was nearing forty, but fighting age with everything she had, including regular visits to the gym that kept her frame lithe and lean, as well as nips, tucks, and color-in-a-bottle that kept the gray away from her otherwise jet-black hair. She and Teri had set up the production company five years earlier, just prior to Teri's second Academy Award, and it had all been downhill from there. Not that it was Mona's fault; that's just the way things had gone.

Teri poured herself a drink then sat on a lounge chair. She took a deep drink, then refilled her glass, leaned her head back, and closed her eyes. They sat in silence for a few moments. The smell of smoke made Teri think of fires in fireplaces, and that made her think of Texas.

"Have you read all the reviews?" Teri asked.

"Yeah."

"And?"

"*Illegitimi non carborundum*. Don't let the—"

"—bastards get you down. I know. But the bastards didn't drag your name through the mud. And what gets me is they act like they enjoy it. It's one thing to be critical. It's another to be so mean-spirited."

"It's what makes them the *illegitimi* in the first place."

Teri combined a swallow with a laugh, followed by a fit of coughing. By the time she was through, both she and Mona were doubled over with laughter. Teri wiped tears from her cheeks and sat up straight. "My side hurts," she said. "And I can't tell you how good it feels."

"It's the first time I've seen you laugh in weeks."

"Let's just hope it's not the last time."

Mona opened her mouth to reply but stopped short at the ringing of Teri's cell phone. Both women froze in place and stared at the phone on the table.

It kept ringing, the theme song from *Magnum, P.I.* Teri looked at the read-out, then at Mona. She nodded.

"You gonna answer it?" Mona asked.

"I'm not sure I want to hear what he has to say." She downed the rest of her drink, then snatched up the phone. "But I guess I better get it over with."

Mike Capalletti's office befit his status as one of Talent Agency of America's rising young stars. He didn't have a corner office yet, but that was just a matter of time. Sitting in the middle of an oversized U-shaped, glass-top desk, his back to floor-to-ceiling windows that overlooked Century City, he wielded multiple phones with the panache of a hibachi chef on steroids. After graduating with his MBA from Harvard, he'd started in the legendary mailroom of TAA, but was now on the cusp of achieving his dream as a full equity partner in the agency. He represented some of Hollywood's hottest talent, both actors and directors, with a sprinkling of writers thrown in. But you were only as good as your A-list clients' last movie. And only one thing could stop his ascent now. Hard to believe, but only one client stood between him and his dream.

He spun in his chair and stared out the window. He had come a long way in such a short time. The tough streets of Chicago's southside seemed but a distant memory now. Sporting the accoutrements of success, such as thousand dollar suits and two-hundred-fifty dollar haircuts, he wasn't about to let anything or anyone drag him down. Not when he was this close.

Silver-haired Bob Keene entered with his strange walk caused by unnaturally bowed legs and small feet. He sat down in one of the plush leather-covered chairs across from the desk. Mike spun around suddenly, startled by the intrusion. He stared hard at the man he idolized and emulated. The man cut from the same pretentious cloth as he, albeit three decades apart in age.

"Are you going to be able to do this?" Bob asked.

Mike spun back around and faced the window. "Don't worry about me."

Teri entered the elevator on the ground floor of TAA's building on Century Park West, in Century City, and took a deep breath. She pushed "12" and the car began its slow ascent. When the doors opened, she got off on TAA's floor and followed the hardwood floors toward Mike's office. Dread tugged at her mind with each step. The sounds of her footsteps, though softened by the rubber soles of her running shoes, seemed to echo just as Poe's telltale heart had driven a man mad. Mike had been close-mouthed when he called. "I just need you to get down here," was all he would say in response to her questions. "We'll talk about it when you get here."

She could almost predict what was coming: She was losing her housekeeping deal at Cinema USA Studios. She'd had the deal since winning her second Oscar and setting up SH Productions with Mona. Cinema USA had outbid several other major studios and given her offices on the lot, a small staff to take care of clerical work, first look at any projects she developed, and agreed to distribute any movies she made. Initially, it looked like a stroke of genius for them when Teri won her second Oscar in relatively short order after the first, but then the drought hit, culminating in her most recent failure. Cinema USA was already bleeding red ink, for a whole list of reasons unrelated to Teri, but her latest movies not only failed to stem the blood flow, they also seemed to open up new veins.

She reached the door to Mike's office, which was uncharacteristically closed. Teri's anxiety kicked up a notch as she knocked.

"Come in," Mike said.

When she opened the door and saw Bob Keene sitting there, she knew instantly things were worse than she imagined. Neither man stood as she entered. Wordlessly, she sat in the guest chair next to Bob, directly across from Mike. Mike looked guilty, Bob looked resigned. Teri wondered if she looked panicked.

"The deal's gone, isn't it?" she asked. Her tone was matter-of-fact, as if this were just another business meeting, even though she knew full well it wasn't.

"You've got to look at it from their perspective," Bob said. "You've lost them a lot of money."

"I made them a lot of money, too."

"Old money is a forgotten memory."

"Then we'll go to another studio."

"No other studio'll take you. Right now, you're poison."

The words stung more than Teri could have thought possible. Her own agents, quoting the press as if it were truth. She looked at Mike, silently pleading with him to come to her rescue.

"You've seen this coming for a long time, Babe," he said.

"Remember what you said just the other day? No studio wants an actor—"

"I don't need you to remind me what I said," she snapped. "I need you to remind the studio who I am."

"What you need is a hit," Bob said.

"Look, Babe," Mike said, "no one believes you're washed up as an actress. The problem's been the movies you made; not you."

"You and Bob were involved in every decision I made. In fact, as long as we're talking about short memories, do you recall that it was you two who brought this last fiasco to me and insisted that I do it?"

"And that was our mistake," Bob said. "But by that point, we were desperate to find something to let you break back out."

Teri tried to make eye contact with Mike, but he seemed more interested in looking at the desktop, the floor, and the ceiling, than at her.

"Look, maybe it's time we switch gears," Teri said. "No more romantic comedies, no dramas, and damn sure no period pieces. How about a thriller? I haven't done a thriller in a long time."

"Do you have a thriller script?" Bob asked.

"Isn't it y'all's job to find one for me?"

She could tell when she said it that, as usual, the "y'all" was like fingernails on a blackboard for Bob. She couldn't help the way she talked. Her Texas roots were deeply engrained, but sometimes, when she was annoyed at Bob, she made it a point to sneak in a few extra "y'alls" and "fixin' to's" just to piss him off.

"Y'all can't tell me there are no good thrillers making the rounds right now."

"Everything out there that's worth a damn has got a male lead," Mike said.

"So we tweak it a bit, turn it into a female lead. Any writer worth a damn can do that. And y'all do rep writers, don't y'all?"

"Sarcasm doesn't become you," Bob said evenly.

His calmness pissed her off even more. "What do I care what becomes me? I'm poison, remember?"

She turned her attention to Mike, banishing Bob to invisibility. "We just need one hit—"

"You mean *you* just need one hit," the refusing-to-be-invisible Bob said.

"No, I mean *we* need one hit. We're a team, aren't we?"

Mike spun his chair around and looked out the window. She glared at Bob, who met her gaze with the same evenness with which he had spoken earlier.

"The executive committee has discussed it, and we think maybe it would be best if you sought representation with another agency," Bob said.

She pulled back and cocked her head, as if she hadn't heard him clearly. "You're firing me?"

"Technically, we're simply exercising the termination provision in your contract. It happens all the time in this business."

She looked at Mike, who still faced the window. "Mike?"

No response.

"Mike, look at me."

He slowly spun his chair back around. She saw nothing in his eyes. Not tears, not remorse—nothing but a blank stare.

"Did you know about this?" Teri asked.

"He was sworn to secrecy until I could tell you," Bob said.

"What did you expect me to do? I've got an obligation to the agency," Mike said.

"You've got an obligation to me. 'Home is here.' Isn't that what you said?"

"It's not personal; it's business."

"Then I guess sleeping with you makes me a whore."

Teri felt tears welling in her eyes, but she willed them back to their ducts. She'd be damned if she was going to cry in front of these two jackasses. The phone on Mike's credenza rang, but everyone ignored it. It stopped on the second ring, and the room went deathly silent. Finally Teri spoke in a low voice, almost a whisper.

"I'm telling you, all we need is the right script."

"It's not about scripts anymore," Mike said. "I hate to say it, but Bob's right. You're box office poison right now. You just don't want to admit it."

Bob stood and clapped his hands, like a football player breaking the huddle. "We'll give you a good referral, Teri. After all, we've had a lot of good years together. Hell, we'll even make it seem like it's your idea. It'll be better for everyone."

"You'll understand if I disagree."

"Think of it as a new opportunity."

Before Teri could respond, there was a knock on the door, then it opened and Philip, Mike's assistant, stuck his head in. He seemed petrified of interrupting the meeting.

"I'm sorry to interrupt, but there's a call for Ms. Squire. It's a lawyer. Something about somebody died."

The words hit hard at Teri's heart. Bingo? Had Daddy had him put down? Then she thought better of that idea. Lawyers didn't call about dead horses.

She walked behind Mike's desk and picked up the phone. Her voice quivered as she spoke. "This is Teri Squire."

"Ms. Squire, my name is Spencer West. I'm Leland Crowell's attorney. I'm sorry to have to tell you that Mr. Crowell has passed away."

"I don't know any Lester Crowell."

"Leland. And he knew you. He's left you a bequest in his will."

CHAPTER 5

WEARING A BLACK dress that stopped just above her ankles, Annemarie Crowell stood alone in a broken-down cemetery just outside of the town limits of Ludlow, California, barely more than a ghost town in the Mojave Desert. The town had once known better days. Founded as a water stop for the railroad, it briefly flourished as a tourist stop on Route 66 before the construction of Interstate 40 drove a spike into its heart.

The cemetery was as sad as the town, brown and barren, devoid of color. There was a scattering of simple headstones, a few wooden crosses and, to mark yet other graves, nothing more than indentations in the ground where the soil had settled over the years. Two elderly Mexican men—illegals, Annemarie was sure—shoveled dirt into a rectangular hole. At the bottom of the hole sat an unmarked pine box. Final resting place for Leland Crowell.

Annemarie stood rigidly as rocks and dirt clods thudded onto the casket. A hot wind blew, its touch like a furnace on her face. A trickle of sweat painted a tiny streak on her left cheek, the only crack in her mask. Her lips pressed tight, gray hair pulled back in a schoolmarm bun, her face revealed nary a hint of emotion. There was no crowd, no preacher, no mourners, no weeping and wailing. Just Annemarie, face painted like a clown, two Mexicans, and her dead son's body.

A helluva send-off into the afterlife.

The last shovel of dirt fell into place, and one of the Mexicans patted the ground with the back of his shovel, then stamped on the dirt to pack it down. Annemarie reached into the pocket of her dress and extracted two fifty-dollar bills. She pressed one each into the hands of the shovelers, who mumbled their *gracias*, then left without looking back.

Annemarie stepped close to the edge of the loose dirt. She glanced around, as if looking for something. Her eye fell on a crude cross on a nearby grave. Made of wood, it was nearly rotten with age and leaned precariously to the side. Inscribed with a simple R.I.P., but no name, it fit her needs. She walked to the grave and pulled the cross out, then returned to Leland's site. She shoved the cross into the loose dirt at one end of the grave, but it immediately listed to the left.

She stepped back and eyed the cross. Another stream of liquid coasted down her cheek. With her index finger, nail long and painted red, she traced it back up her face to its source. She was stunned to find that it originated at her lower eyelid.

She wiped the tear from her cheek, grabbed the wooden cross, and threw it as far as she could.

Then she returned to her car.

CHAPTER 6

TERI DIDN'T CONSIDER herself a snob, and she certainly didn't think of her home in the Hollywood Hills as an ivory tower, but as she wheeled her dark blue hybrid Toyota Highlander SUV past a row of crumbling frame structures wedged one after the other along a street that hadn't seen any tender loving care in decades, she felt as if she had entered another world. Most of the houses were set back mere feet from the curb, some with fading memories of white picket fences. She knew that this had once been a neighborhood of blue-collar workers who took pride in their homes as they raised their families in the shadows of downtown. But urban blight had crept in, families moved out, and now gangs, prostitutes, and drug addicts reigned.

She pulled to a stop in front of a frame house with aluminum siding that flaked huge chunks of paint like canker sores. She double-checked the number on the mailbox with the number written on the notepad in the passenger seat. A perfect match.

She killed the engine and stepped out of her SUV. She looked around, wondering where the roving pack of car strippers lurked that would surely denude her car in a just a matter of minutes, but no one was in sight. She probably should have taken Mike up on his offer to accompany her, but the last thing she wanted from him right then was either his company or his advice. She paused for a moment, debating whether to get back in her vehicle and get the hell out of there. But the siren call of the mystery was too much. She shut the door, punched the remote lock, and headed toward the front walk.

A rusty gate, barely thigh high, swung by one hinge. She pushed it with her foot and stepped inside the gated area that passed for a front yard. Maybe at one time kids had played with toys in this yard, but that would have been a lifetime ago, if ever. She stepped over a broken step at the front porch, sure her foot would punch through and a rusty nail would impale her ankle. The porch creaked, and she wondered whether it would hold her weight any more than the step would have.

A sign on the front door, made of letters nailed to a wooden block, said: SPENCER WEST: ATTORNEY AT AW. The missing L lay on the porch beside the door.

"I'll just bet 'aw,'" she said as she rang the doorbell.

She was surprised to hear it ring somewhere in the house. She would have bet it didn't work. After about thirty seconds of no response, she rang it again then knocked.

Still no answer.

She tried the doorknob and found it unlocked. She turned it and pushed the door open. As she did, a small bell over the doorway rang.

"Hello? Anybody home?" she called.

Silence. She slipped inside, but left the door open behind her. She found herself in a tiny space that passed for an entryway, crowded with a hat rack, a small table with newspapers and magazines piled on top, and an umbrella stand. A lone umbrella rested forlornly inside the stand.

"Hello? Mr. West?"

"Be right there," a voice came from the recesses of the house. A few seconds later, a small man, to the point of looking frail, appeared from the back of the house. He wore creased jeans, a blue button-down dress shirt, and a dark green bowtie. Teri pegged him as fiftyish, but his thinning hair might have added ten or fifteen years to his actual age.

"Mr. West?"

He extended his hand. "Spencer West, attorney at aw, at your service."

Okay, Teri thought, so he's got a sense of humor. But if it was intended to disarm, it failed completely.

"I'm Teri Squire."

"Of course you are. I recognized you right away. Love your movies." He said it almost too glibly, as if he had rehearsed the line.

"Which one is your favorite?" she asked.

He hesitated for a moment then smiled. "Okay, you got me. I never saw any of them. Then again, I don't get out much." He turned toward the back of the house, gesturing with his hand for her to follow. "Come on in."

He led her to what had probably once been a den, but now served as an office. The lighting was poor, but just bright enough to see a gunmetal gray desk stacked with papers, a row of filing cabinets beside it, and a worn leather couch. The walls were obscenely bare, lacking the accoutrements every other law office she had ever seen had sported: diplomas, law licenses, certificates, and pictures of notable clients or acquaintances. She had once heard what some lawyers call their "me" walls referred to as the "proof" wall. By hanging law school diplomas and law licenses on the wall, they proved their legitimacy to clients who sat in their offices. But Spencer West lacked any such proof; only an attorney at aw sign on his front door.

West grabbed a few files from the couch and stacked them on the floor, clearing a spot for Teri. "Have a seat," he said, but Teri remained standing, just in case she needed a quick getaway.

"Mr. West, I think you've got the wrong person," she said. "I've been wracking my brain, and I've never heard of Lester Crowell."

West sat in a wooden chair behind the desk. "It's Leland Crowell. And I hardly think you're the wrong person. Are there any other actresses in this town named Teri Squire who've won two Oscars?"

Her silence provided his answer.

"I didn't think so." He swiveled his chair around and picked up a file folder from a small shelf, then spun back around to face her.

"Please, Ms. Squire, sit."

She slowly lowered onto the couch as West opened the file folder and thumbed through its contents. "Leland was a very troubled young man. He had it in his mind to write the great American novel. Unfortunately, he got writer's block on Chapter One. So he tried his hand at screenwriting. He had a little more luck there. Fewer pages, more white space, and all that. At least he was able to finish one."

"Mr. West, I don't mean to be rude, but could you get to the point?"

"Everyone's always in a hurry. Yes, of course, the point. The point is that he thought you'd be perfect for the lead in his screenplay. I can't say, myself, whether you are or not, since I haven't read it. Nor have I seen your movies. Not my cup of tea—no offense intended."

He paused in his monologue, as if inviting a rebuttal, or at least a defense.

"And?" Teri asked.

"And so he left his screenplay to you in his will." He paused again then added, "Right before he killed himself."

If West expected to shock her with that last revelation, it worked. Her face flushed, the heat rising along with her eyebrows. "That's crazy," she said.

"I'll admit it sounds a bit off, but nevertheless he did it. You are now the proud owner of the sole screenwriting

27

accomplishment of my client, Leland Crowell."

"I don't want a screenplay. I can't even read it unless it gets submitted through my agent—" She stopped, aware that she no longer had an agent. "Or my lawyer."

"That would be true if you were worried about Leland suing you for stealing his screenplay or his idea, but that's not a concern here. He gave it to you, so the screenplay is yours. Legally. You don't have to worry about the deceased signing a release. Which he clearly can't do, anyway."

"What am I going to do with a screenplay?"

West leaned back in his chair, a bemused smile on his face. "Ms. Squire, I'm just a dumb ol' lawyer, and I don't really know what you Hollywood types do with screenplays. I've heard tell, though, that sometimes you read them. Sometimes you even turn them into movies. I happen to have seen some of those movies. Not yours, though. Sorry. But maybe if you make Leland's screenplay into a movie, I'll come see it."

Teri stood. "I don't want his screenplay."

"Please, sit down." The sharp tone in his voice surprised her. When she sat again, he said, "If you don't want it, then burn it, shred it, do whatever you want with it. It's yours, after all, to do with as you please. I guess you could even disclaim it."

"Disclaim it?"

"Yes. Leland has made a bequest to you, and you could disclaim it, if you choose. It's a simple legal matter of signing a disclaimer."

"What would happen if I did that?"

"It would go to his alternate beneficiary. Leland's mother. But if you decide you don't want it, you could always give it to Annemarie, yourself."

"Who's Annemarie?"

"Leland's mother. She wants to deliver it to you personally. Would that be all right?"

Teri shook her head. This was just too frickin' bizarre. First her agents fire her, then some nutcase she's never heard of wills her his masterpiece screenplay—oh, yeah, she was sure it was just great—and now his mother wants to hand-deliver it to her. She felt like she had stepped into an episode of *The Twilight Zone*.

"Have you got it here?" she asked. "Why don't you just give it to me?"

"Annemarie has it. Besides, don't you think it's the least you can do? Come on, she just lost her son. He apparently worshipped you. He said in his will that he wrote his screenplay specifically for you, but that you refused to read it."

"No one ever told me about any screenplay by a Lester—"

"Leland."

"Leland Crowell. It would have gone through my agent or my company or someone else, but it never came to me."

"Well, it's coming to you now. You don't have to like it. You don't even have to read it. But can't you at least be gracious to a poor old woman who's just trying to carry out her son's last wishes?"

Teri stood again. She paused, as if she wanted to say something. But what? The bequest was downright crazy, but the mother's request was imminently reasonable. How could she possibly deny the poor woman something so simple?

"Have her call me," she said at last, as she turned and left.

CHAPTER 7

TERI SAT WITH her legs curled up beneath her on the couch, a stack of screenplays on the coffee table. Through the sliding glass doors, smoke hung heavily on the horizon, obscuring the views of the Santa Monica Mountains with a London-like fog. This was just one more thing that made her long for home in the Hill Country of central Texas, with perennially clear skies and no fear of forest fires, earthquakes, and mentally disturbed screenwriters.

Yeah, about that screenwriter. Lester Crowell, or whatever his name was. When Teri first moved to Los Angeles, seeking a future in film while simultaneously seeking to escape her past, she knew that the movie business dominated the landscape of the city like no other industry in no other town. To use an old Texas expression, you couldn't swing a cat by its tail without hitting an aspiring actor or director. Or, as it turned out, a screenwriter. Teri knew that screenwriters were sometimes the invisible building blocks in the movie business. After all, without a screenplay, there could be no movie. Most movie fans could name the stars of their favorite movies and could usually name the directors. But ask them to name the screenwriter, and their eyes glazed over, as if you had just asked them to explain Einstein's theory of relativity.

You mean somebody writes those things? I thought the actors just made it up as they went.

She looked at the stack of scripts on the coffee table, some of which had been in her hands, yet unread, for months. Mike sent a load over just that morning, his last official act as her agent. And, as far as she was concerned, as her boyfriend. He assured her that, even though he was no longer her agent, he intended to help her find the next great screenplay that would springboard her back to the top. If that actually happened, and if her star should rise again, she had no doubt that he would swoop back in, take credit for it, and demand his cut.

She grabbed the top script on the pile, flipped to the back, and looked at the page number on the last page: 142—too long. It seemed as if everyone in town was writing a screenplay—waiters, bartenders, store clerks, schoolteachers, cab drivers, and suicidal nutcases—but very few of them seemed to know what they were doing. At roughly a minute of screen time per script page, no one wanted anything more than 105 to 115 pages these days.

She tossed the script on the floor beside the couch, grabbed the next one, and looked at the last page: 112. Okay, length was good. How about the story? She flipped to the start and began reading. By page three, she had reached three conclusions: the writer couldn't spell; the writer couldn't construct a reasonable sentence; and the writer didn't have a story to tell. She tossed the script on the floor. Usually Mike had readers at the agency weed out scripts before they reached her, but apparently the readers no longer made time for has-beens. It seemed to Teri as if Mike had simply grabbed a stack of scripts and sent them, then probably checked off "help Teri find a script" on his to-do list.

She grabbed the next script just as the doorbell rang. She wasn't expecting anyone, and she had banned Mike from the premises. Maybe he was sending over another batch of scripts. Or maybe it was Mona. They had talked by phone after Teri's return from the attorney-at-aw's office, and Mona had been just as perplexed as Teri by the bizarre turn of events. "Look at the bright side," she said. "Sounds like you had a potential stalker who decided to take himself off the board. You got lucky."

Teri opened the drawer in the coffee table and grabbed the deadbolt key next to a .22 handgun she had won in the last shooting competition she entered before leaving Texas. The time she entered the mixed division and actually outshot all the men. The prize gun that was now gathering dust, just another memory of a distant past.

Key in hand, she went to the entryway and peered through the peephole. The back of a woman's head, gray hair wrapped in braids, filled the viewfinder. Who the hell was this? Teri punched her security code on the alarm pad, then inserted the key into the deadbolt and unlocked it. The woman on the porch turned as Teri opened the door. Her appearance momentarily shocked Teri, face grotesquely made up with bright red lips. She reminded Teri of Carolyn Jones as Morticia in the old *The Addams Family* sitcom. Or maybe Yvonne DeCarlo as Lily in *The Munsters*.

Then Teri saw the screenplay the woman gripped in her hands, and a light clicked on. "You must be Ms. Crowell."

"Call me Annemarie. Mr. West said you'd see me."

"How did you find out where I live?"

"Some things about Hollywood never change. You can still buy maps to the stars' homes on almost every street corner."

Yet another reminder of how vulnerable Teri could be, or could have been if Lester Crowell had turned out to be a stalker. On the other hand, the way her star was flaming out over the Hollywood sky, it wouldn't be all that much longer before no one knew, or cared, who she was or where she lived.

"May I come in?" Annemarie asked.

"I'm sorry. I wasn't expecting anyone. Yes, please come in."

Teri stepped away and escorted the strange woman inside. Annemarie stood stock still in the entryway and scanned the interior of the house. She seemed to take in a portion of the view, then shuffled her feet and turned a bit, a pattern she repeated several more times, almost as if taking a panoramic photograph for her memory. If the neighborhood this woman lived in was anything like the neighborhood where her lawyer lived and worked, Teri's house must look like pure luxury to her.

Teri led the way to the den, with Annemarie following slowly behind. "Please, have a seat," Teri said as she resumed her place on the couch.

Annemarie perched on the edge of a Queen Anne chair across from Teri, her back rigid, the screenplay held primly on her knees. She looked out the sliding glass door at the smoky horizon then scanned the den, repeating the panoramic routine from a seated position, shifting slightly in the chair as the camera of her mind swept around the room. For a moment, the two Oscars held her attention then her eyes swept across, and locked on, the stack of screenplays. It was as if she were mesmerized by the very sight of them.

"I'm very sorry about your son," Teri said.

Annemarie tore her eyes away from the scripts. "Coffee."

"Excuse me?"

"I believe it's customary to offer a guest coffee. Or tea."

"Well, you can see that I'm very busy." Teri gestured at the stack of screenplays. "I hope you'll understand if I don't."

Annemarie stared at the stack of scripts again, then suddenly met Teri's gaze so sharply that Teri had to look away. The woman's eyes were dark to the point of appearing black, and they were totally devoid of emotion. Annemarie looked at the scripts scattered on the floor, then back to Teri again.

"It must be difficult finding just the right script to suit a woman of your—*talents.*" Annemarie made the last word sound like an epithet, as if talents were a four-letter word.

"It's always tough to find the right script," Teri said. "For any actor."

"Then my loss is your gain."

"Excuse me?"

"My boy Leland wrote this for you. It'll make you famous." Annemarie spoke in a low voice, almost a monotone. She held up the script, clutching it in what Teri could only describe as talons. Long curved nails painted as red as her lips. She began to sway, as if the weight of the screenplay threw her off balance. Unconsciously, Teri watched the movement, her eyes slowly moving back and forth with the swaying.

"Ms Crowell, I don't want to sound conceited, but I'm already famous."

"Leland is a very talented writer."

"I'm sure he was," Teri said, correcting Annemarie's misplaced use of the present tense.

Annemarie's swaying took on more length and momentum. Teri's eyes continued to follow, and suddenly she felt incredibly sleepy, as if the past few sleepless nights had finally caught up with her.

"It's hard for screenwriters to get noticed in this town," Teri said. "There's a lot of competition."

"This will make a lot of money for you."

"Again, Ms. Crowell, I don't want to sound conceited, but I already have a lot of money."

"Yes, you're already famous, and yes, you're already rich. You're also yesterday's news. This will make you tomorrow's headline."

The words stung, more so even than Bob Keene's hanging the "poison" label on her. Bob was a businessman, driven by money, and she could understand his motivation, whether she agreed with his judgments or not. That didn't threaten her ego, though it certainly disrupted her peace of mind. But in Hollywood, perception was everything, and as long as the public perceived her as a talented actress, an Oscar-winning actress, then she could survive the insults of business people who didn't have a single creative bone in their bodies. So for this odd woman to come into her home and tell her she was relegated to the trash heap, with her career hinging on the most likely inane screenplay written by a dead psychopath—and surely the writer didn't fall far from the nut tree that now sat across from her—was more than Teri could bear.

Teri wanted to formulate the words to throw Annemarie out of her house, but all she could come up with was, "I'm sure it's very good."

"Don't patronize me, Ms. Squire."

"I'm not patronizing you."

"I hear it in your tone. You think you're special because you make movies and because you live up here in your fancy house. You don't give a damn about people like my Leland who go to your movies and fawn all over you as if you mattered."

"That's not true. I appreciate my fans. I—"

Annemarie pulled a small photograph from inside the front cover of the screenplay and handed it to Teri. Teri kept her hands in her lap, but pulled her eyes away from Annemarie's swaying to look at the picture. It showed the face of a thin man, drawn and gaunt, with deep-set eyes that had dark circles painted beneath them, and long scraggly hair. A face obviously ravaged by hard living, the kind of face usually associated with the homeless who panhandled the downtown streets in Los Angeles. She found herself strangely hypnotized by the photo, yet at the same time, tearing her eyes away from Annemarie's sway seemed to have lifted the sense of drowsiness that had overtaken her earlier.

"That's my boy," Annemarie said. "You should at least know what he looks like. She gestured toward Teri with the photo, but Teri kept her hands in her lap. Annemarie placed the picture back inside the screenplay.

"You read this screenplay," Annemarie said, "then you make this movie. You owe it to Leland."

"Why do I owe it to Leland?"

"Because he wrote it for you. And because he died for you."

"Ms. Crowell, Jesus died for me, but Leland didn't. I don't know why he killed himself, but it wasn't for me. I didn't even know him."

Annemarie slid back in her chair and stopped her swaying. "Making money in the movies is all about making a big splash and getting attention. I read the papers. I know all about the 'buzz.' A movie doesn't have to be good if there's enough hype. But my boy's screenplay is good. It's better than good. And what better hype than playing up a story about a writer who died just so you would read his screenplay? It's got blockbuster written all over it."

"If you think I would take advantage of your tragedy—"

"I think you'd be a fool not to."

Teri stood. "Ms. Crowell, I know you've suffered a loss, and I'm sorry for that. I've tried to be respectful, but I'd like for you to leave now."

Annemarie stood and stared at Teri, the intensity of her gaze finally forcing Teri to look away. She extended the script to Teri.

"Please take the script with you," Teri said. "It should be yours. You're his mother; you shouldn't have been just an alternate beneficiary."

"I'm not an actress. I can't do anything with it, but you can." Annemarie gently, almost tenderly, laid the script on top of the pile on the coffee table. "Read it. Then call your agent. Call the studio. Call your publicist. Get the buzz going right now. Leland would have wanted it that way."

She paused, then added, "Leland died so it would happen. He's your Jesus; he gave his life for you."

Annemarie turned and walked out. Teri dropped back onto the couch in stunned silence. She listened to the echo of the woman's footsteps, then the sounds of the front door opening and closing. She had once heard it said that the difference between fiction and real life is that fiction has to be believable. But who would ever believe what had just happened?

She leaned forward and looked at the cover of the screenplay: THE PRECIPICE, a Screenplay by Leland Crowell.

She took it in both hands, without opening it, and tossed it on the floor with the other rejects.

She grabbed the next one in the stack, opened it, and began reading the first page.

CHAPTER 8

ANNEMARIE CROWELL ENTERED her apartment, dropped her purse on a flower-print couch, and went to the bathroom. With a tissue and cold cream, she wiped the heavy layer of make-up from her face. It was not an easy task, given the thickness with which she had applied it in the first place. She turned on the hot water, which took several minutes to heat up, then soaked a washcloth and scrubbed off the remnants left by the tissue. Beneath the mask of make-up lay a face equally hardened, the harshness merely enhanced by the make-up as opposed to created by it.

A ringing sound interrupted her before she was finished. She tossed the washcloth in the sink, then returned to the den and extracted her cell phone from her purse. She eyed the readout then answered with two words: "It's done."

In his darkened apartment office, Spencer West pushed the disconnect button on his desk phone, and then dialed a number he had written on a piece of notepaper. After three rings, a woman's voice answered.

"L.A. Entertainment Weekly. How may I direct your call?"

"I need to speak to one of your reporters," Spencer said. "I have a helluva story for you."

After Spencer filled in the press on that helluva story, he sat at his desk in near darkness, with only a small desk lamp offering any light. His body rigid, as if in a catatonic trance, he moved only his right arm, and even that like a robot. He pulled the middle desk drawer open and, without looking at its contents, took out a .38 handgun.

He held the gun upward and pressed the barrel against the underside of his chin.

He smiled.

And pulled the trigger.

CHAPTER 9

TERI FINISHED LOADING groceries into the back of her Toyota SUV. She didn't ordinarily do her own shopping, but usually let her housekeeper take care of that chore. Some days, though, she just wanted to feel normal, even if that meant taking care of mundane chores herself and risking the stares of other shoppers. In her pocket, the strains of the *Magnum* theme announced a call on her cell. She slammed the rear of the vehicle, extracted the phone, and looked at the read-out: MIKE. She clicked off the phone and slid in behind the steering wheel.

Back at home, she unloaded the groceries and carried them inside. The message light on the kitchen phone blinked urgently, but she knew whose voice was on the message. After all, Mike had left one on her cell, as well. Still, it could be Mama with news of Bingo.

She pushed the playback button and listened. Sure enough, Mike Capalletti's voice.

"Teri, please pick up if you're there." A pause, then, "I think this is what we've been looking for. The one to put you back on the map."

Intriguing. She grabbed the phone and picked up, her finger poised to dial, but thought better of it. She hung up and unloaded the grocery sacks, then headed through the den toward her bedroom. On the floor, as she passed by, lay Leland Crowell's screenplay. She stopped and looked down at it. It was almost as if it reached out and grabbed her by the ankle, so strong was its pull. She picked it up and looked at the cover. No change since the last time she had seen it: THE PRECIPICE, a Screenplay by Leland Crowell.

She grasped the cover page between her index finger and thumb, ready to open it. But she knew that if she did, she might be pulled in, not by the quality of the work but by the sordid and bizarre set of affairs that had landed it on her den floor. She dropped it back on the carpet and continued to her bedroom.

Mona and Teri cleared away dishes from a less than satisfying meal of spaghetti and marinara sauce, with no support foods other than sliced cucumbers. Mona opened a wine cooler for herself and a diet soft drink for Teri then ushered her outside to the deck. The smell of smoke still hung in the air, but seemed to be dissipating somewhat. Teri sat on a lounge chair while Mona sought out her usual loveseat.

"I hear the fire's just about out," Mona said.

"God, I hope so. I'm good for about fifteen minutes out here, and then I have to go back inside. I hate losing my outdoor time."

They sipped their drinks in silence for a few moments.

"Have you heard anything from Mike?" Mona asked.

"He called, but I haven't called him back."

"You going to?"

"I don't know yet." She paused then asked, "Would you?"

"Not a chance in hell."

"That's what I thought. And I've still got my invisible WWMD wristband."

"WWMD?"

"What would Mona do?"

"If you'd been wearing that, you'd have dumped his ass years ago."

Teri laughed. "Yeah, I should have been listening to you all along."

"Does he know about the nutcase who left you his script?" Mona stood and went to the rail. She set her wine cooler on top and turned to face Teri. "It's just the kind of thing he'd get all hot and bothered about if he knew."

"That's why I haven't told him."

"Have you read the script yet?"

"No. And I don't intend to."

Mona leaned against the rail and polished off her drink. "What if it's good?"

Teri looked hard at her business partner for a moment, and then burst into laughter. Mona joined in, both of them laughing until tears ran down their cheeks.

The ringing of the doorbell from inside the house interrupted their laugh-fest. "Wait here, I'll go see who it is," Teri said.

She left Mona on the patio, grabbed the deadbolt key from the coffee table, and went to the door, surprised to see that the alarm had been turned off. She looked through the peephole and sighed heavily. She stood stock still, as if hoping the person on the porch wouldn't hear her and would go away. The doorbell rang again, followed by banging on the door.

"Come on, Babe," Mike called. "My key won't work."

Because I had the lock changed, Teri thought. Too bad I didn't think to change the security code, too.

The knocking continued. "I won't go away until you let me in," Mike said.

Mona appeared at the edge of the entryway, wine cooler in hand. "Are you going to let him in?"

"I have to."

Mona put her drink down on an end table. "Then I'm leaving. I don't want to say something I'll regret tomorrow. Or won't regret."

Teri unlocked the door and opened it. Mike Capalletti breezed in as Mona rushed out beside him, two ships passing at breakneck speeds in the night.

Mike continued into the den, straight to the stack of scripts on the coffee table, and began rifling through them.

"Where is it?" he asked.

"What are you doing here?"

Mike looked over his shoulder at her as she entered the den. "My key doesn't work, by the way."

"I changed the lock."

His expression never changed as he stared at her for a moment, then he turned his attention back to the stack. "Where's the script the dead guy gave you."

"How do you know about that?"

"Not from you, that's for damn sure."

He grabbed a script, read the title, and tossed it on the couch. "Is it one of these?"

"How do you know about the screenplay?"

Mike ignored her, still frantically sorting through the stack. She grabbed his arm and spun him around.

"Mike, I asked you a question. How do you know about the screenplay?"

"My phone's been ringing off the wall. I've had reporters calling all day. You're happy enough to let them know, but not your agent."

"I haven't told anyone but Mona. And I just told her about a half hour ago."

"Well, someone did. It's already on the Internet. And when it breaks in the trades tomorrow, it's gonna snowball. It doesn't matter how bad it is—it is bad, isn't it?"

"I haven't read it."

"Doesn't matter. We'll get one of our writers to do a rewrite then we'll have the studios begging us for it. It'll be a bidding war to end all bidding wars. The buzz'll freaking blow up the box office."

He turned away from Teri and started shuffling through the scripts again.

"Stop," Teri said.

"What?"

She grabbed his arm again. "I said stop."

"What the hell's the matter with you?"

"Somebody died, Mike."

Mike straightened, bowed his head, and put his hand over his heart. "Yes, let's have a moment of silence for the dearly departed."

After two seconds, he went back to shuffling the scripts. So far, he had failed to notice the screenplays on the floor by the sliding glass door.

"Now let's see if we can't save your career before it dies, too," he said.

She grabbed his arm again and yanked hard, spinning him around. His eyebrows shot up in surprise. He looked at her hand on his arm, fingers white with tension from her grip on his bicep. She let go.

"Get out," she said.

"You're kidding, right? Just still a little pissed?"

"I've never been more serious."

"You've been pissin' and moanin' about something to put you back on the map, and now it's dropped right into your lap. And what do you do? You want to ignore it."

"I don't want to take advantage of someone's death."

"You didn't kill him," Mike said. "This guy killed himself, and he gave it to you in his will. He knew what he was doing."

"You just said it, Mike: He killed himself. Does that sound like someone who knew what he was doing?"

"Look, Babe, he was looking for a way to get his script in

your hands. He also had to know what a firestorm this would kick up. Dead man wills famous actress his screenplay. Yeah, I think he knew exactly what he was doing."

"But he's dead, so what good does all this do him now?" she asked.

"It's like a posthumous medal of honor. Or like John Kennedy Toole's Pulitzer for *A Confederacy of Dunces*. That only got published because he killed himself. Maybe this guy was a Toole fan."

"It just doesn't feel right."

"As your agent—"

"You're not my agent anymore. Remember?"

"Did you ever get a formal termination letter from the agency?"

"No."

"Read your contract. We're still your agents until that happens. And as your agent—"

Teri walked to the front door. Opening it, she said, "I want you to leave."

"And I want that script."

He tossed the last script on the couch and scanned the room. His eyes fell on the scripts scattered on the floor. He took one step that way, but Teri ran across the room. She snatched up the scattered scripts and held them to her chest.

"Get out, Mike. Now."

"You're serious, aren't you?"

"What was your first clue? Maybe when I told you I was serious?"

"Come on, Babe, don't be an idiot."

She marched back to the front door and stood silently. After a moment, Mike headed that way, refusing to make eye contact with her. As he brushed past and out the door, he said, "Better read your contract."

She slammed the door after him. She tried to blink the tears away but with no success. She looked at the scripts she held. The top one was *The Precipice*. She dropped the others on the entryway floor and stared at it. Maybe she should read it. Just a few pages, anyway. Didn't she owe at least that much to the man who bequeathed it to her? Her fingers flicked at the cover. She tried to will them to open it, to reveal the first page, but it was as if they had a mind of their own.

She carried the script to the fireplace and tossed it inside. Ashes puffed and fluttered from the last fire she had started months earlier on a winter's day when the temperatures had plummeted into the 50s. Okay, so maybe it wasn't Texas, with its freezing winter days, but she always loved a crackling fire, and any excuse would do to start one. Maybe even burning a screenplay.

She knelt and turned the key to start the gas. She grabbed a fireplace match from the container on the hearth, struck it on the bricks, and opened the screen. The gas was flowing, the noise a soothing sound. She extended the flaming match toward the gas.

Almost unconsciously, she turned the key and extinguished the gas, blew out the match, and closed the screen, leaving the script, possibly along with her career, face up on the ash heap.

CHAPTER 10

CHAD PALMER KNELT beside an aging horse lying on its side on a bed of hay in a barn on the outskirts of the Texas Hill Country town of Bandera. Behind him in the airy barn, dimly-lit by a single bulb hanging from a wire, stood Tom and Mary Tucker, Teri's parents. Dressed in bedclothes and robes, they watched and waited for Chad's report.

Still fit, in his mid-forties, Chad's sun-weathered face showed concern, his eyebrows knitted, his mouth pressed in a thin line. He turned to address the Tuckers. "I don't think we can wait any longer."

"You're sure?" Mary asked, tears already streaking her face. Beside her, Tom stood stoically, emotionless.

"She's suffering, Mrs. Tucker. It's the humane thing to do."

"Do it," Tom said in a cold monotone. Purely a business decision for him.

Chad looked at Mary. "Does she know?"

Mary was frozen in place, unable to move, unable to respond.

"Mrs. Tucker, does she know?"

The words shook Mary from her trance. She slowly shook her head as she pulled a cell phone from her pocket and punched a number on speed dial.

To call Teri's slumber "fitful" would be a gross understatement.

She thrashed about, entangled in sheets, and had been doing so for the past two hours. Moonlight streamed in through open shades, almost like a spotlight singling out a star on stage. But Teri felt as if her star had burned out, along with Leland Crowell's. She didn't know how Leland had died, how he had taken his own life, but still she dreamed about it. Snippets of dreams, actually, covering every possible form of suicide: The Leland from the picture Annemarie Crowell had shown her putting a gun in his mouth; Leland jumping off a bridge; Leland swallowing an overdose of pills; Leland in a running car in a closed garage. Each time, she saw his ravaged face. Each time, the clown woman Annemarie Crowell stood in the shadows, watching, a screenplay gripped tightly in her hands.

The *Magnum* theme roused Teri just as Leland was about to drive a car at full speed into a concrete pillar, while Annemarie stood curbside and watched, screenplay in hand. Teri kicked the sheets from around her legs and looked at the bedside clock: 12:46 a.m.

She grabbed the phone and looked at the read-out, then answered. "Mama, what's wrong?"

"It's Bingo, Baby. Chad's got to put her down."

Teri sat bolt upright in bed. A quiver gripped her voice. "No, Mama. You can't do that."

"It's for the best. Chad says—"

Mary's voice was cut off, replaced by Tom's. "It's done."

"You can't do that, Daddy. Bingo's not your horse. You don't get to decide when to put him down."

"And Adam wasn't your son, but you damn sure decided without my input."

It was as if the words had punched her in the stomach. She bent over and gasped for breath, unable to formulate a response.

"You gave up your right to complain a long time ago," Tom said.

"But Daddy—"

The hang-up tone rang in her ears and jostled her brain.

She got out of bed and stood, stretching as tall as she could, fighting for air. Hot tears tingled on her cheeks. She paced the length of the room, struggling to understand. Her life that had, at one time, seemed to be the stuff of dreams, had crumbled into a nightmare. And a nightmare from years ago had resurfaced to join the new nightmare. How could everything have gone so wrong so fast?

She threw on a robe over her flannel shorts and t-shirt, stuck the cell phone in her pocket, and hurried straight to the kitchen. Almost as if on autopilot, she filled the coffee maker with water, measured coffee into the filter, and pushed the "on" button. As the water boiled and coffee dripped into the pot, she stared out the kitchen window at the blackness that seemed so fitting. She didn't know how long she stood there, but when she turned back around, the coffee was finished.

She filled a cup, then went into the den and curled up on the couch in the dark. Her gaze drifted to the fireplace, the white cover of *The Precipice* barely showing in the shadows, face up. Just as, earlier, it had seemed to reach out and grab her ankle as she walked by, it felt as if it were calling to her yet again. This time, though, she answered the call.

She set her cup on the coffee table and approached the fireplace, opened the screen, and took out the script. She dusted a few stray ashes off and then returned to the couch, turned on a lamp and, for the first time, actually opened the cover.

And began reading.

An older model Chevrolet sedan sat curbside in front of Teri's house. A lone occupant sat behind the wheel: Annemarie Crowell. Annemarie watched the house as lights came on, first in what she remembered as being the kitchen from her prior visit, then a softer, fainter light from the living area. The light by the couch. Annemarie knew the actress was sitting on the couch, Leland's screenplay in hand. Reading it.

At long last, reading it.

An hour and a half later, Teri turned the last page. A cup of cold coffee sat untouched on the table before her. She sat silently, digesting what she had read.

She pulled her cell from her pocket and dialed a number. After several rings, Mike Capalletti's sleepy voice answered. "Hello? Teri?"

"The script is brilliant," she said. "What's our next step?"

PART TWO:

THE PRECIPICE

CHAPTER 11

ONLY ONE WORD could adequately describe the look on Teri Squire's face: fear. What the hell was she doing there, so far from the comforts of her own home? This was not the kind of house she made a habit of going to. The last one like this had been Spencer West's so-called office, dark and drab, filled with cast-off furniture. She stood silently in the entryway, just inside the front door, head cocked, as if listening.

"Hello? Anybody home?"

Nothing.

She stepped deeper into the house, across the entryway and stopped at the edge of the house's living area. Torn wallpaper hung from the wall beside her and the roof sagged directly above her head, spotted with yellow watermarks. She heard scampering sounds in the attic, too heavy for mice, too light for raccoons. Probably squirrels.

At least she hoped it was squirrels.

She hesitated for a moment, allowing her eyes to adjust to the blackness of the house, which was darker than outside, even though it was a moonless night. She pulled a scrap of paper from her pocket, held it close to her face, and squinted. This was the address she had been given, but there was nothing familiar about the house or its contents, at least to the extent she could see them.

She tucked the paper back in her pocket then reached inside

to the den wall and felt for a light switch. She flipped it, but no light came on. She took out her cell phone, pushed an app button, and it lit up. She held it out, its light meager but at least allowing her some field of vision. Directly ahead was a fireplace with a barren mantel above it. She moved the phone around, trying to gauge the rest of the room. A couch, stick-legged coffee table, recliner, television—all aged, all ragged, and all there was. The walls were barren, striking in the absence of any signs that this house was lived in.

A dark spot in front of the couch drew her attention. She walked closer and knelt beside the darkness, about the size of a manhole cover on the threadbare carpet. She extended her phone to see better, then gasped. It was reddish in color. She felt it with her free hand, jerked it back at the wetness. She held her fingers next to the phone. No mistaking the liquid at the tips: blood. She held the phone about a foot from it and snapped a picture.

A creaking sound came from behind her, then a shadow appeared, recognizable only by a deepening of the darkness in the room. She stood and turned, cell phone hand outstretched. There he stood. She couldn't see his face, but she instantly knew the shape and form of his body, standing well over six feet tall, his broad shoulders nearly touching both sides of the doorway to the den. She pushed the video button on her phone and began recording what she saw.

"I knocked," she said, "but no one answered. The door was open."

No response. She couldn't make out the features on his face. His eyes were like caves, dark black against a charcoal face. He stood with his hands behind him, as if hiding something.

"I just want to talk," she said.

Still no response.

She looked at the screen on her phone to view what she was recording. All that was visible was the silhouette of this very large, very disturbed man.

"What have you got behind you?" she asked.

He moved one hand around and waved it in front of his face. Nothing.

"Your other hand."

He moved it around. Even in the dark, she could see the outline of a knife. A hunting knife, maybe, or a kitchen knife. Maybe even a Bowie knife.

"I know it's not your fault," she said. "I know about your mother. I can help you."

The man stepped forward.

Teri stepped back.

He stepped again. She backed up again, the backs of her knees pressing against the couch. She heard squishing sounds as she stepped in the pool of blood on the carpet. With nowhere to go, she sat down on the couch. Arm still extended, still recording.

The man kept coming forward, until he completely filled the screen on the phone.

He extended the knife.

Everything went black.

A screen disappeared behind an overstuffed chair where Teri sat, wearing jeans and a button-down Oxford shirt, next to *What's Up in Hollywood?* host Carl Price's desk. A full studio audience applauded, led by Price.

As the applause died down, the rubber-faced Price said, "Boy, how're you going to get out of that one?"

"You'll just have to watch the movie when it comes out and see."

"Was that guy, like, a zombie?"

Teri smiled mischievously. "Again, you'll have to watch the movie. I don't want to give away all the secrets."

"We can keep a secret, can't we folks?"

He led the audience in another round of applause.

"Patience, Carl, patience. The movie will be out next month."

"I'm not giving anything away, though, if I say it's about a serial killer who is also a hypnotist?"

"Say no more."

"My lips are sealed." Price turned an imaginary key at his mouth. "I've got to tell you, though, this is one of the most fascinating stories of how a script made it to the screen Hollywood has ever seen. For those in our audience who have been living in caves for the past two years—"

He stopped and looked across the stage to his bandleader, Archie Soocher.

"You listening, Archie?"

"Yeah, I'm listening."

Laughter from the audience. Even bigger, more exaggerated laughter from the band members.

"The screenwriter actually willed this to you, right?" Price asked.

"Right. And then he took his own life. His mother brought me the script."

From across the stage, Archie said, "Man, I've got to get out of that cave more."

"I think we're all better off, especially the women, if you stay there," Price said. When the laughter died down, he turned back to Teri. "It reminds me of John Kennedy Toole, the author of *A Confederacy of Dunces*."

"Believe me," Teri said, "we've all talked about that parallel. A novel writer who took his own life because he was so despondent that he couldn't get his book published—"

"Then ended up winning a Pulitzer Prize when his mother got it published after his death. What kind of prize are you hoping to win?"

"Let's just say I've got room for something else on my mantel. I've always thought three was a nice round number."

That set off a wild round of applause from the studio audience packed with Teri Squire fans. Price and Archie joined in, while Teri smiled. It was good to be back in Hollywood's good graces again. It had taken two years, but Hollywood memories were short and all was forgiven. For now.

"Ladies and gentlemen, two-time Academy Award winner Teri Squire," Price said. "The movie is called *The Precipice*, and it opens soon at a theater near you."

CHAPTER 12

TERI LOOKED AT herself in the bathroom mirror. An unusually harsh critic, she took one more stab at her hair, then double-checked that her dress, specially created by Montavo, Hollywood's newest one-name-designer flavor of the month, didn't reveal any unflattering cleavage or cling too tightly to hips, love handles, or buttocks. Makeup effectively covered the crow's feet that radiated from her eyes. She had always heard that exposure to sun would age your skin, but growing up in Texas, it was impossible to avoid sun, especially for a ranch tomboy who spent more time out of doors than in. Crow's feet were badges of character where she came from, instead of the beginning of a countdown to the ends of careers, as they were in Hollywood. Fittingly enough, if they ran amuck, she would soon move from leading lady to character actress.

Mike entered and stood behind her. He put his arms around her waist, clasped his hands on her stomach, and pulled her close. "You about ready, Babe?"

She pulled at her bangs, spreading them evenly across her forehead. "Does my hair look stupid?"

"No."

"Does this dress make me look fat?"

He gave her a once-over in the mirror. "Like anything could ever make you look fat."

She unclasped his hands from her waist, turned, and sighed.

"Well, if I don't look fat and stupid, then I guess I'm ready to go."

Mike laughed, and Teri smiled to see it. Throughout their relationship, she had always been able to make him laugh. That is, until the "troubles," the term he used to describe the firing/unfiring of her by her agents, the way some older folks in the Deep South still referred to the Civil War as the "recent unpleasantness." Teri thought that using that word was Mike's way of marginalizing what had happened, and his part in it, as if the whole sequence of events had merely been an uninsurable force of nature or an act of God, as opposed to a calculated decision by Bob Keene, supported—or at least acquiesced in—by Mike.

Even now, with her career apparently back on track, things were not what they had once been. If the future of their relationship was to be dependent on the fickleness of a Hollywood career, things most likely would never be the same. But things were good for now, and that was as much as Teri could hope for. She had long ago shelved the marriage hopes she once harbored. There might still be marriage in her future, but she knew it wouldn't be with Mike, or anyone else in "the business," for that matter.

They drove to the Beverly Hilton in silence. Teri kept her face to the window as Mike drove down Coldwater Canyon Drive, across glitzy Sunset Boulevard where Coldwater Canyon became Beverly Drive, and on to Wilshire Boulevard. Limos and luxury cars were already lined up in front at the valet stand of the Hilton, the car-parkers working in overdrive. Rope lines had been set up alongside a red carpet, from the curb to the entrance, and crowds of fans and onlookers gathered on both sides, cameras and cell phones in hand, ready to snap shots of celebrities.

Mike pulled in at the back of the line, waiting to edge up one car at a time.

"You nervous?" he asked, the first word spoken since they

got in the car.

"Yes. Are you?"

"No."

"Your reputation's on the line, too." She knew, though, that he'd be ready to bail out at a moment's notice, just as he had before. She was sure he had already re-packed his parachute after aborting his last bailout in mid-jump.

"We're going to do a hundred mil opening weekend," he said. "And that's if a natural disaster cuts into the box office. I've never seen buzz like this on a movie before."

They moved forward another car length. Teri let out a big sigh.

"What are you worried about?" he asked.

"What if the movie's no good? What if I was just so desperate for a hit that I let all the weirdness of suicides and wills and crazy mothers influence my judgment?"

"I read the script, too, Babe. It's good, damn good."

"You read the scripts on the busts, too. You're the one who told me to do them. Do we trust your judgment?"

"Trust Doug Bozarth and his people who thought it was good enough to sink seventy-five million dollars into. And you've seen the final cut of the movie. You know it's good, Babe. The hype may bring in the audience the opening weekend, but word-of-mouth's going to give it legs. We're going to set records with this one."

"If you say so." But Teri wasn't so sure. She had seen can't-miss turn into what-were-you-thinking before. Sure, opening weekend should be good, but word-of-mouth, while it could give the movie legs, could also cut it off at the knees. Twitter and Facebook and other forms of social media, with the instant gratification they brought, could kill it before the first Saturday matinees were over if the Teri Squire haters started texting in darkened theaters.

They pulled up another car length, and a young man in black pants, white shirt with tie, and tennis shoes opened the passenger door. The murmur from the crowd opened up to a roar. Teri could just make out her name being spoken over and over, sometimes a whisper, sometimes a shout, as the crowd recognized who was in the car.

Mike took her hand in his. "You ready to do this?"

Teri took a deep breath, squeezed her eyes shut for a moment, then opened them and smiled. She nodded.

"Then let's go greet your fans," he said.

She gave the valet her hand and allowed him to escort her out of the car while Mike hustled around to take the handoff and lead her to the door. Excited fans surged forward against the rope line. Hands extended holding paper, pictures, napkins—anything she could autograph. She took the first one and signed her name, then took the next.

"Babe, we gotta get inside," Mike said.

"Just a few more," she said. "You'll notice these folks don't think I'm toxic." She reveled in the attention and adulation of the crowd. It had been a long time since she had felt like this. And with her track record, there was no guarantee she would ever feel it again, so she wanted to enjoy it while she could.

Mike held her elbow and tried to hustle her along, but she insisted on signing everything that was thrust her way. Exasperated, he grabbed her hand as she reached for a glossy shot of her from her first Oscar-winning film. She got only a glimpse of it, but something about the photo troubled her. She couldn't quite put her finger on it. Maybe not the photo, exactly, but the hand that held it.

"Now," Mike said. "Inside."

She looked at the person who held out the photo. "I'm sorry. If you'll still be here later, I'll be happy to sign it."

The man was thin-faced with longish greasy hair and a gap-toothed smile. His appearance startled her. There was something troubling about his face, just as something troubled her about the hand that held the photo. She glanced down just as the man withdrew the offer. It was a fast move, too fast for her to be able to make out any detail of the tattoo on his bare forearm. She could see just enough to tell there was something there, crude and simplistic. And vaguely familiar.

She looked back at the man, whose smile lingered but his eyes showed no mirth. They were dark and flat and emotionless, almost reptilian. A cliché villain. And yet, a fan.

"I'll be waiting," the man said. "I have been for two years."

Teri allowed Mike to pull her away, her mind troubled by the encounter. Something continued to nag at her mind. Who the hell was that guy? Did she know him? She was pretty sure she didn't, but there was no denying a familiarity that was more than just a fleeting sense of déjà vu. Something about those eyes, especially. The frozen smile beneath lifeless eyes. She couldn't shake it.

"What's the matter, Babe?" Mike asked. He led her inside as uniformed doormen opened both doors to allow them to enter.

"I just wish I could have signed some more autographs. It seems like it's been a long time since anybody wanted one from me."

"They'll be there later. But remember, sign and move on. We've still got to get over to the theater."

Teri kept thinking about the man with the tattoo as Mike escorted her to the ballroom. As they neared, music and the dull roar of voices from inside greeted them. The pre-premiere party was in full swing, the room full of loud, boisterous people chatting, drinking, and some even dancing to a live band.

Bob Keene, wearing a black tuxedo with tails, saw them as they entered. He left the group of people he was talking to and strode toward them, beaming. Teri didn't know when she had ever seen such a big smile on his face, and she wanted to slap it off. Something about him always made her want to whip his ass—and that was before he tried to sink her career.

"One of the best pre-premiere parties I've ever been to," Bob said. "Expectations are sky high."

Great! Teri thought. Nowhere to go but down. She preferred lower expectations, where it took less to be considered a success, to high expectations, where even a success by any other standard could be deemed a failure.

Bob shook hands with Mike, then extended his hand to Teri, who gave it a tiny shake and let go almost instantly.

"Are the angels happy?" Mike asked.

"The angels are ecstatic. We'll hit a hundred mil the first weekend, maybe one and a quarter, but we're thinking three or four or maybe even five hundred domestic before it's over, and who knows how much in foreign. By the time all the income streams are tapped out, the angels'll probably quadruple or quintuple their money."

"Isn't that great?" Mike said to Teri, who stood with an almost stoic countenance. Yeah, it was great, but she would be damned if she'd give Bob Keene any satisfaction.

"Teri, what can I say?" Bob said, beaming at her. "You were right, I was wrong."

"About what, specifically?" She knew what he meant, but she wasn't going to make it easy for him. On the other hand, it was a legitimate question. Bob had been wrong about a whole litany of things, so it seemed fair to ask him to narrow it down. Maybe it should even be a multiple-choice exam.

Bob dipped his head in a sort of bow. "I apologize for doubting you."

"I told you all I needed was the right script."

"If you'd also told us you needed a dead screenwriter, maybe we could have accommodated you sooner. I know a few who need killing."

That drew a brown-noser laugh from Mike, but barely a smile from Teri. The truth was, she was still troubled about taking advantage of tragedy to benefit herself. That might be the way of the Hollywood world, but it went sharply against the grain of her Texas upbringing. She had experienced tragedy in her own life, even been responsible for some of it, and she would be damned if she would ever sit still for someone to profit from her and her family's loss. Yet here she was profiting from Annemarie and Leland Crowell's misfortune.

"Is Annemarie Crowell here?" she asked. She had not seen Annemarie since she had delivered the script to Teri's house two years earlier.

"Are you kidding?" Bob said. "Why would that nutcase be here?"

"Because it's her son's script."

"It's your script," Mike said. "Her son gave it to you, and she's got no interest in it."

"Mike, we talked about this. She should be here for this. And for the premiere."

"We'll send her a DVD," Bob said.

If Bob actually did send her a DVD, it would be the only thing Annemarie would see from her son's work. She was a strange woman, creepy, in fact, but Teri felt she deserved something more than a token acknowledgement that the screenwriter had been her son. Teri had vowed to share her profit participation with Annemarie, though she had not yet told anyone. In fact, she would likely never tell anyone. Her plan was to handle the payments anonymously through her personal attorney to Annemarie via Spencer West, attorney-at-aw.

Bob nodded across the way at three well-dressed men huddled in a tight group. All relatively young—early to late 30s—all slick, all polished. One of them stood a head taller than the other two, his black hair slicked back Mike Capalletti-style, longish in back. His jaw was square, a three-days growth of beard worn for effect. And it worked, giving him an aura of calculated nonchalance. He was clearly the alpha dog of the pack. Nearby stood three women, dressed to the hilt, champagne glasses in hand, eyes glassy and star-struck as they pointed out celebrities and whispered excitedly among themselves. Wives.

"I don't think you ever met your angels, did you?" Bob asked. "The tall one is Doug Bozarth. He's the real angel. I think at least fifty of the seventy-five is his personal money."

"Maybe I'm his angel," Teri said.

"She's right, Bob," Mike said. "When the dust settles, those three rich dudes are going to be three filthy rich dudes."

"They're already filthy rich," Bob said. "But they'll be obscenely rich."

"What's the difference?" Mike asked.

"A decimal point or two."

"And it'll be a good payday for you, too," Teri said, "especially considering it all dropped right into your lap."

"Off a cliff and into your lap," Mike said. He and Bob laughed, caught up in the moment, but Teri stayed silent. Death wasn't funny to her.

The band launched into a reggae arrangement of a Lady Gaga number, the calypso sounding as if it belonged organically to the pop star's music. Teri grabbed Mike's arm and dragged him toward the dance floor.

"Come on, I want to dance," she said, as much to get away from Bob as anything.

"And dance you shall," Mike said. He handed his glass to Bob and followed her onto the dance floor.

Teri glanced over her shoulder at Bob as she and Mike moved off. He ignored her but raised his glass at the angels. Doug Bozarth raised his glass back to Bob in a silent salute, then turned to the dance floor where he locked gazes with Teri. After a brief moment, he smiled, but Teri thought it stopped well short of his eyes. She had seen smiles like that before, including one along the ropeline just moments earlier.

She looked away.

CHAPTER 13

LIMOUSINES STRETCHED FROM the front of the Beverly Hilton, down the street, and around the corner. Uniformed, and sometimes tuxedoed, chauffeurs stood beside their cars, some smoking, but all talking amongst themselves, no doubt regaling each other with tales of the absurd about the conduct of the rich and famous in the back seats of limos. Stories ranged from the overt sexual to illegal to flat-out gross. Celebrity and fortune had imbued many in Hollywood with the notion that rules of decency and courtesy simply didn't apply to them. The chauffeurs who drove them may have been silent while transporting their charges, but they weren't deaf and blind.

If anything, the crowd gathered along the rope lines had increased in size and sound, no doubt fueled by curiosity seekers who had joined their ranks and others who simply had nothing better to do with their time. The scraggly-haired man with the tattooed forearm hugged the rope, fighting to keep position in front. He had to occasionally push back with an elbow to force others away, but for the most part the crowd avoided contact with him. Although they pressed against each other, hips brushing hips, shoulders against shoulders, a small bubble seemed to have encompassed the man. Perhaps the ragged teeth and greasy hair sounded hygiene warnings that the others subconsciously heeded. Joining the adoring fans were scores of paparazzi, cameras at the ready, prepared at a moment's notice to catch smiles, frowns, and awkward short-skirted entries into vehicles.

A shout went out as the front door of the hotel opened and the first wave of celebrities began exiting. They came in small groups, usually two or three at a time, a few seconds apart, as if wanting to ensure that no one else intruded on their limelight as they walked to their waiting limos. The scraggly-haired man gripped the velvet rope with one hand. With the other, he clutched the Teri Squire glossy. He kept his eyes fixed on the front door, oblivious to the glitz and glamour that exited. As far as he was concerned, the beautiful people were a dime a dozen. Only one of them mattered to him.

And there she was, her boyfriend in tow, making her way toward the curb. She smiled, chatted with fans, and signed autographs while the boyfriend talked on his cell phone. The scraggly-haired man wondered if there was anyone on the other end of the call, or if it was all just for show. He had his money riding on the latter.

He strained against the rope, eager with anticipation as she drew closer. Although she was Hollywood royalty, albeit minor royalty these days, he had to admit there was a freshness, almost a wholesomeness, about her. The kind of innocence that was usually accompanied by naïveté, and which would play right into his hands She was ten feet away, now eight, now five—and now right in front of him. He thrust the picture toward her. As she took it, he saw her look at his forearm with the blue tattoo of a football helmet, a star inside the outline. She froze for a brief second, staring at it.

"Sign it 'To Leland, who gave his life for me. From Teri, with all my love,'" he said.

Something about the tattoo nagged at Teri. She knew the familiar Dallas Cowboys logo by heart—what Texan didn't?—but she tried to remember where she had heard about a tattoo like that.

Then the man spoke, and the name he used churned up a memory. Terror gripped her. She stared at his face, which looked remarkably like the one in the photo that Annemarie Crowell had shown her when she first brought over the screenplay.

But that was impossible! Leland Crowell was dead.

"I knew you'd like my script," the man said.

"It's my script," Teri replied, though she knew her words, which nearly choked off in her throat, were barely audible over the din of the crowd. And, she had to admit, there was no conviction behind them.

"Hmmm. Wonder if dear old mom actually probated my will. She's forgetful sometimes." He smiled then added, "And if I'm not really dead, does it matter?"

Teri felt strength drain from her legs, and she sagged, fighting to stay afoot. Mike grabbed her elbow and whispered into her ear. "You okay?"

Teri ignored him as she tried to give the photo back to the man, who pushed it into her hand. "Have your people call my people," he said. "We'll do lunch. *Ciao!*"

Then he disappeared into the crowd.

Almost in a daze, unblinking, mind not fully grasping what had just happened, Teri made her way to the limo with Mike's help. In her hand, she gripped the glossy photograph of herself. As she settled into the back seat, Mike clambered in beside her.

"What happened back there?" he asked. "Who was that guy?"

Teri shook her head. Mute, she turned and stared out the window.

Mike punched in a number on his cell phone. "Check out a guy on the rope line," he said. "Tall, thin, long hair. Looks like a homeless guy."

Teri looked at the headshot. It had been taken just prior to her first Oscar. It was wrinkled and worn along the edges, with what appeared to be a greasy thumbprint on the left side. Teri's stomach roiled at the thought of the greasy-haired man holding the photo with one hand.

She turned it over to see if there were additional finger stains on the back side. In small, neat handwriting, there was a single inscription: CRESCENT HOTEL 324.

Teri folded the picture and glanced at Mike. He was still on the phone, face pressed to the window, searching the crowd. He hadn't yet noticed the picture in her hand. She folded it and tucked it under the seat.

"No," she said.

"What?" he asked, pulling the phone away.

"It was nothing. Forget about it. Let's just go to the theater."

Mike put the phone back to his ear. "Find him." Then he hung up and looked at Teri.

She stared straight ahead.

There was a packed house for the movie, just what every actress wants. The audience seemed captivated by the action on the silver screen, collectively gasping at the right moments, tittering and giggling with relief at others, but hanging on every word spoken by the characters, drawn into a story of breathtaking suspense and psychological terror. Teri looked good up there, her face reflecting the same emotion as the audience, or maybe it was vice versa. No one in Teri's camp questioned that they had a *bona fide* hit on their hands. No, not just a hit; a blockbuster.

But Teri didn't seem to notice any of that. She couldn't even watch herself on the big screen. She had seen a rough cut on a smaller screen at the studio, but this was her first chance to watch the story play out on this big a scale. Yet her mind was elsewhere. She couldn't get the scraggly-haired man out of her mind. His thin face, his vacant eyes. Dead eyes. And that damned tattoo.

Other memories rushed back. The freakish Annemarie Crowell, her face pale, lips bright red, all made up as if for the circus. Eyes so dark they looked black. Emotionless. The grieving mother who didn't grieve. Sitting in Teri's den, talons clutching her dead son's screenplay as she subtly swayed, perched on the edge of a chair. The words that stung: "You're yesterday's news." Shoving that picture of her dead son in Teri's face.

Yeah, the dead son who looked remarkably similar to the man outside. And who shared his mother's dead eyes.

Just what in the hell was going on?

Teri turned and glanced at the row behind her, where her "angels" sat with their wives. Their attention was riveted to the screen, counting dollars in their heads, most likely. All, that is, but Doug Bozarth. His eyes locked with hers. She was suddenly struck by the deadness in those eyes, even in the darkened theater. Eyes that could have belonged to Annemarie Crowell or the man on the rope line.

Bozarth nodded his head ever so slightly. She couldn't be sure it had moved at all. She nodded back then turned to face the front.

"You okay?" Mike whispered.

"I'm fine." But she could tell he didn't believe her. Hell, she didn't even believe herself.

CHAPTER 14

THE CRESCENT HOTEL not only looked like a place that probably rented rooms by the hour, it actually *was* a place that rented rooms by the hour. A neon light alternately flashed green and purple, announcing vacancies, which was no surprise to any passersby. Two stories fanned east and west from the office, the façade a fading beige. Only a handful of cars dotted the parking area, the newest at least a decade old. A certain kind of person inhabited places like this. The kind of person you didn't want to meet on a dark street, and the kind of person you certainly didn't want to see in your respectable neighborhood or take home to meet mom and dad.

A checkered taxi pulled up in front of the office, sat for a moment, then disgorged that very kind of person. The scraggly-haired man slammed the door shut, then went to the stairs and ascended to the second floor landing, taking the stairs two at a time. At the far end of the landing from the office, he unlocked the door to Room 324 and went inside.

The man flipped a light switch just inside the door, which illuminated a dim lamp on a nightstand that perched on matchstick legs. The bed had not been made, likely for days, the threadbare bedspread in a pile on the floor and the sheets swirled into a tangled mess in the middle of the mattress. A non-matching nightstand on the other side of the bed held empty soda cans, a Styrofoam container of taco crumbs in which two roaches cavorted, and a cigarette lighter.

The most disturbing thing about the bed, though, sat perched on the side nearest the cockroach playground: Annemarie Crowell, with her painted face.

"How'd you get in?" he asked.

"Is it done?"

"Answer my question."

"Does it really matter how I got in?"

"It does to me."

She shrugged, and one corner of her mouth raised a fraction. "It'll just have to be one of life's little mysteries."

He walked to the dresser, just as mismatched as the rest of the furniture, extracted a thin wallet from his back pocket, and put it on top. He grabbed an open can of orange soda and took a swig.

"Is it done?" Annemarie asked again.

"I gotta tell you, it's weird coming back from the dead."

"Did she know who you were?"

"She knew."

"How can you be sure?"

"Trust me, she knew."

He set the can down and went into the tiny bathroom. Remnants of whiskers and shaving cream scum decorated the sink, although they were not nearly as eye-catching as were the orange streaks of rust. He stripped off his shirt, revealing a dangerously thin torso with ribs punched out against the skin. The kind of body prisoners-of-war often returned home with after months or years of incarceration—or drug addicts too strung out to eat.

Annemarie swiveled her head to watch him as he splashed water on his face and dried it with a towel he picked up from the floor. He looked at himself in the mirror, ran a hand through his hair as if it made a difference, then turned toward Annemarie.

"Just baited the trap. The little mousey will come for the

cheese soon enough."

"Good."

He turned back to the mirror and studied his reflection. Annemarie stood robotically then went to the bathroom. She entered and stood directly behind him, looking over his shoulder. In the mirror, it appeared to him as if he had two heads.

He turned the water on again and took a can of shaving cream from the medicine cabinet behind the mirror. As he lathered his face, Annemarie put her arms around him. Her hands caressed his chest, her fingers tangling in a thin nest of graying hair.

Against his will, his nipples sprang erect and his groin stirred. She slid one hand down across his stomach as she gripped a nipple with the fingernails of the other.

She squeezed the nipple, pinching hard with her nails. The other hand slipped inside the waistband of his pants and found the handle it sought.

She kissed him on the back of the neck, purred softly in his ear.

For a moment he stood still, his eyes closed. The pain in his nipple gave way to pleasure as her other hand moved up and down.

He opened his eyes and looked in the mirror. She stared at him, no pleasure on her face. Rather it was the look of a worker dutifully going about her chores.

"Enough," he said.

He grabbed her wrist at the waistband of his pants and pulled her hand out, then spun around and evaded her grip on his nipple.

Her lips curled again, ever so slightly. She held her fingers to her mouth and licked the tips of her fingernails.

"She'll be here soon," he said.

"Can you be sure?"

"I saw her face. She'll be here."

Annemarie turned and left the bathroom. As soon as she cleared the doorway, the man slammed the door shut. After a few seconds, he heard the sound of the outside door open and close.

He opened the bathroom door and looked out. Sure enough, she was gone.

He glanced down at his chest, where a line of blood trickled from his nipple. Further down, he saw the bulge at his crotch.

He spun and punched his fist into the mirror.

CHAPTER 15

TERI RODE SILENTLY in the passenger seat of Mike's Mercedes SUV, face pressed to the window, looking out at the world the same way she did when she was a little girl back in the Texas Hill Country. By all accounts, the premiere had been an overwhelming success. Bob was happy, and that meant Mike was happy. The angels were happy, and that meant the studio was happy. Everybody was happy except Teri. Oh, sure, she put on a good face, smiling at everybody, laughing at all the right lines, and accepting congratulations left and right, but the scraggly-haired man haunted her.

"You sure you're okay?" Mike asked. "You haven't said two words since the limo dropped us off back at the hotel."

"I'm fine. Just tired. It's been a long night."

"It was that guy on the rope line, wasn't it? What did he say to you?"

"It wasn't anything he said. It was just..."

"Just what?"

"He reminded me of somebody, that's all."

"Who?"

"I don't know."

Mike blew a puff of air through pursed lips. "You're not making a damn bit of sense. This should have been one of the biggest nights of your life—it's your comeback, for God's sake—

and you act like you've seen a ghost."

"Maybe I have."

"What?"

"Nothing. Like I said, I'm just tired."

Not another word was spoken until Mike pulled into the circular drive in front of Teri's house. He put the vehicle in park, then turned the key to shut off the engine.

"I'm going to bed," Teri said.

"I'll come in with you."

"Alone."

Mike looked at her, creases forming on his forehead as he scowled. "I don't get you. We should be celebrating."

"I know, I'm sorry. I just don't feel well."

He placed his hand on her cheek, but she pushed it away. "Please, Mike."

"All right, fine." He started the car and looked straight ahead.

"Please don't be mad."

"I'm not mad."

She leaned over and kissed him on the cheek. He made no move away from her, but he kept staring out the front windshield.

She opened the door to get out then looked back at him one more time. "What if something goes wrong with the movie?"

That got his attention. He looked at her, eyebrows raised. "Like what?"

"I don't know. Just something."

"Is that what this is all about? Fear of success?"

"You've got a lot riding on this, don't you? You and Bob, both."

"A lot of people do."

"So what happens if it all goes bad?"

"Now you're just being crazy. You saw everyone tonight. A hundred million the first week; I guarantee it. Even if it tanks after that—and I'm not saying it will, but if it does—it's still a home run. Nothing can go wrong. We can't lose. You can't lose."

She nodded at the words, which all made sense in her head, yet at the same time didn't make sense in her heart, where she knew something, indeed, could go wrong. And she worried that she was about to find out what.

The night crew at Hollywood Luxury Cars and Limos had its work cut out for it. The limousines had returned from the premiere of Teri Square's comeback movie *The Precipice* and, by all accounts, everyone had had a good time. Washing and waxing the exteriors of the cars wasn't nearly as demanding a chore as cleaning the interiors, which were stained by everything from alcohol to seminal fluid. As Pablo Hernandez went to the next car in line, all he could think about was how money can buy just about anything except class.

He opened the front passenger door and quickly wiped down the dashboard. He glanced over toward the back seat, ready to be repulsed at what he might find but saw that it was remarkably clean. He slipped out of the front, opened the back door, and crawled inside. The dome-light illuminated black leather, which appeared spotless. Either this limo had gone unused or it carried AA members or married couples. Not a single spot of alcohol or splash of bodily fluids to be found. A sober, chaste evening was had by the passengers.

Pablo took a clean cloth from his back pocket, sprayed it with a leather care product, and began wiping the seats. As he leaned across to the far side, he saw the corner of something sticking out from beneath the seat. He pulled it out and found it to be a folded headshot of the famous actress Teri Squire. He admired her picture. She was beautiful.

But the greasy fingerprints on the glossy photo seemed out of place. Whoever had put them there had not been in this car, because there were no such greasy prints anywhere on the seats or windows.

He turned the photo over and saw something scrawled in an uneven handwriting: CRESCENT HOTEL 324.

Strange. Very strange, indeed.

He backed out of the car and headed for his supervisor's office.

CHAPTER 16

SLEEP WOULDN'T COME to Teri. The scraggly-haired man haunted her every time she closed her eyes. At last, at nearly two a.m., she got up and turned on her laptop then connected to the Internet. A few minutes later, she had directions to the Crescent Hotel. Dressing hastily in jeans, tee-shirt, running shoes without socks, and a green "University of Hawaii Rainbows" baseball cap from her most recent trip to the islands, she grabbed her purse and left the bedroom. She stopped in the den just long enough to transfer her .22 from the coffee table to the purse then she went to the garage, started her SUV, and backed out.

Twenty minutes later she found herself trolling parts of Los Angeles that she had heard about only in news reports, usually involving stories of murder, mayhem, and gang violence. Storefronts were gated and barred, topped off with gargantuan padlocks. The rare buildings unmarked by graffiti stood out, conspicuous by the absence of street artwork, just as her SUV was conspicuous by its newness. Even at the late hour, gangbangers, mostly Hispanic, milled about on street corners and greedily eyed her vehicle as it passed. Fortunately the windows were tinted or they would have been able to see a lone, terrified Anglo woman behind the wheel. That would have been like ringing a bell for Pavlov's dogs.

Up ahead, a "vacancy" light flashed in purple and green, beneath a larger sign that proclaimed "Crescent Hotel," along with a sliver of a moon outlined in fluorescent paint. The light in the office was on. As she turned in, she looked through the glass doors at a man who appeared to be either asleep or dead at the front desk, facedown on the counter. She hoped it was the former.

Barely idling, she drove along one wing of the hotel, scanning the doors for numbers. Just as she neared the end of the building, she spotted 324 upstairs. Lights were on behind thin curtains. The fabric pushed back and a man looked out. Waiting. Watching. She couldn't tell much about the man's features in the darkness, but she knew it was the scraggly-haired man. And she knew the scraggly-haired man knew it was her. She wondered how many times he had looked out tonight before she arrived.

There were no stairs at this end, so she circled about and headed back toward the office, where she parked her SUV at the foot of a flimsy steel staircase. She locked the doors but kept the keys gripped tightly in one hand. In the other, she carried her purse by gripping the outline of the .22 inside, finger pressed against the trigger guard. The material was flimsy enough that she would be able to fire the weapon without even removing it from her purse.

At the top of the stairs, she turned slowly and approached the room at the end. The door opened before she reached it. She closed the last few feet then stood in the doorway and looked inside. The scraggly-haired man stood by the bed, shirtless, but at least wearing pants. She glanced at his forearm at the football helmet tattoo. It appeared a little smeared, but that fact didn't register.

"Well, well, well," he said. "If it isn't my favorite beneficiary." He bowed and gestured in a grand sweeping motion for her to enter. "Welcome to my humble abode."

He sat on the end of the bed, expectantly. Teri stepped inside, purse and keys still tightly clutched in her hands.

"Close the door," he said.

"I think I'll leave it open."

"Well, that's really not very safe. Not in this neighborhood. I'd hate for something to happen to you just because some pervert saw a beautiful woman like you standing in the open doorway to a hotel room."

Good point. Teri cut a look outside to the street below. She closed the door but stood with her back pressed against it.

The man reclined on the bed, propped on one elbow. His eyes scanned her from head to toe and back again, lingering on both passes at her breasts and her crotch. He was obviously having fun toying with her.

"You ever talked to a dead man before?" he asked.

"What do you want?"

"Well, for starters, I want to know if you've ever talked to a dead man before."

"You're not dead."

"Not now. But I was. My mother even has the death certificate to prove it."

"It won't be the first time a death certificate was wrong."

He laughed. "No, I suppose it won't. But past mistakes will pale in comparison to this one."

"Whose body was that they fished off the rocks?"

"Why, didn't you hear? That was me. Leland Crowell."

"Maybe it wasn't. Or maybe you're not."

"Didn't Mom show you my picture?"

"Pictures don't mean anything."

He pointed at the dresser on the far wall. "My wallet's right there."

She glanced at it but remained frozen to the door. The last thing she wanted to do was move any farther into this snake den.

"Go ahead," he said. "It won't bite."

Teri tucked her keys into her pocket, then hustled over, grabbed the wallet, and returned to the door. Awkwardly, using one hand since the other still clutched her purse, she flipped the wallet open. Sure enough, the scraggly-man's unsmiling face stared at her from a California driver's license, which bore the name: Leland J. Crowell.

"J for Joseph," he said.

"Again, doesn't prove anything."

"Boy, you're a tough nut." He leaned his head back, as if deep in thought. Then he rolled across the bed and grabbed an olive green backpack on the floor next to the nightstand on the far side. In one motion, he swung it upward and tossed it toward Teri. It landed at her feet with a soft thud.

"Feel free to look in my filing cabinet," he said. "You'll have to forgive my filing system, though. I'll admit it's not very organized."

Teri bent at the knees, laid the wallet on the floor, and opened the backpack. She reached in and pulled out a stack of paper clipped together at the top. A screenplay: *The Precipice*. She dropped the screenplay on the floor and two pages fluttered loose. She picked them up one at a time and looked at them. One was a certificate of registration for the screenplay with the Writers Guild of America. The other was a certificate of registration from the United States Copyright Office.

She looked from the copyright document to the man on the bed. "You can ask your lawyers, but I think that does prove something," he said. "In fact, it'll be all I need when I walk into court to get an injunction to stop the release of your movie."

"It doesn't prove you're Leland Crowell."

"You got any proof I'm not?"

Teri stood silently, pondering how best to answer that question. In fact, pondering if she had any answer at all.

"Then I believe we're at a stalemate" he said. "Or maybe we're not. I'm not a lawyer, but I don't think it's gonna be my job to prove I'm me; it's gonna be your job to prove I'm not. And who's a judge going to believe is best suited to say who Leland Crowell is? Me, the California Department of Motor Vehicles, and dear ol' Mom? Or you?"

Teri remained mute. She had no good answer to that question, either. Damn if he didn't ask some good ones.

"What's the matter? Cat got your tongue?" he asked.

Still nothing in response. After all, what could she say?

"Yeah, that's what I thought," he said. "Then again, maybe we can work something out."

So that's what this is all about, she thought. Money. Isn't it always?

"How much do you want?" she asked.

"Who says it's about money?" It was as if he had read her mind. "Maybe I want my fifteen minutes of fame. Or maybe I want a screenwriting career. Or—"

"I can give you that. Under a different name, though. I have a new studio deal, and I can use the writer of my choice."

He smiled, showing brown teeth. "Or maybe you were right all along. Maybe it is money I want." He gestured around at the room. "Maybe I want a nicer place to live. I could use an upgrade, don't you think?"

He sat back up, perched on the edge of the bed. "Or maybe it's all of the above. The options are limitless, and I'm in the catbird seat."

"Cut the bullshit and just tell me what you want."

He stood. She hadn't realized how tall he was until he did. She certainly hadn't noticed it at the theater.

He moved forward a few steps, until he was a mere arm's length away. Something on his chest caught her eye for the first time. A tiny rivulet of dried blood tracked down from his left nipple. As she looked at it, something below his waist brought her glance downward, but her eyes immediately bounced back to his face, repulsed by the bulge in his jeans.

"This is kind of romantic, don't you think?" he asked. "You and me, alone in a hotel room. I've never had a movie star before."

"And you're not going to start now."

He reached forward and ran his hand through the hair on the side of her head. "Are you sure?"

She pulled the .22 from her purse and pressed the barrel against his solar plexus. "You've got three seconds to tell me what you want or I'm leaving."

He backed up then looked down at the small red circle the gun barrel left on his chest. "Now look what you've done."

"Two seconds."

"Why would someone like you have a gun?"

"I'm from Texas; it's a birthright. One second."

He backed away farther and sat on the edge of the bed again. "You've got quite a dilemma, don't you? You're about to open a movie that was made from a screenplay you don't own. My screenplay."

"You willed it to me."

"So now I am Leland, huh?"

"If you say so. And you willed it to me."

"But I'm not dead. You don't get it unless I die."

She waved the gun at him then aimed at his face. "Easily enough done."

For a moment, she thought she'd broken him. She thought she could smell fear emanate from him. Until he laughed at her.

"Priceless," he said. "Just priceless. You almost had me going there."

"What makes you think I won't shoot?"

"Let's see. What makes me think you won't shoot an unarmed man in cold blood? How about because you also don't get the bequest if you kill me."

"Who's gonna know it was me?"

84

"You know, there's a solution to this whole thing. For both of us. I keep on letting people think I'm dead and—"

"How much do you want?"

"I want a cut."

"How much?

"Fifty percent." He paused, then added, "Of the gross."

Teri was stunned. Was he kidding? Or merely negotiating? "You're crazy."

"And you're a thief. You stole my screenplay. So we're right back to my injunction."

"A judge will never let you get away with this."

"I'm willing to risk it. What have I got to lose? But how about you?"

Teri lowered the gun. She had blinked first, and he knew it.

"Fifty percent," he said. "You've got twenty-four hours to decide. After that, I go to the courthouse."

"Do I get in touch with you here?"

"How about I get in touch with you? I may be moving soon."

He smiled, and she looked away. She stuck the gun back in her purse, opened the door, and bolted outside into the fresh air.

Panic overtook her as she raced along the landing to the stairs. She had her head down, trying to concentrate on the concrete stairs lest she miss one through the blurring of tears forming in her eyes. She didn't see the black Mercedes SUV pull into the space by her Highlander, nor did she see the tall man in blue jeans and tennis shoes get out and quietly ascend the stairs to meet her.

It was only when she nearly plowed right into him that she looked up. She immediately burst into tears.

Mike wrapped her in his arms and pulled her to his chest.

CHAPTER 17

MIKE AND TERI sat in a corner booth at a well-lit Denny's restaurant on Wilshire Boulevard, where Mike nursed his coffee but Teri speared pancakes from her Grand Slam and ate with gusto, hoping to bury fear with food. She was also in no mood for Mike's lecture, which had continued unabated via cell phone as they drove their respective vehicles back to civilization from the desperate neighborhood inhabited by the likes of Leland Crowell—if, indeed, that was who he was.

"I still can't get over it," Mike said.

"So I gathered."

"What were you thinking?"

"Look, Mike, you can keep asking the same question over and over again, but the answer won't change. I had to find out what he wanted. I *had* to. That's what the hell I was thinking."

"That doesn't mean you go to war zone areas of this God-forsaken city by yourself in the middle of the night. And you damn sure don't go into hotel rooms with strange men by yourself. Who knows what might have happened!"

"What the hell were you thinking?"

The voice belonged to Bob Keene, who trudged across the restaurant toward them. Even with a golf shirt thrown over sharply creased jeans and deck shoes, he looked slick, with every hair in place. Even his stubble of beard seemed calculated to scream "casual." Mike slid over as Bob sat next to him.

"I've already asked her that," Mike said.

"Five times," Teri added. "And the answer was the same all five."

"Well, I haven't heard it, so what was it?"

"I saw that tattoo on his forearm, and it triggered something in my memory. I had to find out who he was."

"And it was Crowell?" Bob asked.

"I have no idea. Remember, I never met Leland Crowell in my life. But he said he was. And he looked like that picture his mother showed me. And I remember he was supposed to have had a tattoo like that."

A waitress appeared and Bob ordered coffee, then sent her on her way. "So it was Crowell."

"Damn it, Bob, the answers to your questions don't change either just because you ask them again. I'll say it real slow for you: I don't know if it was him."

"But it could be him."

"Of course it could be. And could just as easily be someone else."

"It really doesn't matter if it's him or not. If he's got a copyright certificate and we can't prove he's not, he wins."

"We can trump that if we've got an order from a probate court giving the script to Teri," Mike said. "Dead or alive, if the court—"

"Is that really the law?" Bob asked. "Or is that just wishful thinking?"

"Look, if there's a court order—"

"I don't know if there is one," Teri said.

The reappearance of the waitress with Bob's coffee was all that stopped him from exploding. After she left, he leaned across the table, red-faced.

"What the hell are you talking about? Are you saying there's no probate order?"

"I'm saying I don't have one, and I've never seen one."

"Surely you at least had a copyright assignment. Something—anything that makes it yours legally."

"Just a lawyer who said Crowell willed it to me, and a mother who showed up at my house and gave it to me. You're the one who had the lawyers working on all this, clearing the chain of title. I just assumed they'd cleared everything. Isn't there a clearance letter for the E and O carrier?"

"There has to be," Bob said. "No way the studio would release the movie without it."

"So send the lawyers back in there to look at everything. I'm not saying there's no probate order; I'm just saying I've never seen it if there is."

"I think we're overlooking the obvious here," Mike said. He pushed his cold coffee away and rubbed his eyes. "If the guy's not dead, does it really matter if we've got a probate order or not?"

"That's what I was just saying a while ago," Bob said. "Now you act like it was your idea all along. But surely an order has to mean something, at least for chain of title."

A sound at the front entrance drew their attention that way. The hostess pointed them out to Doug Bozarth, who had just entered. Like Bob, his appearance was slick, dressed in business casual. Unlike Bob, he had bothered to shave before arriving.

He pulled a chair up from a nearby table and sat between Bob and Teri, who occupied the ends of the benches on their respective sides of the booth.

"I understand we have a problem," Bozarth said.

"Nothing we can't handle," Mike said.

Bozarth stood. "Good. Just let me know what the plan is so I can go back to bed."

Silence from everybody.

"That's what I thought." Bozarth sat back down. "Okay, let's start over. I understand we have a problem."

"We were just wondering, if the guy's not dead, whether he has a legal claim on the script," Mike said. "I don't know a lot of probate law, but I don't think you can inherit something if the guy you inherited it from didn't die."

"We can win that lawsuit," Bob said. "No court's gonna let this guy fake his death then suddenly pop up and grab his script back."

"That misses the point," Bozarth said. "I don't give a rat's ass about winning a lawsuit. I care about not getting sued. My people have got seventy-five million dollars tied up in this movie, and I'll be damned if I'm going to let Lazarus screw that up."

"I'm betting the publicity'll drive the box office even higher," Mike said.

"That's only if we get to release it. But if this guy gets an injunction, we've got a real problem. And, long shot or not, what if he wins? What then?"

"If he wins, he gets a cut," Mike said. "How is that any worse than paying him off now?"

"The last thing we need is the finances under a microscope on this deal," Bob said.

Teri perked up at that. For a while, she felt as if she didn't belong in the conversation, but now her antennae quivered. "Why? Where did the money come from?"

"You waived your right to ask that when you dragged everyone into a movie you don't have the rights to," Bob said.

"I have the rights," Teri snapped.

"Do you really?" Bob asked.

Teri felt the heat rise and knew that her face had turned sunburn red. "You didn't seem to have any problem with rights when people were throwing money at us, Bob. People like Mr. Bozarth, here." She turned to focus on Bozarth. Her voice rose an octave as fear and outrage waged a war within her psyche. "You came to us, Mr. Bozarth, remember? The way I understand it, you were begging us to take your money. And maybe this is a question I should have asked a long time ago, but where did that money come from?"

In contrast to Teri's agitation, Bozarth's voice was calm. Almost unnaturally so. "It's too early to worry about that right now. If we can head this off—"

"I think right now is a helluva good time to worry about it."

"If we can head this off, it'll be a non-issue, and we'll all be happy. We've got two things to do for starters. First is to find out where the rights to the script are, legally. I'll get my lawyers working on that. The second thing is to find out what'll it take to make this guy go away."

"And we've got to find out who he is," Mike said.

"If we can make him go away, it doesn't matter who he is."

"How can you make sure he goes away?" Mike asked.

"Leave that to me," Bozarth said. "Teri, how'd you get the script in the first place?"

"His lawyer called me about it after Leland Crowell died. Then Leland's mother brought it to my house."

"Who was the lawyer?"

"Spencer West, attorney-at-aw."

"What?"

"Nothing."

"Go see him tomorrow. See what you can find out about the probate. Go see the mother, too. We need to know if they're all in this together with the undead."

"She's a little creepy for my taste."

"Any creepier than the dead writer coming back to life?" Bob asked.

"Doesn't matter," Bozarth said. "Talk to her anyway. Then make contact with Crowell."

"Or whoever he is," Mike said.

"For now, let's assume he is who he says he is," Bozarth said.

"We can't afford to underestimate him or make any miscalculations. There's too much at stake."

"I agree," Mike said. "But there's no way we can give this guy what he wants."

"What does he want?" Bozarth asked.

"He said he wants fifty percent of the gross."

Bob dropped his head on the table with a loud *thunk*. It had the desired dramatic effect of drawing everyone's attention his way. "That could be over a hundred million," he said. "If this thing hits, it could be hundreds of millions."

"He knows it's ridiculous," Bozarth said. "He's just negotiating."

"How do you know?" Bob asked. "This guy doesn't know anything about the business. He doesn't know what costs are involved and how profits get split up. He probably doesn't know gross from net from his ass from a hole in the ground. For all we know, when he says fifty percent, he means fifty of the box office. First dollars."

"People like this are always negotiating," Bozarth said. "You just said it, Bob, he has no idea how the business works. I doubt if he even understands what fifty percent of the gross means or how much it could be. He's fishing for a number, so we'll give him one."

By now, Teri realized the truth of what Bozarth was saying. This man, whether he was really Leland Crowell or not, had just enough knowledge to be dangerous. He knew he could claim ownership of the script and cause a few heart palpitations, maybe milk a dollar or two out of the producers, but he had no idea of the real value of what he was doing.

"I think Mr. Bozarth is right," she said. "From what I've seen of this guy, he wants money now. He *needs* money now. He's not going to wait for the back end, even if we promised it to him."

"How do we know that?" Mike asked. "And what happens if

we give him money now, then he shows up again on the back end."

"He won't." Bozarth said the words with a surety that sent a shiver coursing through Teri's spine.

"How do you know he won't?" Mike asked.

"It's my business to know."

"You mean it's your business to make sure," Teri said.

"Take it however you want," Bozarth said.

He met her eyes evenly. She searched his face for signs of humanity, but found none. Just a blankness that would make any poker player proud. And in that instant she knew, without knowing, that Leland Crowell, or whoever the scraggly-haired man was, was living on borrowed time.

"Teri, do you think you can do all that?" Bozarth asked. "Talk to the mother and the attorney and then—"

"Just because I'm an actor doesn't mean I'm stupid," she said.

"Of course not." But his tone said the opposite. Unspoken was the rebuke that she was the reason they were in this mess in the first place. How smart did that make her?

Bozarth scooted his chair back and stood. "Well, I think that's all we can do for right now." He pulled a business card from his shirt pocket and handed it to Teri. "Call me after you've talked to the lawyer and the mother. Then we'll decide how to handle the writer."

"Are you sure you haven't already decided?" Teri asked.

Bozarth smirked, the only emotion he had shown all night, then turned and left.

The others waited until Bozarth was out the door then Bob turned to Teri, barely able to suppress his anger. "You remember that apology I gave you? Well, I take it back."

With that, he abruptly lurched to his feet and stormed off.

CHAPTER 18

MIKE WALKED TERI out to her car, which was parked next to his in the parking lot. He put his arm around her waist and pulled her close, but she felt no warmth from the closeness. All she felt was the chill that Doug Bozarth's words, both spoken and unspoken, left in her heart. The truth was that, when she first realized the implications of Leland Crowell's resurrection, her next thought was how much better off she would be if he were dead. Then, when she pulled the .22 from her purse and aimed it at him, thoughts of pulling the trigger tickled her consciousness. No one knew she was there—or so she had thought at the time. And surely no one would actually *believe* she had been there. What would Teri Squire be doing in a squalid hotel room in that part of town?

Yes, it would have been easy enough to dispatch the man back to the great beyond from whence he had apparently returned. She could have taken the screenplay and its registration documents, slipped his drivers license into her pocket, and no one would have been the wiser. It would be quite unlikely that the man could even be identified. After all, he was already dead, and had been for two years. How can you kill a dead man?

But as soon as those thoughts entered her mind, she banished them. Killing a man eroded one's soul, no matter how pure the motive might be. That was more than esoteric bullshit. Teri knew it *for a fact*. And she also knew that money—and surely that was

what this was all about—was never a pure motive. Yet that was
Doug Bozarth's motive. He hadn't actually said he was bent on
killing Leland Crowell, but everyone at the table knew that was
what he meant.

The question that nagged at her was whether it was just talk,
or whether Bozarth was actually capable of killing a man over
money. The answer should have been obvious. Every day,
newspapers carried stories of people who killed over Dallas
Cowboys jackets, basketball shoes, and even parking spaces. Doug
Bozarth had seventy-five million dollars on the line, and that was
motive in anyone's book. If he carried out his promise to "know"
that Crowell would not show up on the back end with his hand
out, could she live with that? Or did she have an obligation to stop
him? And if so, how? She couldn't very well go to the police and
tell them that Bozarth had indirectly threatened—very indirectly;
so indirectly, in fact, that it took considerable interpretation in
her overactive mind to reach that conclusion—to kill a man who
was already dead. They would laugh her out of the police station,
lumping her in with other Hollywood crazies and their insane
rantings.

Mike must have sensed her thoughts. "He's not going to kill
anybody," he said.

"I know *he's* not going to, but that doesn't mean he won't
have it done."

Mike turned her around to face him, but she refused to make
eye contact. "Look at me," he said. "Teri, look at me."

When her gaze finally settled on him, he continued. "He's a
businessman. He travels in circles we can only read about, but
they're still business circles. He's not a killer."

"How do you know?"

"Because I just know."

Again, with the "knowing."

"That's not good enough."

"Look, our lawyers vetted him. Remember, we've got to comply with the Patriot Act, so we've got to know where the money comes from, especially foreign money. Everything passed muster."

"So where did the money come from?"

"I didn't say *I* knew. Like I said, the lawyers vetted him, and they say everything's aboveboard."

"Are these the same lawyers who vetted the chain of title on the script?"

"Look, don't make waves on this," Mike said. "Let's just do what he says. It's a business decision for him. He'll figure out how much to pay to make this guy go away, and that'll be the end of it. He'll consider it just part of his investment. Hell, he'll probably even write it off on his income tax. Don't read anything more into it than that."

She looked at him for a good fifteen seconds, debating how to respond. At last she chose acquiescence—at least on the surface. "I guess you're right. I'm tired, and I'm still a little scared, that's all."

"What you need to do is go home and go to bed. Your mind will be clearer tomorrow."

She unlocked her car with the remote, and he opened the door for her. She slid in behind the wheel and started the engine.

"You want me to come home with you?" he asked.

"Like you said, I need sleep."

"All right." He leaned in and kissed her lightly on the lips. "Sleep good. Call me tomorrow when you get up."

Two hours later, Teri was still wide awake, sitting cross-legged on the bed, hunched over her laptop. All her research had turned up a big zero. Although she considered herself an expert at Internet research, Douglas Bozarth remained as big a mystery as when she started. He had made money in real estate development in

Colorado then parlayed that into oil and gas, building up an oil exploration company that had international contracts in the middle east. He sold the company for over a billion dollars, earning him a place on the *Forbes* list of richest Americans. Since then, it looked like he had just played with his money and his contacts, putting together investment groups in various ventures, home and abroad, including this virgin foray into the movie business. But other than generic, publicist-blessed releases and stories, she could find virtually nothing about his personal life.

The good news, though, was the absence of certain kinds of stories: no arrests and convictions, no SEC investigations, no sex scandals, no bankruptcies—and no murders. Ultimately Teri determined that, in this case, no information was good information. Either he was a good, clean upstanding businessman or he was very discreet, or both.

She looked at the clock on her computer screen. Nearly four a.m. Not entirely satisfied, but too tired to continue, she shut down the computer and set it aside, turned off the light, and crawled beneath the sheets. Five minutes later, she was asleep.

A thin man slumped in a leather chair in the middle of a U-shaped computer table. Monitors faced him from all three sides. He stared intently at the monitor directly in front of him, then picked up his cell phone and hit a number on speed dial. After four rings, a male voice answered.

"Learn anything?"

"Internet research. Lots of Internet research."

"What was she looking for?"

"Lots of searches, but all of them had the same two words. Douglas and Bozarth."

"She find anything?"

"Nothing she was looking for."

"Let me know if she ever does."

* * *

It seemed as if Teri had barely closed her eyes when an unending buzzing sound filled her ears. At first she thought it was a dream, then the alarm. After knocking the clock to the floor, but with no success at stopping the sound, she realized it was the door buzzer. She was going to have to replace that with a kinder, gentler ring tone.

She sat on the edge of the bed and rubbed her eyes. At the same moment, the *Magnum, P.I.* theme music blared from her cell phone. She snatched it up and looked at the read-out. The first thing that struck her was the notice that she had four missed calls. How had she slept through those?

Then she focused on Mona's name as the caller. She accepted the call and held the phone to her ear. "Hello?"

"So you're still alive."

"Just barely."

"I've been ringing your doorbell for five minutes."

"Well stop it, damn it."

"Then let me in."

"Give me a minute."

Cell phone in hand, Teri staggered to the front door and opened it to greet her producing partner. Mona brushed past her and on to the kitchen. Teri followed meekly. As Mona set about making coffee, Teri sat at the kitchen table and held her head in her hands.

"What the hell were you thinking?" Mona asked.

"That seems to be the consensus."

Mona spun around, her brow knit, her lips pursed. "I'm serious. When Mike told me you went to that hotel room at night, all alone, I couldn't believe it. Who knows what could have happened."

"The fact that I'm sitting here, listening to you lecture me, is proof that nothing did."

"That's not the point."

"I know, I know." Teri shrugged. "But I can't change it now, so let's move on."

They waited silently for the coffee to brew then, when they had filled their cups, they adjourned to the deck, where a smoky haze hung in the air.

"How bad is it?" Mona asked.

"I don't know."

"But bad?"

"Maybe. I don't know."

"What do you think this guy's gonna do?"

"I'm more worried about what we're gonna do."

Mona sipped her coffee and appraised her friend. "You look tired."

"I didn't get much sleep last night. And I've got a busy day ahead of me."

"That's what Mike said. I want to go with you."

Teri shook her head. "I need you doing something else for me."

"Name it."

"Find out everything you can about Leland Crowell and his will. Was there anything strange about the probate? Was there an order that allowed me to take the script? I need to know everything, and I don't trust the lawyers to do it."

"Okay."

"And I need to know as much as I can about Doug Bozarth and his money. I want to know where it came from. And I want to know what he's capable of."

"What does that mean?"

"It's just a hunch, but I think that we may end up having more to worry about from him than we do from Leland Crowell."

Mona stopped in mid-sip. "What are you talking about?"

"That's what I need you to find out."

Then Teri got up and went inside, leaving Mona slack-faced on the deck.

CHAPTER 19

THE NEIGHBORHOOD WHERE Spencer West, attorney-at-aw had maintained his home office had not changed in the two years since Teri's first and only visit there. She pulled up in front of the house and killed the engine on her SUV. She checked herself in the rearview mirror. With her hair pulled back in a ponytail, wearing faded jeans and a golf shirt, a Texas Rangers baseball cap, and sunglasses, she thought herself passably disguised.

As she approached the front porch, the first thing she noticed was the absence of West's "shingle" out front, pathetic though it had been. She had not heard from him since that prior meeting, so she had no way of knowing if he had moved or simply shut down his practice. She pushed the doorbell, but heard no sound inside. She knocked on the door, her knuckles causing the flimsy wood to wobble with each rap. After a moment, she heard shuffling sounds from inside, then the thin curtain over the window in the door moved aside. A few seconds later, the door cracked open about ten inches and an elderly Hispanic woman peered out, her eyes wide behind thick glasses lenses.

"Can I help you?" the woman asked, in perfect, unaccented English.

"I'm looking for Mr. West."

"There's nobody here by that name."

"Is this no longer his office?"

The door opened wider, to reveal a diminutive woman, no more than five feet tall, wearing a threadbare flowered housecoat. Her hair was shoe polish black, though surely she was approaching her eighties.

"You looking for the lawyer?" she asked.

"Yes, Spencer West."

"He's dead."

"Dead?"

"They say he killed himself," the woman said. "I don't know for sure. I just know he died in here."

"How long ago did this happen?"

"Oh, two years ago, maybe." The woman pulled her glasses down on her nose and peered over them at Teri. "Do I know you?"

"No, I don't think so."

"Sure I do. You're that actress."

"I get that a lot, but no, I just look like her."

"No, you're her. I know."

Teri backed away and down the steps. "I'm sorry to have bothered you, ma'am."

She turned and headed for her car as the woman stepped outside onto the porch. "You're the one that writer killed himself over. Did the lawyer kill himself over you, too?"

Teri got in the SUV and locked the door. She squeezed the steering wheel with both hands and leaned her head back. "Lady," she said softly, "that's starting to look like a really good question."

"I've got a new research assignment for you," Teri said.

On the other end of the call, Mona answered, "I guess I've got nothing better to do."

Teri slowed and peered at a street sign. The letters were obscured by rust and spray paint, the name of the street barely discernible. She turned left.

"Find out what happened to Spencer West, Leland Crowell's attorney. He died a couple of years ago. Might have been suicide."

"What difference does it make?"

"Because if he was part of a scam, or even if he wasn't, but found out about it and ended up dead under mysterious circumstances, then that tells us something."

"Tells us what?"

Teri saw a crumbling apartment complex ahead on her left, with a sign out front that proclaimed it the "Paradise Arms." She figured that, even in its heyday, the name must have been some kind of inside joke.

"For one thing, it tells us if this is more than just a scam. If this thing is going to get dangerous, I'd like to know."

"Don't you think you're being a little melodramatic?"

"What you find will tell us whether I am or not."

She pulled in to the Paradise Arms parking lot and stopped in front of the staircase. It all seemed eerily reminiscent of last night's visit to the Crescent Hotel. Apparently rundown structures in bad parts of town had a limited number of building plans to choose from. She climbed the stairs and went to the apartment number she had been given by Bozarth's office, but no one was home. Back downstairs, she located the management office, opened the door, and went inside.

To call it an office was to be kind. It was actually a darkened studio apartment that doubled as the residence of the complex manager, a rail thin black man who sat at a card table, eating cereal and watching a tiny television. Behind him was a filing cabinet, and next to it a sofa bed, opened and unmade, which rounded out the furnishings.

The manager looked up in surprise when Teri entered. "Don't you knock?" he asked.

"I'm sorry. I thought this was the office." She took off her sunglasses and allowed her eyes to adjust to the dim light.

"It's also my home."

"You might want to put a 'please knock' sign outside."

"Yeah, I'll do that," he said, obviously with no intention of doing so. His eyes narrowed, then widened in recognition. "Hey, I know you."

Two for two; so much for thinking she had adequately disguised herself.

"I'm looking for one of your tenants. Annemarie Crowell in apartment—"

"She moved out yesterday." He turned in this chair and shuffled through a haphazard stack of papers and envelopes on the floor beside him. "But she said you'd come looking for her. I thought she was lying, but damned if you aren't here."

He grasped a legal-sized envelope from the stack, turned, and handed it to Teri. "She said to give this to you," he said.

Teri took it and looked at the careful handwriting on the outside, the name PEGGY TUCKER in all capital letters. She flinched just briefly at the name, but quickly recovered.

"Who's Peggy Tucker?" the manager asked.

"I don't know."

He grabbed a notepad from the floor, along with a pen, and thrust it at Teri. "Can I get your autograph?"

"No."

"Just say 'To Rondell, my biggest fan.'"

Teri put on her sunglasses, turned, and left with the envelope in hand. As she closed the door behind her, she barely heard Rondell's last words: "Sorry to bother you, your royal highness white bitch."

Teri ran to her car, gasping for breath. It seemed as if every inhale she took was a desperate struggle for life. A vise gripped her chest, and a deep freeze settled into her soul. She jumped in the car and slammed the door.

"Easy, easy," she said to herself. A few deep breaths, blowing air out through pursed lips, and she felt her heart rate slow. Not yet back to normal, but getting there. She stared at the name on the envelope. *Peggy Tucker.* Peggy had been dead and buried for nearly twenty years. How did Annemarie Crowell know about her? What the hell was going on?

With trembling fingers, Teri tore open the envelope. Inside was a single sheet of yellow paper from a legal pad. In the same handwriting as the name on the outside were the words: CALEB'S DINER—MIDNIGHT.

She crumpled the page into a tiny wad in her right fist and threw it over her shoulder into the back seat.

She gasped for breath again.

CHAPTER 20

THE SAME GROUP that had met at Denny's after Teri's encounter with Leland Crowell had reassembled, this time at Doug Bozarth's Malibu home, perched above the beach overlooking the ocean. Mike seemed almost giddy when he explained to Teri that this was Bozarth's "beach house," complementing his three acre estate in Brentwood, his mountain resort in Vail, and his four-thousand-square-foot vacation home on Anini Beach, on the north shore of Kauai. And, oh, yes, there was also that small island he owned in the Caribbean and the villa overlooking the Mediterranean in Italy. Not yet forty years of age, and Doug Bozarth had done quite well for himself.

Although Teri had never been overly impressed with the accumulation of wealth and assets, Mike made no secret of his own aspirations in that regard. He relished his newfound association with Bozarth and his ilk, to the point, Teri thought, of shutting down his mind and stifling any inclination to ruin a good thing by even considering the possibility that matters were not as they should be with Bozarth. Mike's villains of choice remained Leland Crowell and his mother. Teri had a more expansive list.

The four sat around a patio table on a teak deck that resided on stilts above the beach. Mike and Bob enjoyed beer, Bozarth his Scotch, but Teri stuck to water, wanting to keep her mind one hundred percent clear. Although to any passerby below, it would appear to be a casual gathering of friends, the atmosphere was anything but casual. The mood was tense, even grim. The centerpiece on the table was the uncrumpled yellow page with Teri's rendezvous instructions, and it was the focused topic of conversation.

"I don't want her meeting alone with this guy," Mike said.

"How do you know it's Crowell?" Bob asked. "Maybe it'll be the mother. After all, she's the one who left the note for Teri."

"I don't care which one it is. They're both nuts. And I think that makes them both dangerous."

"It'll be the writer," Bozarth said. "The mother is just the messenger. But what this proves is that they're both in it together, and they have been from the start."

"I can't get over this whole thing," Teri said. "Do you know how much patience it takes to run a scam like this? They've been waiting for over two years, and they had no way of knowing at the start that it would ever pay off. What were the odds that I'd even read that script, much less like it?"

"Maybe it was just luck, and now they're taking advantage of it," Mike said.

"Spencer West died right after I got the script. If his death is connected, then that's a plan."

"And that means there's more to it than we know," Bozarth said.

"Do you think the lawyer was in on it, too?" Mike asked.

"Probably. They figured they couldn't trust him to keep his mouth shut."

"I think I've missed a step here," Bob said. "Are you saying they killed him? I checked with the police, and they're pretty sure the lawyer was a suicide."

"But I did some checking of my own," Mike said, "and I'm pretty sure he's the one who spilled the story to the trades. Like I told Teri back then, it really didn't matter if the script sucked, because we could rewrite it into something worth a damn, and the buzz would carry it from there. I'm with Teri on this; it's all part of a plan."

"The police were also pretty sure that Leland Crowell took a swan dive off that cliff up at Big Sur," Bozarth said. "But we now know he's alive and well. That spells plan, too. A lot of thought went into this. I don't believe in happenstance."

"Somebody damn sure jumped off that cliff," Mike said.

"But not Leland," Teri said.

Bozarth riveted his attention on Teri. "So you see what we're dealing with: people who are willing to kill to scam us." The subtext wasn't lost on her: We've got to be willing to kill to protect ourselves.

Then a sudden thought hit her. "It is a scam."

"Welcome to the conversation," Bob said. "Try to keep up here."

"No, I mean what if that really was Leland Crowell who jumped off that cliff? Annemarie identified his body; what if she wasn't lying? What if that really was her son?"

"I'm not following what you're saying," Bob said.

"I've been sitting here trying to understand how anyone, especially someone who needs money as badly as Annemarie and the 'undead,' as Doug calls him, could sit back and wait two years for their scam to pay off. That doesn't make sense to me. I don't buy it. So what if this isn't a two-year-old scam, but it's a brand new scam made out of opportunity?"

Bozarth furrowed his brow. "I think I see where you're going. You're saying that the newly resurrected Leland Crowell isn't Leland Crowell at all. But he and Annemarie see a chance to get in on the money, so he shows up claiming to be the dead man. Or maybe it was all part of a plan, but Leland is still dead."

"Exactly."

"That would make sense."

"So if we can prove it was really Leland Crowell who died,

whether he killed himself or not, then the script is legally mine. And even if it turns out that the will wasn't legally probated, that's just a formality."

"How do we prove that it was Crowell who died?" Bob asked.

"We don't have to," Mike said. "We just have to prove that Lazarus is someone else."

"Go there tonight, Teri," Bozarth said. "If it is Leland, or whoever the hell he is, who shows up, we'll have someone watching. We'll take it from there."

There was that subtext again that bothered Teri. And again, it was nothing you could take to the bank, but she heard it as a mortal threat. Maybe Annemarie and the scraggly-haired man were killers, or maybe they were just scam artists. Either way, that's what courts were for. Taking the law into your own hands left scars; all this talk was picking at the scabs over Teri's scars.

She stood and walked to the edge of the deck and gazed at the ocean. On the beach below her, a blonde-haired girl and a small dog that looked like a Sheltie passed by. Carefree, a day on the beach. Teri wondered what dreams and aspirations the little girl had. Did she want to grow up to be a doctor or lawyer? Or an actress?

With her back to the others, even though she knew they were all watching her, Teri said, "What do I tell him?"

"Tell him he's not getting a damn dime," Bozarth said.

She spun around to face him.

"Are you crazy?" Mike said. He got up and walked to Teri, then stood beside her, as if lending support.

"It'll rattle him," Bozarth said.

"That's what I mean," Mike said. "We already know these people are willing to kill, and now you want Teri to go in there alone and deliberately piss him off?"

"He needs to know he's not the only one willing to kill."

The words hit Teri like a tidal wave.

There, he had flat out said it!

She supposed she should give him credit for honesty, but things seemed to be spiraling out of control.

"What the hell is that supposed to mean?" Mike asked.

Bozarth answered Mike, but looked at Teri as he spoke. He wanted to be sure she knew he was talking to her.

"What I'm saying is that people kill for lots of reasons. Sometimes it's for money. Sometimes it's for love. And sometimes it's just plain ol' self-preservation."

He nodded almost imperceptibly when he spoke the last words. She knew exactly what he meant.

"If he's willing to kill, he knows others might be, as well," Bozarth continued. "There's one other thing he knows. If he should suddenly disappear, no one would miss him. After all, he's already a dead man."

"I don't like the sounds of this," Mike said.

"You don't have to like the sounds of it," Bob said. "It makes sense."

"Look, Mike, don't go getting all Grassy Knoll on me," Bozarth said. "He just has to *think* we'd kill him. It'll put him off-kilter so he'll make a mistake. Then we can wrap this up."

"Wrap it up, how?" Teri asked.

"Let me worry about that."

CHAPTER 21

BETWEEN SPENCER WEST'S former office, Annemarie Crowell's apartment complex, and the Crescent Hotel, Teri had seen enough rundown, ragged structures in the last couple of days to last her a lifetime. These weren't the charming "holes-in-the-wall" that she learned to love back home in Texas, the quaint ranch and farm houses and classic cafes. These were the kinds of places that testified to a world of sadness and poverty that she and her friends only read about in newspaper articles or saw on television or the big screen. The world that she subconsciously hoped she would never know about firsthand. The world that she had somehow been drawn into against her will by a bizarre sequence of events that even the most creative screenwriter might have dismissed as not being credible. But before she could put that world of rundown structures behind her, she had one more to visit.

Caleb's Diner.

At exactly midnight, Teri pulled her SUV into the sparsely-populated parking lot and stared at the building, constructed in the style of a railroad car, or maybe Airstream trailer, with windows lining the front with a row of booths. What looked like a narrow aisle separated those booths from stools at a counter. Through the windows, she saw that all booths were vacant at the end away from the front door, and only a couple of the stools at the counter supported diners. No Leland Crowell, as far as she could tell.

She got out of the car, wearing her same unsuccessful disguise from the day before: baseball cap, ponytail, and sunglasses, despite the lack of sun. Given the location, the hour, and the shadows, she hoped it would be more effective than it was the last time. She stood beside her car for a moment, steeling her nerves. She had to restrain herself from looking around, searching for Doug Bozarth's men, who surely were out there somewhere. She would feel better if she knew exactly where they were, but she would have to be satisfied with the sure knowledge that they were, in fact, there.

Or would she actually feel better if they weren't there at all? She wasn't entirely sure.

She entered the diner with a façade of bravado. "Show no fear," she thought, although she was painfully out of her comfort zone. The trick, though, was not to let anyone know that. She stood in the entryway for a moment and let her eyes adjust to the light. It would have made sense to take off her sunglasses, but she opted against that.

A waitress approached, dressed in a dirty tan uniform, decorated by the various foods and drinks she had served that day. When she smiled, she revealed a black tooth in front that almost made it look as if the tooth were missing.

"How many?" the waitress asked.

"I'm meeting someone here," Teri said, "but I don't see him."

"Some guy just went to the men's room."

"What does he look like?"

"Oh, I don't know, thin, longish hair."

"That sounds like him."

"I'll take you to his table."

The waitress led her to the back of the diner, the last booth against the wall farthest from the door. As Teri passed a scattering of late-night customers, she wondered if any of them could be Bozarth's men. None paid her any attention as she walked by, but then again, a good surveillance man would ignore her. The faux leather seats on the rear booth, colored a sickly orange, were split, with tufts of foam rubber sticking out. A half-empty cup of coffee sat on the far side of the booth, so she slid in across from it.

"Need a menu?" the waitress asked, as she set a glass of water on the table.

"No, thank you."

The waitress left, and Teri sat rigidly, posture ramrod straight, and looked out the window. After a few minutes, she heard footsteps behind her. She refused to turn her head as a shadow loomed, then Leland Crowell—or whoever he was—slid into the far side of the booth. He wore tattered jeans, his bony knees poking out, and a long-sleeve blue denim workshirt that was so faded as to be nearly white.

"Ms. Squire, how good of you to come," he said.

She said nothing in reply, but simply stared at him.

"Are you hungry? Let me get you a menu."

"This is not a date. I don't need a menu."

"No reason we can't be pleasant."

"Actually, there's every reason we can't be pleasant," she said, "so let's just get this over with."

"Ahh, *tsk tsk*, so little manners today. Okay, fine, let's have it your way."

They sat in silence for a moment, each acting as if expecting the other to talk first. Finally the thin man said, "Well, have you got something to tell me?"

"Who are you?"

"Oh, dear, are we back to that again? You know who I am."

"I know who you *say* you are."

"And I know who you say you are...Peggy."

She tried hard to maintain her composure, but still blinked.

The question was whether he noticed it. "My name is Teri."

"Credibility is a fragile thing."

He had noticed.

"I've got a question for you," Teri said. "Something I've always wondered about the script. Why did you end the first act the way you did?"

For a moment, she sensed that she had shifted the momentum. This time, he blinked. Like a frog, with lifeless eyes, his expression totally blank.

"It just seemed like it was the best way," he said. A bead of perspiration popped out above his right eye then trickled down his jawline despite the coolness of the diner. The question obviously made him uncomfortable.

"Yeah, but what made you think that would work as a plot point?" she asked. "You developed the set-up so well, but then you had your protagonist—" She stopped, almost ready to laugh at the blankness that had replaced cockiness on of his face.

"You don't have any idea what I'm talking about, do you?" she asked. "You don't know what a plot point is or where the act break is, or anything."

Silence, the frog blinking in rapid succession.

"Leland Crowell would know," she said. "The writer would know exactly where the act break was and why he put it there. But you don't have a clue."

"I don't have to have a clue. I've got a copyright certificate."

"But the certificate says that Leland Crowell owns the copyright, and you're not Leland Crowell. You just proved that. Did you kill him? Huh? Did you throw him off that cliff?"

The man leaned back in his seat and stared out the window for a moment. Then he rolled up his shirtsleeve and stuck his arm across the table, with the blue football helmet tattoo directly under the light. He pressed his lips together, as if to say, "There. That proves it."

For just an instant, Teri flashed back to the Crescent Hotel, straining for a memory that lurked deep in the recesses of her mind. What was it? Oh, yeah, now she remembered: The tattoo was smudged.

Wordlessly, she took her water glass and poured a few drops on the tattoo, then rubbed it with her thumb. She had to swallow the bile that rose up in her throat as she touched his bare arm, but her little gambit did the trick: the tattoo smeared.

"I'm not a lawyer, but I think I can help you get your money back from the tattoo parlor," she said. She kept her eyes locked on his face, but he wouldn't meet her gaze.

"Let's say, for the sake of argument, that you really are Leland Crowell," she said. "You know what's really pathetic about that?"

Now he met her eyes. For the first time, emotion filled his. A mix of rage and fear, and she wondered if she was pushing him too far. But she also knew she couldn't stop now. She felt that she was on the verge of something.

"What?" he asked.

"You're already dead."

"Big threat from such a little girl."

"It's not a threat; it's a fact, isn't it? Leland Crowell already jumped off a cliff, so if he disappears again, who's going to miss him?"

The mix of rage and fear turned to pure rage. He leaned across the table and spoke in what could only be described as a growl. "I want my money."

"You're not getting anything."

He pulled away, his back rigid against the booth.

"That's right; not a damn penny." She stood and looked down at him. "See you in the funny papers."

Then she turned and headed for the door, fighting to keep her head high and her mouth set. From behind her, she heard the

man's shouts. As he yelled, customers turned and looked at her
    And recognized her!
    "You come back here. You can't threaten me, Miss Bigshot
Actress! I want what's coming to me. You hear me? You won't
get away with this."
    She picked up her pace, but kept it to a walk, albeit a fast
one.
    Then she was out the door.

He sat frozen to his seat as the actress disappeared out the door.
How dare she! Didn't she understand what was going on here? He
was in charge, not her. He called the shots, not her. Or did he?
She had been scared the last time he saw her, in his hotel room,
but tonight she showed little of that fear. In fact, she seemed
almost emboldened as she sat there, grilling him about the
screenplay. Then that parting shot, threatening him. That's what
it was, wasn't it? A threat. Letting him know that she, or
someone, had *carte blanche* to take him out of the picture. That
could mean only one thing: It was a death threat.
    He scrambled from his seat and bolted for the door. He
pushed his way outside and scanned the parking lot. A dark blue
Toyota Highlander SUV idled in a space near the building, its glass
tinted to prevent anyone from seeing inside. As people inside the
diner stared out the window, he raced to the SUV, snatched open
the passenger door, and jumped inside.
    The vehicle drove off.

CHAPTER 22

AS SHE LEFT the dismal part of town that housed the diner, Teri found herself in a daze. What had started as merely strange had grown more fantastic almost by the hour, culminating in what now seemed like surreal territory. She didn't know if the man in the diner had been the real Leland Crowell any more than she had known that night in his hotel room. It had taken all her nerve—and she had plenty; history proved that—to call his bluff, because she knew that not meeting his demands probably offered greater danger than caving in to him.

Part of her felt comforted knowing that Doug Bozarth was waiting in the wings should things go wrong. Another part of her, though, knew that Doug Bozarth might prove to be an even bigger risk than dealing with Leland Crowell, or whoever he was. If anything happened to the scraggly-haired man, anything at all, she knew two things with certainty: (1) Doug Bozarth would be the man behind it; and (2) she would be a co-conspirator, even though she had no idea what he might do.

There was also a third thing she knew: Whatever might happen, it would be untraceable to Bozarth but, if traceable at all, would likely lead to her own doorstep. She felt sure Bozarth would see to that. And she would be powerless to do anything about it, since there were witnesses who could testify that they had seen the two of them together. Ponytail, baseball cap, and sunglasses notwithstanding, she was a recognizable figure in this town. Her visit to Spencer West's former office proved that. In fact, she was not just recognizable in this town, but internationally. Her face was her calling card and now might be her undoing if anything happened. People had seen her and recognized her. And they had heard raised voices. Harsh voices. How many movies had she seen—hell, had she made—where the victim and the suspect had argued before the murder, and that argument had been hung around the suspect's neck like a millstone?

But wait. If anything happened. There was a clue there, provided she could call it to mind. If *anything* happened…If anything *happened*…*If* anything happened.

If. That was the magic word. The uncertainty of danger from the man in the diner was more than counter-balanced by the certainty of danger if something happened to him. She had to make sure that nothing happened. If she could head off anything unfortunate from happening to the scraggly-haired man, she could achieve a small measure of comfort, perhaps even salve her conscience a bit. Not that she wanted to become this extortioner's bodyguard, but she realized that her own welfare was in play. Self-interest was a bitch.

She had barely gone two blocks when she swung her SUV around in a sharp U-turn in the middle of an intersection and headed back to the diner. She had no plan in mind, no course of action. But if nothing else, she would wait and watch. Information was power, and what she really needed right now was information. Not only on the scraggly-haired man, but also on Doug Bozarth. She had struck out on her own research, but maybe Mona had been more successful.

She pulled out her cell phone from her purse and was just about to hit Mona's speed dial number when she saw a Toyota SUV that looked remarkably similar to hers, right down to the color, idling in the parking lot of Caleb's Diner. She couldn't be sure, but it sure as hell looked as if the scraggly haired man had just jumped into the passenger side. Could it just be coincidence that the car he was in looked just like hers? She didn't think so. And who was driving? Here was a chance to find out who was in cahoots with whom. The SUV pulled into traffic.

She dropped the phone in her lap and followed.

Mona Hirsch scrolled from link to link on her laptop, curled up in her queen-size bed with a notepad beside her and a Diet Coke on the nightstand. She had tried to sleep earlier, but sleep wouldn't come. Not until she heard from Teri and knew that she was all right after her late-night visit to meet the purported Leland Crowell. She had Googled the name and found the man to be, or have been, a mere cipher. Other than news stories about his strange bequest and the imminent release of *The Precipice*, with the inevitable comparisons to John Kennedy Toole and his *A Confederacy of Dunces*, the information superhighway was more of an information trickle. There wasn't even an obituary from his death two years earlier. As far as the Internet was concerned, he had neither been born nor died, nor lived in between. It was as if he had never existed except as a character in a bizarre drama that was even now playing out.

She glanced at her notepad, struck by how empty it was. Nary a single note, fitting, perhaps, as the sum of Leland Crowell's pitiful existence.

She grabbed her Diet Coke and took a sip. After she set it back on the nightstand, she keyed in a new Google search: Douglas Bozarth.

Teri maintained a discreet distance from the SUV, staying far enough back to only be seen as headlights in a rearview mirror, but close enough that accelerating to clear intersections on yellow or red lights would not seem suspicious to the lead vehicle. She had tailed cars before, but only under the glare of spotlights with cameras rolling and a director ready to yell "Cut!" if anything didn't look right. The worst that could have happened, then, was another take. But tonight, there would be no second takes if the driver up ahead realized he or she was being followed.

And just who was the driver? Who was the scraggly-haired man's partner in crime? What she wouldn't give to know the answer to that.

Then a thought hit her: What if the driver was on the payroll of Doug Bozarth? She had already thought through the notion that, if anything happened to the thin man, it would be made to look as if she had a hand in it. Was that what was going on here? Was that why a car just like hers had the thin man in it? Had he sought to join her in her vehicle as she left, only to discover he had been lured into a trap?

Then she thought back to seeing the SUV pull out of the parking lot. If, indeed, that was the scraggly-haired man in the passenger seat—and she was pretty sure it was—he didn't seem distressed. He appeared to be simply riding along just like any other passenger in a vehicle. And that could mean but one thing: He knew the driver.

CHAPTER 23

MONA PULLED UP yet another website that told the same generic story about Doug Bozarth that Teri had recited to her following her own research. She didn't really expect to find anything, but at least it killed time since she couldn't sleep anyway. No, the real inside scoop on Bozarth, if there was any to be found, would come from the computer major at USC she had emailed earlier, who was far more adept at research than Mona and Teri put together. That had less to do, Mona supposed, with surfing the Web than it did with the student's ability to access databases supposedly impenetrable to hackers. Databases that had all kinds of initials and acronyms associated with them, including CIA, NSA, FBI, and DOD, just to name a few.

She was surprised, though, that she had not yet heard a response from the student, who usually was glued to his computer at all hours, including while he was in class. She was sure her email would have gotten his attention, with the subject line of "Help" and the simple message: *Need dirt on someone; will pay premium rates.* And yet nearly two hours had gone by and no response. She had sent it, hadn't she? She opened the Sent file on her email program and scrolled down. Yep, there it was, transmitted one hour and fifty-seven minutes earlier.

A tone announced the arrival of a message. She switched back to the Inbox and saw the response she had been waiting for. She opened the message and read: *Just got this, but there was no message. I see it was sent hours ago. Don't know why it was delayed. Is someone monitoring your email? Was there supposed to be a message?*

She typed a reply: *Why do you ask? And, yes, there was a message.*

His response: *Sometimes hackers get into mail programs. They can divert mail or delete messages. Sometimes that delays the delivery; sometimes it prevents delivery altogether.*

A noise from the far reaches of the house pulled Mona's attention away from the laptop screen. It could have been just one of the normal "things that go bump in the night." It might even have been the return of that nasty family of raccoons that had done almost two thousand dollars worth of roof and attic damage to her house just a few months earlier. And if it was the latter, Mona was prepared. She pulled open the drawer in her nightstand and took out a BB pistol. She had bought it after a "critter catcher" had advised her that it was as good a way as any to chase off unwanted animals.

"You don't need anything more powerful," he said. "You don't want to kill it or injure it badly. If that happens, it might crawl between the walls to die, and you wouldn't know it until it stunk so bad, you'd never get the smell out."

She held the pistol in her right hand, slid her legs over the side of the bed, and stood. She cocked her head and listened. Nothing. She walked softly to the doorway to her bedroom and listened. She had learned to distinguish the sounds she often heard in this hilly and tree-lined neighborhood of Beverly Hills. Skittering sounds generally meant squirrels on the roof. Louder skittering meant squirrels in the attic. But pounding and banging, like a mini-construction project—that meant raccoons in the attic, treating the soft insulation as their own private latrine and ripping their way in and out through the shake roof.

But there was only silence.

She had just turned and was headed back to bed when she heard it again. Not a skittering sound, or a banging sound overhead. This was a very distinct sound. One that she knew meant trouble.

It was the sound of a footstep. Inside the house.

And it was close.

Suddenly the questions about delayed emails and deleted messages made sense. Frightening sense. Teri had told her to be discreet in her search but never really explained why; no specifics, anyway. All Mona knew was that, for some reason, Teri was uneasy about Doug Bozarth and his money. Now Mona realized that Doug Bozarth might be just as uneasy about Teri Squire and her questions.

She grabbed the door and swung it closed, but it caught with a sudden jolt. Gloved hands appeared on the edges, and she knew that a rubber-soled shoe had braced against the bottom to keep it from closing.

She screamed then turned and leaned her back against the door. She spread her legs, dug in her bare feet on the carpet, and pushed. For a moment she made progress, closing the door until it appeared it might cut off the fingers on one of the intruder's hands. Then her feet lost their tenuous grip on the fabric. The person on the other side of the door pushed it open six inches, then ten. Her feet continued to slide.

"What do you want?" she screamed. "Who are you?"

No answer from the intruder; just a redoubled effort to force the door open.

"Please, what do you want?" Her voice sounded shrill. Even as she spoke the words, she knew they were meaningless. Besides, she thought she already knew what the intruder wanted, though she found it hard to believe. Was Doug Bozarth really the kind of man who would kill just to squelch an investigation into his business? If so, that meant there was something to be found that Bozarth wanted to keep buried.

The door was open maybe a foot now. A hand slipped all the

way inside and clamped around her throat. She felt the leather grip her skin. The intruder pressed forefinger and thumb on either side of her trachea and squeezed. At first it was the pain that weakened her, but then came the lack of oxygen. Her feet slid further, and the door opened wider. The man was able to force his shoulders into the opening now. She felt his breath on her cheek, the sound of his breathing muffled by something. A mask probably.

She suddenly remembered that she was still holding the BB pistol. How could she have forgotten that? She raised her right hand, her wrist turned unnaturally as she tried to point it at the intruder's face.

The hand on her throat lurched away, and air flowed into her lungs. The hand grabbed at the gun.

She pulled the trigger. A voice screamed, the sound deep and guttural. She didn't know where she had hit him, but she knew she had. His hand let go of hers. She pulled the trigger again. Another scream.

Then the door slammed shut, her body weight full against it. She gathered her feet under her, ready to brace again if he renewed his assault. But there was nothing. Only silence.

And her own ragged-sounding breaths.

She willed herself to stop breathing, to hold her breath and listen. Was he still there? How bad was he hurt? She cocked her head to listen, but heard nothing.

The silence was suddenly filled with Hawaiian music. *Drums of the Islands* by the Makaha Sons. She glanced at her cell phone on the nightstand. Did she dare chance it, to dart to the phone? What if the man wasn't hurt bad but was simply waiting for a chance. A chance she would give him if she went for her phone.

The music ended, the caller having hung up. There was silence again.

Then she heard another sound, one she had heard before on

movie sets. The sound of a slide being racked on a gun. But she knew this one didn't contain blanks.

The last thing she heard before she felt a burning pain in her back was the roar of the weapon as it was fired through the door.

CHAPTER 24

TERI DROPPED THE phone on the passenger seat, her attention still riveted to the SUV up ahead. Why wasn't Mona picking up? If she was out somewhere, surely she had her phone with her. And if she was asleep, well, she always kept her phone on the nightstand.

The SUV had gone north on the 405, hit the 101 west and north, and then connected with the Pacific Coast Highway in Ventura. Teri stayed with it, just two lonely cars on the California coast. Occasional traffic passed by the other way, heading toward Los Angeles, but other than that, Teri felt totally alone. The moon was partially obscured by clouds, forcing her to concentrate on the road. Fortunately the taillights of the lead vehicle clued her in to curves ahead. To her left, the ocean glittered an inky blackness, topped by occasional whitecaps. The actress in her said this was a great setting for a movie murder. The mood was ominous, the road treacherous, and the audience would be on the edge of their seats. Not even Leland Crowell could write a better scene.

As they passed the turn-off to William Randolph Hearst's castle at San Simeon, she wondered how much farther they would go. And just where in the hell were they going? Ahead was a small parking lot for a convenience store. She eased her foot off the gas. The distance widened between her and the scraggly-haired man's SUV. She had to decide now.

The hell with it. She turned into the convenience store parking lot, whipped around, and pulled back out onto the highway heading south.

The SUV rounded a curve then eased to the side of the road at a particularly sharp drop-off near Ragged Point. The identical spot where Leland Crowell had met his demise. The passenger door opened and the scraggly-haired man stepped out. He walked around to the cliffside and stepped over the guardrail. He perched precipitously on the edge, never looking down, his back to the open driver's side window of the SUV. The roar of the waves wafted up and a breeze mussed his hair, but he heard and felt nothing. He stood riveted to the spot. Frozen. Almost zombie-like.

A gunshot echoed from inside the car, briefly lighting the interior like a firecracker.

The bullet slammed into the scraggly-haired man's back, driving him forward.

Off the precipice.

Head first, into the blackness below.

CHAPTER 25

IN THE IMMORTAL words of Yogi Berra, it was like déjà vu, all over again, as California Highway Patrol detectives Howie Stillman and Jeff Nichols pulled their Chevy Tahoe behind a cruiser, its rear passenger door open, lights striking against the darkness of the early morning sky. A paramedic unit was parked in front of the cruiser and several utility vehicles from the power company rounded out the group. Both men looked puffy-eyed, as if they had just been awakened, both carrying cups of coffee. Just as they had two years earlier, they watched as a crane pulled up a paramedic riding a basket, perched next to a body in a rubber bag.

A CHP officer, whose name tag identified him as "Gerrit," approached. He was young, almost baby-faced. He pointed up the steep inland hillside. "We got a report of a suspicious vehicle from some hikers who were camping up there."

"Suspicious, how?" Nichols asked.

"They said they heard the vehicle slowing down, then it pulled over to the guardrail and just sat there. Someone got out on the passenger side, but they couldn't tell anything about him in the dark. Just a shadow. Then whoever it was walked around to the cliffside. At that point, they lost sight of him, but the vehicle pulled away in a hurry."

"What kind of vehicle?"

"They said it looked like an SUV."

"Where are these hikers?"

"Back seat of the cruiser."

Stillman and Nichols approached the opened rear door of the cruiser, where two young people, probably no more than twenty or twenty-one sat. The male had close-cropped hair, while his female companion was frizzy-haired and freckled. They huddled against each other, as if they feared they were about to be implicated in this whole mess.

They slid out of the cruiser when they heard the detectives approach.

"I'm Detective Nichols, this is Detective Stillman," Nichols said.

"Billy Williamson. This is my girlfriend, Sheri Slade."

Nichols gestured up the hillside. "We understand you folks were camping up there?"

"We know we're not supposed to, but we were hiking and it got kinda late on us, so we decided to stay the night," Billy said. "That's why it took us so long to call anyone. We were afraid we'd get in trouble, but after we saw what had happened, we knew we had to."

"Nobody's in trouble," Nichols said. "But why don't you walk us through what you saw."

"Well, like I told the other officer, we heard a car that sounded like it was going pretty slow. Sound really carries up here, so when the noise stopped, we figured the car stopped. Then—"

"We got that part already. Fast forward a little bit."

"Okay, well, like I said, we were afraid we'd get in trouble, and besides, it didn't seem like anything had really happened, anyway. We thought it was kind of strange that the passenger got out and we didn't see him get back in, but he could have gotten in on the other side of the car."

"You said 'him' and 'he.' Was this a male?"

"We couldn't tell. We just sort of assumed that, but I don't know why."

"Could you hear anything? Voices, anything like that?"

"No, just a popping sound."

Stillman and Nichols exchanged glances. "Popping sound?" Stillman asked. "What kind of popping sound?"

"It wasn't loud, but, I don't know, just a popping sound. Anyway, this morning, when it got a little bit lighter, we decided to come down and see if we could see anything. All we saw were some tire tracks at first, so we were about to go back up, but then Sheri saw footprints on the other side of the guardrail."

"I wasn't sure at first," Sheri said, "so I shined my flashlight over there and you could see them pretty clear. That's when I also saw some red splashes on the guardrail."

"We didn't know if it was blood or not, but it was all getting a little too weird. That's when we decided we had to call someone."

"Detectives." Gerrit called from the edge, where the basket was reaching the top.

"Wait here," Nichols said. He and Stillman hustled over and stood next to Gerrit, by the guardrail.

"Give me your flashlight," Stillman said to Gerrit.

The young officer dutifully unholstered it from his belt and handed it to him. Stillman shined the beam on the top of the guardrail and both detectives bent close to study the metal. And there it was. The red splashes the girl had mentioned. They had both seen enough blood splatter before to recognize it immediately.

"Make sure no one disturbs this until the techs get here," Stillman said, and Gerrit nodded.

The basket had reached the top, and the paramedic scrambled off as his colleagues hauled it over the guardrail.

"Can you tell anything?" Nichols asked.

The paramedic unzipped the body bag, to reveal a pulpy

mess of a face. Again, shades of déjà vu. "But that's not the interesting thing," the paramedic said.

"What is?"

Using both hands, he twisted the torso onto its side. "Look in the middle of his back."

Leaning close again, using the flashlight, there was no mistaking what they saw: a bullet hole.

As the paramedic rolled the body back over, one arm flopped free and dangled over the side of the basket. Both Nichols and Stillman froze at what they saw: a blue tattoo, smeared but clearly distinguishable as the shape of a football helmet with a star in the middle.

"Well, son of a bitch!" Stillman said.

"Amen, brother," Nichols replied. "Amen."

CHAPTER 26

AFTER RETURNING HOME at close to 9:00 a.m., Teri stripped to her underwear and a tee-shirt and crawled into bed, but sleep did not come easily. Who was driving the look-a-like SUV? Was it all part of an elaborate ruse perpetrated against her by the scraggly-haired man and his mother? And where was Mona? Teri had tried her cell phone time and again on her way home, but finally concluded that Mona's battery must have died without her knowing. After all, that phone was Mona's lifeline to the world, and she wouldn't be caught dead without it.

Between long periods of lying awake and staring at the ceiling, Teri thrashed and flopped like a fish on a deck. It wasn't until the sun was fully up that she finally succumbed to exhaustion. Even then her dreams were haunted by visions of the scraggly-haired man, his faded blue tattoo, and the screams he hurled at her as she left Caleb's Diner.

The buzzing of the doorbell roused her from her shallow slumber. She wiped sleep from her eyes and glanced at the clock. Nearly three in the afternoon. It was probably Mona at the door, apologizing for not answering her phone. Teri snatched hers off the nightstand to see if she had missed any calls from Mona, but there had been none.

Teri disentangled herself from the sheets, slipped on a pair of gym shorts, and staggered to the front door. She put her eye to the peephole and looked out, shocked to see three men she had never seen before on the front porch—two relatively young and an older man with gray hair.

"Who is it?" she called.

The older man held a badge in front of the peephole. "Police, ma'am," he said.

She slid the chain-lock off and opened the door. The three men stepped back almost as one.

"Sorry to disturb you, Ms. Squire," said the man with the badge. "I'm Detective Walter Swafford, Beverly Hills PD. These are Detectives Stillman and Nichols with CHP. May we come in?"

"Why? Is something wrong?"

"Ma'am, do you know a Leland Crowell?"

Teri hoped she didn't react at the sound of the name, but the whole affair with the screenwriter had been in the media, so there was no use denying it. The real question wasn't whether she knew who Leland Crowell was; the real question was whether these cops knew about last night's shouting match with the resurrected Leland Crowell at Caleb's Diner.

"Yes," she said. "I mean, no. I know who he was, but I've never met him. He died a couple of years ago. I'm sure you must have heard about it."

"Yes, ma'am, we know the legend," Swafford said.

"Legend?"

"Let's just say there are some unanswered questions that we'd like to clear up. That's what we want to talk to you about."

Teri stood rooted to the floor for a few beats, conscious of the pounding of her heart. She was an actress, trained to fake emotions and put up façades, but the rush of blood in her ears and the tingle in her cheeks told her she was failing miserably.

She stepped back. "Come in."

As the men crossed the threshold, they gathered in the entryway, as if waiting for still another invitation. She appreciated their restraint. She had seen on the news and read in the Los

Angeles papers every day about over-the-top searches and aggressive interrogations. She'd even conducted one or two herself playing a cop on the big screen, and she had been the subject of one years ago back in Texas. Now was the time to marshal her thoughts and remember what police consultants had told her about strategies and mind games in interrogations. She was starting to wish she had played more cops and fewer romantic leads, and gotten into the heads of more detectives and fewer love-starved professional women.

Wordlessly, Teri closed the door and led the men to the den. The room was still darkened by closed drapes, but she pulled the curtains back in front of the sliding doors to illuminate the sitting area. Her spirits were dark enough without the gloom.

None of the men sat. The one identified as Stillman went to the sliding doors and stared out at the hills, wisps of smoke still hovering on the horizon.

"Do you mind?" he asked.

She shook her head, and he unlocked and slid the door open. He stood in the doorway, his frame blocking the entire opening. "The fires are completely out now," he said.

"It looks that way," she said.

"I bet it worried you for a while."

Tired of waiting for the men to sit, Teri perched on the arm of the couch. "I'm sure you didn't come over here just to talk about wildfires," she said. "You were asking about Leland Crowell."

Swafford leaned against the mantel, while Nichols stood to the side, as if on guard duty. "Yes, ma'am," Swafford said. "You said he died a couple of years ago?"

"I'm sure you already know all this. It's been the biggest Hollywood story in years. He killed himself and willed his screenplay to me. I got it from his mother, but I never met him."

"Why do you suppose he willed his screenplay to you?"

Nichols asked.

He stepped forward, as if he was assuming control of the conversation, while Swafford seemed to fade into the background. The fact that there were two CHP cops and only one Beverly Hills cop told her that Swafford had just been brought in as a courtesy, to preserve jurisdictional niceties. She had learned that, too, from playing cops in the movies.

But why in the hell was CHP here? Unless something had happened farther up the Coast Highway after she had turned back last night. Was that it? She shifted uncomfortably on the couch arm, pulled a leg up beneath herself, and waited for the other shoe to drop.

"Believe me, I was the most surprised person around when I found out that he had willed it to me. His mother even said that he wrote it for me. I guess he was a fan."

"I am, too," Swafford said. "And so is my wife. She's not going to believe it when I tell her I met you."

He smiled at her, but she didn't return it. She figured out by now that he was the good cop, Nichols was probably going to be the bad cop, and the other guy by the open glass door—well, she guessed he was going to be the silent cop. She glanced his way and saw that he was still in the middle of the doorway, staring straight ahead at the hills, but she could also tell by the tilt of his head that he was carefully listening to everything that was being said.

"Didn't that strike you as odd?" Nichols asked. "Him leaving his screenplay to you?"

"It struck me as weird as hell," Teri said. "I've had people try all kinds of things to get scripts to me. I had one delivered once with a singing telegram. Another time, someone threw one in my open car window when I was stopped at a red light. I've even had people—men, in fact—follow me into the ladies room and slide one under the stall door. But this is the first and only time someone left me one after he died."

"Do you know how he died," Nichols asked.

"I was told he jumped off a cliff up near Big Sur. And that's what the papers all say."

"Stillman and I worked that case. We were there when they brought up his body."

"Then you already know all this."

Stillman turned around and lasered his focus on Teri. "What we know is that *somebody* jumped off that cliff back then. It might have been Leland Crowell; might not. We sure thought so back then, but now we're not so sure."

Teri felt her antennae start quivering. Something did happen last night, but what? "What do you mean, you aren't sure?" she asked.

"Because he went off that same cliff again last night," Stillman said. "This time with a bullet in his back."

She felt her pounding heart suddenly stop. The blood rushing in her ears drained away, and the tingle extended all the way down her neck and shoulders, to her fingertips. "I don't understand what you're saying."

"What we're saying," said Nichols, "is that we're no longer sure the man who jumped off that cliff a couple of years ago was Leland Crowell."

"Then who was he?"

"We're still working on that."

Lightheaded, Teri slid off the couch arm and onto the seat. She needed the back of the couch for support.

"What does this have to do with me?" she asked.

"Well, Ms. Squire, we know you talked to this man—I'll call him Leland Two—last night at Caleb's Diner," Stillman said. "What did you talk about?"

Teri felt as if she might throw up. Her words froze in her throat.

"Ms. Squire, you okay?" Nichols asked. She detected genuine

concern in his voice.

"I'll get some water," Swafford said, heading for the kitchen. In a moment he was back with a glass half full and handed it to her. She took a small sip, just enough to wet the inside of her mouth.

"Ms. Squire," Stillman said, "what did you talk about last night?"

"I told you I've never met Leland Crowell."

"Okay, let's go with the idea that it wasn't the real Leland Crowell. But you were at Caleb's Diner last night, weren't you? And you talked to somebody. The same somebody that our witnesses say threatened you. And they also say he left the diner with you."

"That's impossible."

"I'd love to hear why."

Teri remained silent, trying to process what she had been told with what she had seen last night. Who had been driving that SUV, the one that looked exactly like hers? Whoever it was had killed the scraggly-haired man and was doing exactly what she feared: trying to frame her.

"Ms. Squire, I'm kinda like Detective Swafford's wife," Stillman said. "I'm a big fan of yours. And I keep up with all the movie gossip. So, yeah, I know all about your big movie about to open up from Leland Crowell's screenplay."

"Everyone knows that," she said.

"But here's what I keep asking myself: What if it turned out that Leland Crowell wasn't really dead? What if he was still alive? Would you still own his screenplay?"

"I'm not a probate lawyer, detective. I don't know what the law is about people faking their deaths. Assuming your scenario is correct, of course."

"But it would sure solve a lot of problems for you if he turned up dead before he could make a stink about it, wouldn't it?"

"And wouldn't it open up a whole lot of new questions?" she asked. "Like just exactly who was it who went off that cliff two years ago?"

"Another question for another day," Nichols said. "Our question for today is who put a bullet in that man's back last night."

"Ms. Squire, do you own a handgun?" Stillman asked.

"You don't ask many questions you don't already know the answer to," Teri said. "I'm sure you already know I have a registered twenty-two. I keep it in the coffee table."

She leaned forward to grab the drawer. As if in one motion, all three cops grabbed for their weapons. She froze, her hand just inches from the handle.

"Maybe one of you would like to check," she said.

Swafford stepped over and grabbed the handle. Teri leaned back as he slid the drawer open.

To reveal nothing.

Teri looked at Swafford, who met her gaze with a skeptical eye. "That's where I always keep it."

He straightened and backed away.

"When's the last time you saw it?" Stillman asked.

"I don't remember. It's always in there, so I hardly ever notice it or even think about it."

"Well, here's what we know so far," Stillman said. "You argued with Leland Two last night at Caleb's Diner. Leland Two then got into a car that witnesses describe as looking exactly like the one that's registered to you. Then someone put a bullet in his back. A twenty-two. You have a twenty-two registered to you, and it's missing. Do you have any conclusions you suggest we draw from all that?"

Teri felt numb. Everyone in the room knew the conclusion to draw. The unspoken line was that she had motive—a multimillion dollar motive; she had means—a missing .22; and she had opportunity—witnesses who placed her with the victim last night, and even placed him in her car.

"Do I need a lawyer?" she asked.

Stillman took a deep breath then paused, as if weighing his next words very carefully. "I suspect that would be a pretty good idea, don't you?"

CHAPTER 27

MONA DIDN'T KNOW what time it was or how long she had been lying there. All she knew when she regained consciousness was that the pain was like nothing she had ever felt before. Not even the skiing accident four years ago when she leg-whipped a pine tree at sixty miles an hour. Every time she replayed that one in her mind, nausea roiled her stomach as she slowed down the picture and watched her lower leg snap like a pencil, bending ninety degrees sideways. Nor the time she was texting while driving and plowed into a parked car on Wilshire. The airbag punched her texting hand into her face and the corner of the phone gouged her cheek. That one had required sixteen stitches to close.

And not even the emotional pain when she had come home early from a shoot and found her first and only husband in a three-way with her two sisters. In fact, she had been able to excise that pain painlessly with just a few signatures on court documents that cut the bastard permanently loose. And as for her sisters, well, what sisters? They were now dead to her.

She wondered how long before she would be dead to them.

In fact, she wondered simply how long before she would be dead.

For a few brief moments as she cleared the cobwebs from her mind, she couldn't even remember where she was or what had happened. All she knew was that she found herself lying face down on her bedroom floor, unable to move. Barely able to breathe. And with a deep pain in the middle of her back.

It slowly came back to her. The sounds in the house, the man on the other side of the door, the sound of gunshots. And then the pain.

She turned her head, a simple motion that upped the intensity of the searing hot sensation in her back. She could see three holes in a triangular pattern on the wooden door and shards of splintered wood that marked the paths of the bullets. It was a big triangle, isosceles in shape, the pattern made by a man who couldn't be real sure where she stood and was shooting blindly and hoping to make contact. She didn't know how many bullets were in her back, but the pattern suggested no more than two, maybe only one. That uncertainty on the part of her assassin might be the only reason she was still alive.

What was puzzling, though, was why he had not entered the room after firing. Once she no longer blocked entry, he could easily have pushed the door open, stepped inside, and emptied his weapon into her. Then she remembered that she, too, had been armed, albeit with just a BB pistol. She also remembered that she had fired it, and she remembered groans—or were they screams?—from the other side of the door. She couldn't imagine that BB wounds would be fatal, but maybe they had been strategic enough to drive him from the house.

Unless he was still inside, playing cat and mouse, and waiting for her to exit her hole.

She redirected her focus to her cell phone on the nightstand. If she could just get there without too much pain. It wasn't the hurt, itself, that worried her; it was the idea that too much would shut down her mind, sending her back to blissful unconsciousness. And if she blacked out, if she couldn't get to the phone first, she might never wake up again.

She raised up onto her elbows and dragged herself forward.

The carpet burned on her skin, but she paid it no mind. Carpet burns were no more than hiccups in a hurricane compared to the pain in her back. She moved forward what seemed like only an inch at a time, the nightstand growing tantalizingly closer with each pull of her elbows. The black waves seemed held at bay as they crashed on the shore of her consciousness, driven back by her sheer will power.

At last she reached the nightstand. She paused for a moment, as each breath came in a ragged gasp. At times she felt as if she were drowning, and she wondered if the bullet had punctured a lung. She pushed up as high as she could on her left elbow and reached with her right arm. Her hand danced around on the surface of the nightstand until she found the phone.

With a sigh of relief, she rolled onto her side as best she could, but even that small pressure on her back sent lightning bolts through her body and into her brain. She pressed the first number in her "favorites" and held the phone to her ear.

After a moment, a familiar voice answered.

"Teri," she said, her voice weak and breathy. "Help me."

"Where are you?" Teri asked.

Mona gasped, spit out a wad of phlegm onto the carpet beside her face. Dark red, glistening in the glow of the lamp from the nightstand.

"Bedroom."

Then she blacked out.

CHAPTER 28

"MONA?—MONA!"

Teri looked at Stillman, her face a pale spectre. He read her look instantly.

"Everything okay?" he asked.

"We have to go to Mona's," Teri said to the three detectives. "Something's wrong."

"Give me the phone," Stillman said.

Teri complied and watched as he raised it to his ear. "Mona?" He looked at Teri and shook his head. "The line's still open."

"Can you hear anything?"

"Nothing. Who's Mona?"

"Mona Hirsch. She's my producing partner. I tried to call her all night, but she wouldn't answer."

Swafford took his own cell phone from his pocket and dialed a number. "This is Swafford. We need a unit to respond to..."

He looked at Teri. "What's her address?" he asked Teri. She told him and he repeated the address, then said, "I don't know. Just have someone get there ASAP. I'm on my way."

Teri led the way in her SUV, followed by Swafford in his car and the two CHP detectives in their Chevy Tahoe. She tried to make some sense of events over the past twenty-four hours, but none of it lined up.

She knew she had been recognized at the diner. Los Angeles

and its environs were used to celebrity sightings of disguised and camouflaged movie stars, and only rarely did disguises work. Just as some people supposedly had "gay-dar," able to pick out those still hidden deep within their closets, and others could spot toupees at a hundred paces, Angelenos knew their celebrities when they saw them. Half of them might not know who the President of the United States was even if you spotted them the O and the bama, but flash a picture of a sunglasses-and-baseball-cap-wearing two-time Academy Award winner, and ninety percent of them would nail the identity in a split second. The other ten percent would simply mistake her for Sandra Bullock, Hilary Swank, or Angelina Jolie.

She wished now that she had kept following the look-a-like vehicle north on the PCH last night. Maybe things would make more sense to her if she had actually seen what happened up there, but common sense told her that would only have made things worse. Someone might have spotted her in the vicinity, which would have gutted her already nearly worthless alibi.

But then she remembered calling Mona last night. Was there technology that would allow the police to figure out where she had been when those calls were made? Seems like she had seen that at least once on a cop show on television, but then again, how much of what you saw on TV could you actually believe? Still, it was worth a shot. If so, it would show that she had been working her way home when she had called, and maybe it could provide her an alibi for the exact time Leland Crowell, or whoever the scraggly-haired man was, took a header off that cliff.

But the real nagging question, the one that was now gnawing at her heart, was why Mona hadn't answered last night. If she had been home, she would have had her cell turned on. If the battery was low, she would have had it charging, but still turned on. Mona never turned her phone off. It was her umbilical to the world.

Then Teri thought of the ragged gasps and the nearly guttural sound of Mona's voice on the phone. "Help me."

She pressed harder on the gas, took the turn onto Sunset on two wheels, and accelerated. Behind her, the detectives did the same, keeping a close tail on her. Within a matter of minutes since receiving the call, she turned onto Mona's street. It was a stereotypical Beverly Hills residential neighborhood of luxury homes from another era, many gated or walled off by hedges, usually some variety of free-blooming hibiscus bushes, yards neatly trimmed, high-priced cars in circle driveways. The air was sweet with the fragrance of a hundred varieties of flowers, and not a soul was on the sidewalks other than the hired help with gas-powered edgers, leaf blowers, and hedge trimmers.

A Beverly Hills PD squad car sat at the curb in front of Mona's house, which was more modest than those of her gaudier neighbors. Teri remembered the first time she had been here, meeting Mona who had just put a down payment on the house. It was with the joy of a child getting her first bicycle that Mona led her through the vacant structure, pointing where she was going to put this and where she was going to put that, and what she was going to have to buy to fill this room, and the artwork that would hang on this wall and that wall. When their financial success as a producing team snowballed for a brief while, Mona had done exactly as she said, filling her house to fit the exact parameters of her dream.

Teri wondered what nightmare they would find inside now.

She got out of her car as the detectives pulled up behind her. Two uniformed police officers stood at the front door, looking back at the sound of the arriving vehicles. Teri rushed to the door, Stillman hard on her heels.

"Is this your home, ma'am?" one of the young cops asked, recognition in his eyes, but professionalism in his voice. He looked as if he had come straight from a *GQ* modeling shoot, with every hair in place, his skin bronze from the sun. His partner, a slightly older but equally gorgeous cop, nodded toward Swafford, who brought up the rear, as if they knew each other.

"Anything?" Swafford asked.

"We just got here," said the first cop, whose nameplate identified him as S. Baskind. "We rang the bell, but there's no answer. And the door's locked."

"I have a key," Teri said. Her fingers trembled as she struggled to single one out on her key ring. She had just managed to grasp it when it slipped through her fingers. She knelt to pick the ring up, her eyes suddenly filling with tears.

"Let me help you, ma'am," Baskind said. He picked up the key ring and extended the one she had been trying to grasp. "Is it this one?"

She nodded.

He inserted it into the lock and turned. The deadbolt slid back, and he slowly pushed the door open. The only sound was an urgent beeping from the security system in the entryway.

"Alarm is set," Baskind said.

"I know the code," Teri said as she tried to squeeze by. He stepped aside and allowed her to enter. She punched in the four digit code, and the beeping stopped.

She took a quick step toward the interior of the house, only to be stopped by Stillman grabbing her arm. She looked back at him, startled by the suddenness of his movement.

"Stay behind us," he said.

She nodded then noticed Swafford squatting at the threshold. "Check this out," he said.

All eyes turned to the area indicated by his extended index finger, on the entryway floor just inside the door. Guns were drawn as they recognized the unmistakable droplets of blood. Looking outside the door, Teri saw additional droplets on the porch that she had not noticed before.

Swafford pointed toward the interior of the house. "They're coming from there, leading out to the door."

"Oh, my God," Teri said, her words barely audible. "Mona."

"Go wait by your car," Stillman said. Then, to Officer Baskind, "Wait with her."

"And call for Crime Scene," Swafford said.

Baskind nodded. "Let's go, ma'am," he said to Teri.

Teri felt numb as the officer gently grasped her elbow and escorted her to the curb.

CHAPTER 29

STILLMAN LED THE way toward the interior of the house. "There's more here," he said.

A thin but clearly defined trail of blood led in a zig-zag pattern deeper into the house, as if someone had carried a bucket of red paint with a tiny pinprick hole in the bottom. "And you're right, whoever was dripping was moving this way. They weren't moving too steady, though. At least they couldn't walk a straight line."

Swafford stopped at the entrance to the living room, still shrouded in darkness despite the brightness of the day outside. He reached inside, felt along the wall, and flipped the light switch. A chandelier clicked on as a ceiling fan slowly revved up. He crossed the room and opened the drapes, allowing light into the room. The blood trail glistened.

Stillman looked back at the others. "Follow the yellow brick road."

Baskind had told Teri to sit in the back seat of the car, which he turned on and cranked its air conditioning, but she found it impossible to sit still. She joined him beside the car as he finished calling for Beverly Hills crime scene technicians.

"Friend of yours live here, ma'am?" Baskind asked.

"My best friend."

"I'm sure she's okay."

"You wouldn't say that if you had talked to her."

He nodded but said nothing in reply.

She paced the sidewalk while he watched her every move, likely aware that she was a suspect in a murder. That much had probably been communicated to him by the detectives during the drive over. And now more cops were on the way. She had wanted to leave her cell free during the drive in case Mona called back, but now she wondered if it was time to make the call to a lawyer.

She pulled her cell from her pocket and hesitated briefly to see if Baskind would stop her. When he didn't, she hit a number on speed dial.

"I'm at Mona's," she said when Mike Capalletti answered. "I think something's happened." She paused, but before he could respond, she added, "I need you here as my lawyer."

The blood trail stopped briefly at the foot of a broad stairwell, but Swafford spotted it again on a step about halfway up. "Someone's trying to stop the blood flow, but it's not working too well," he said. "It did slow down some, though."

Sure enough, the blood trail was thicker and more distinct farther up the stairs. Whatever happened had happened up there.

"Ms. Hirsch?" he called. "Police, Ms. Hirsch. Are you up there? You okay?"

Silence.

Nichols joined him at the top of the stairs, while Stillman squatted on the steps behind them, studying the blood splatter.

"You think this movie star killed that guy up the highway?" Swafford asked.

"I don't know. I hope not."

"You think she did something to her partner?"

"I don't know. I hope not."

"Is that all you can say? 'I don't know. I hope not.'?"

"I don't fucking know. I fucking hope not."

Swafford smiled. "Okay. Just wanted to make sure you Chippies don't have limited vocabularies."

Nichols smiled back. "Well, now you know I know at least one two-syllable word."

"And one three-syllable word, if you count 'syllable.'"

Then, as if someone had flipped a switch, they turned grim as they followed the blood trail down the hallway. Stillman hustled to catch up, taking the steps two at a time and staying close to the side so as not to step in the trail. At the top, he looked back down.

"Blood on the banister," he said.

Nichols and Swafford turned and looked. Sure enough, a slick of blood ran down the top of the banister for a length of about 18 inches.

"Someone leaned on it for balance," Stillman said. "Might be able to find some prints."

"That only matters if it's not Hirsch," Swafford said.

"I know."

"And if it's not Hirsch, that probably means we're not going to like what we find up here."

"I know."

Swafford turned to Nichols. "Did he forget how to say 'don't,' or is he just your opposite?"

"I don't know."

Swafford took a deep breath and wiped his smile away. "All right, damn it, let's keep going."

He led the way to the end of the hallway and turned the corner, with the two CHP detectives close behind. "Here's where it happened," he said.

When the others had joined him, they saw what he meant. They faced a closed door with a triangle of holes in it, about chest high. A small pool of blood had collected on the floor just outside the door, clearly the spot where the trail originated.

"Whatever we're going to find, we're going to find on the other side of that door," Stillman said.

With Swafford leading, the three men inched toward the door, then paused again. Weapon in front, Swafford slowly pushed the door open with his free hand. The first thing to get their attention was blood-soaked carpet directly in front of the open door, littered with tiny shards of wood. Lying on the edge of it was a BB pistol.

"Looks like someone might have got off a shot or two with that," Swafford said. "It would explain the blood trail down the stairs."

But the next thing to get their attention was a much broader blood trail that led around the edge of the bed to a foot just visible on the side nearest the wall. Swafford stepped over the BB pistol and looked into the face of Mona Hirsch.

Her eyes were open, her lips moving as if trying to speak. He holstered his weapon, squatted down beside her, and leaned close to hear.

"Help me."

CHAPTER 30

TERI HEARD SIRENS then saw Detective Stillman exit Mona's house and head toward her. She rushed to him, just as he waved the occupants of an arriving ambulance to hurry. Officer Baskind followed close behind.

"Crime Scene's on its way," Baskind said to Stillman.

"Good."

"Who called an ambulance?" Teri asked. "Is she okay?"

"She's in pretty bad shape, but she's alive," Stillman said. "She's been shot."

Teri froze. "Shot?"

"Looks like someone was trying to get into her bedroom and she blocked the door. Whoever it was shot right through it."

Teri tried to move past him, but Stillman grabbed her arm and stopped her. "I can't let you go in there. It's a crime scene."

"She's my friend."

"I know she is, but let's let the paramedics do their job and get her to the hospital."

As he spoke, two paramedics, hands full of gear, moved across the front yard toward them. "Upstairs, back bedroom," Stillman said.

"Teri."

She and Stillman looked to the curb, where Mike had just arrived. He looked as if he had just come from the country club, wearing creased khakis and a polo shirt.

"What's going on?" he asked.

"It's Mona. She's been shot."

The words seemed to have very little effect on Mike. His face was impassive as he looked at Stillman. "Who are you?"

"Detective Stillman. CHP."

"You don't have any jurisdiction. This is Beverly Hills."

"Mike, nobody gives a damn about jurisdiction," Teri said. "Didn't you hear what I said? Mona's been shot."

"I'm just looking out for you. I am a lawyer, you know."

"Is he the lawyer you were going to call?" Stillman asked.

"You still haven't answered my question," Mike said. "What's CHP doing here?"

"They were at my house," Teri said. "Then, when Mona called, we came here."

"Look, I don't mean to seem obtuse," Mike said, "but all you said when you called was that something was wrong at Mona's and you needed a lawyer. Now I get here and find out you've had state cops at your house, and I don't have a clue why."

"They're here about Leland Crowell."

"What about him? He's dead."

"Yes, sir, he is," Stillman said. "But the question we're trying to answer is when he died."

"Two years ago."

"Or maybe it was last night."

While the news of Mona's shooting had little impact, those words seemed to shake Mike. He looked sharply at Teri then looked away, as if he'd been caught in front of the computer with porn on the screen.

"Maybe you'd better start at the beginning," Mike said to Stillman, an edge to his voice. "And go slow. I'm a little dull-witted sometimes."

"I can see that," Stillman said.

"You—"

"Not now, Mike," Teri said. "All I care about right now is Mona."

The words seem to soften Mike a bit. "How is she?"

"Paramedics are with her right now," Stillman said. "She lost a lot of blood, but she was conscious when we got here."

"Please let me see her," Teri said.

"I'm sorry, Ms. Squire, but I can't. I'll find out what hospital they're taking her to, though, so you can meet the ambulance there."

The dam that had been holding back Teri's tears burst. Mike pulled her close, wrapped his arms around her, and held her as she sobbed.

Teri hated hospitals. Always had, always would. Some people thought of hospitals as places people went for healing; Teri thought of them as places people went to suffer and die. Both of her grandparents had. Her best friend back home, Suzette, had. And her brother Adam had. Was her new best friend, Mona, also going to die? Right then, thoughts of movies, screenplays, and Leland Crowells didn't matter. All that mattered was Mona.

As she paced in the Emergency Room waiting area, Mike sat on a small couch across from the two CHP detectives. He watched them with steely eyes, as if taking their measure. They, on the other hand, talked to each other and steadfastly ignored his stare. It was as if, to them, he didn't exist.

The elevator bell sounded its tone. The doors opened and Doug Bozarth stepped off, impeccably dressed in a tailored, gray pin-striped suit, with a pale blue dress shirt open at the collar and no tie. Casual day for him, obviously. Close by his side was Bob Keene with his bow-legged stride, wearing creased designer jeans, a tan camp shirt, deck shoes, and no socks, an outfit designed to look thrown-together but that screamed calculated, as usual.

They approached Mike, not Teri, something that the

detectives seemed to take note of as they watched, then signaled to each other with glances.

"What's going on?" Bob asked.

"Cops," Mike said, nodding toward Stillman and Nichols.

"Is there some place we can talk?" Bozarth asked. His tone was strictly professional, his words generic in the presence of the police.

"Cafeteria is downstairs," Mike said.

"Let's go."

Teri continued to pace.

"Teri," Mike said. "We're going to the cafeteria."

"I'll be here."

"You need to come with us."

"I need to be here if the doctors come out."

"I'm sure CHP will get a message to you," Mike said. "Won't you, officers?"

"Actually, we'd prefer that she stay here," Stillman said.

"I'm her attorney," Bozarth said. Teri cut him a sharp look. That was news to her.

"I thought Mr. Capalletti was," Nichols said.

"Great country, the United States," Bozarth said. "They let you have as many lawyers as you want."

"Or need."

"So you'll understand if we'd prefer to talk in confidence," Bozarth continued.

"Just don't leave the hospital," Stillman said. "We still have more questions for Ms. Squire."

"Is she under arrest?" Bozarth asked.

"No."

"They're CHP, not local," Mike said.

"Is that so? Well, then it seems that their jurisdiction ended at the freeway."

"Common mistake," Nichols said. "Mr. Capelletti made it

earlier, as well. Actually the California Highway Patrol acts as the state police and has jurisdiction to enforce all state laws anywhere in the state. But I'm sure you didn't come here for a civics lesson."

"But speaking of civics lessons," Stillman said. "Are you a licensed attorney in the state of California, Mr. Bozarth?"

"So you know who I am."

"I've seen your picture in the papers. And I know you're not from here. Pennsylvania, right?"

"I live here now."

"But you haven't answered my question: Are you licensed to practice law in California?"

"Information easily enough found," Bozarth said. "I'd suggest you check with the California Bar Association. But for now, my client and I need privacy to talk. You have my word that we won't leave the hospital."

Dismissing the detectives, he turned and walked to the elevator. Bob followed close behind, with Mike and Teri at the rear. They found a corner table in the hospital's basement cafeteria. Mike got coffee for all of them and then sat next to Teri.

"Now tell me very carefully just what in the hell is going on here," Bozarth said.

"Someone broke into Mona's house and shot her," Teri said.

"Back up a bit. We'll get to that, but I want the full narrative. You met with this imposter last night at the diner, right?"

"They're saying I killed him."

"That's just plain crazy," Mike said.

"What have you told them?" Bozarth asked.

"Nothing. Just that Leland Crowell died a long time ago and that I never met him."

"The report I get is that they've got witnesses who say you and someone else argued at the diner last night."

"How do you know that?" Teri asked.

"I've got my sources."

"You were supposed to have your people there last night. What do they say?"

"The same thing the police say. That you and Leland argued."

"So they were there," she said, more of a question than a statement.

"Of course. Just as I said they would be. They also said the man you argued with got in a late model SUV, same color as yours, and left."

"But not mine. I had already left."

No response from Bozarth.

"Did they see that?" Teri asked. "Did they see me leave?"

"What about your gun?" Bozarth asked.

"Answer my question. Did your people see me leave ahead of Leland, or whoever he is?"

"Was," Bozarth said.

"Whatever. Did they see me leave?"

She held Bozarth's eyes for a long moment, her personal lie detector at work. He met her gaze evenly, spoke deliberately. "They say he got in your car and left with you."

"That's bullshit!"

"They have no reason to lie."

"Unless they're setting me up."

"And they have no reason to do that. We don't need the scrutiny." He paused then added, "*I* don't need the scrutiny."

Teri's alarms starting going off again. He had a good point, but it was hardly one that could be raised at this stage. *We didn't kill anyone because we're committing fraud, so we want to fly under the radar.*

"What about the other people at the diner?" Bozarth asked. "They also say he got in your car. Why would they lie?"

"I'm not saying they're lying; I'm saying they're mistaken. I had already left, but there was another car there, just like mine. That's the car he got in, not mine."

"How do you know?" Mike asked.

"Because I came back. I saw the other SUV in the parking lot, and he got in it."

"Driving?" Bozarth asked.

"Passenger side."

"Did anyone see you leave?"

"How should I know?"

"Why did you come back?" Mike asked.

"I don't know. Just a hunch, I guess. I wanted to see if anyone came to meet him. That's when I saw them leaving, going the other way. So I followed them."

"Goddamn!" Bob said. "You followed them? Are we going to find out other witnesses saw you in the vicinity of the murder?"

"I don't know what we're going to find, Bob," Teri said. She'd had as much of him as she could tolerate over the past couple of years, and if ever there was a time to assert herself with him, it was now. Besides, did it really matter if she pissed him off? The way things were going, he was the least of her worries. Prison was more at the forefront of her mind. Someone was setting her up, and they were doing a damn good job of it.

"Did you see what happened?" Bozarth asked.

"Once they got up north, past San Simeon, I turned around and came home. I don't know what happened after that."

"It's a shame you didn't go just a few miles farther. You might have found out how the dead guy got dead."

"Yeah, maybe next time."

The group lapsed into a silence for a few minutes, mulling over what they knew and fretting over what they didn't.

Bozarth broke the silence. "Back to my earlier question about your gun. My sources tell me the dead guy had a twenty-two bullet in his back. You own a twenty-two. Where's your gun?"

"Why do we keep calling him 'the dead guy'?" Mike asked.

"Because he's the dead guy."

"How do you know I have a twenty-two?" Teri asked.

"The question is whether the police have it and whether it matches the bullet."

"I don't know where it is," Teri said. "They asked me for it, but it wasn't where it was supposed to be."

"Let's just hope they don't find it. If someone's setting you up, I'd bet my last dollar the bullet will match."

"So they can't ever prove anything without the gun, right?" Bob asked. "And in the meantime, it's just more publicity for the movie."

"Haven't you been listening?" Bozarth said. "It's publicity that'll call into question whether Teri ever rightfully owned the script in the first place. And if the dead guy really is the writer, she didn't inherit from him if he didn't die before, and she can't inherit from him now if she killed him."

"I didn't kill him." She glanced at Mike then turned her attention back to Bozarth. "Are you a criminal lawyer?"

"I'm whatever I need to be."

"Why don't I feel reassured?"

"Look, even just an arrest will throw the bequest into question. A conviction will invalidate it. That much criminal law, I do know. So you see, Ms. Squire, I am highly motivated to do whatever it takes to see to it that you never get so much as charged. And *that* ought to give you great comfort."

Somehow it didn't.

CHAPTER 31

CHAD PALMER TIGHTENED the cinch on Hansel, his chestnut quarter horse with a star on his nose and black socks. He put one boot in the stirrup, threw his other leg over the horse, and settled into the saddle. Gretel, Hansel's sister, snorted in the adjacent stall, unhappy that Hansel was going out while she had to stay behind. Temperatures seemed to have hit a slump, dropping to just above 100 degrees. Twenty-five days in a row of triple digits, but still not as brutal as the prior week, when the mercury topped out at 109 degrees for three consecutive days.

Chad pulled the reins to the side, turned Hansel, and headed out of the barn, across the corral, through the gate, and off into the trees. Ever since he was a little boy, Chad sought the comfort of the woods to think and clear his head in times of trouble. Today was no different. The news reports he had heard were disturbing. Not a lot of detail, just enough to signal trouble for an old friend who had already seen more than her fair share of trouble. He wanted to reach out to her, to offer his assistance, but what could he do? He was just a lowly Texas Hill Country veterinarian, a decade her senior, who had hoped to wait for her to come of age, but she left years ago and never looked back.

Not that he blamed her. There were too many sad memories associated for her with everything in Texas. And even if she came back, he was now divorced, closer to fifty than forty, and hardly a catch, his skin leathered and tanned by years in the sun.

Still…

He moved through an arch of willows that grew together overhead, creating a tunnel of trees. As kids, he and Adam Tucker had ridden their horses here, pretending they were entering a cave or playing Butch and Sundance, running from the Pinkerton posse led by Joe Lefors. Sometimes Peggy, Adam's little sister, followed them, wanting to play with the big kids, only to be sent packing by Adam. The trail ended at a ledge overlooking the Medina River, not nearly as high as the cliff in the movie, but enough of a drop to create an adrenaline rush as they held hands and jumped off into the cool, clear waters below. Adam was always the one who wanted to mimic Sundance's famous yell as they fell. Sometimes Peggy only pretended to go home, then followed and jumped right behind them, mimicking Adam's "Ohhhhhh shiiiiiittt!!!" Chad wondered if she was saying that same thing today.

His thoughts were taken back to the present by Waylon Jennings singing *Are You Sure Hank Done It This Way?*, his cell phone's signature ringtone. Chad was surprised by the tone, cell reception being so spotty on his ranch. The farther he rode from the house and the barn, the less likely he was to have service at all. In the trees along the ridgeline, near the meadow at the entry to his property, there was no prayer of reception. And yet he carried his phone with him everywhere he went. You never knew when a patient was in trouble and his owner urgently needed the doctor.

He answered without checking the read-out to see who the caller was. "Hello."

The next words he heard chilled him. He had heard the same words spoken nearly twenty years ago by the same voice, with the same tremulous tone:

"Chad? It's Peggy. I'm in trouble."

There was something comforting to Teri in Chad's voice, even though he had spoken but one word. There was strength in hearing the one person in the world who had believed in her and stood by her in her time of need, when she felt her whole life coming apart, as if she stood on a precipice of her own. Now that she found herself perched there again, she reached for the same lifeline he had thrown her once before.

Window down, breeze rustling her hair and drying tears on her cheeks, Teri maneuvered her SUV up Coldwater Canyon Drive, her thoughts wandering to Mona lying helpless, but at least alive, in her hospital bed. It was a classic good news/bad news situation. The bad news was that her friend was barely clinging to life, but the good news was that at least it took Teri's mind off the fact that she was a murder suspect.

She glanced in the rearview mirror and saw a boxy sedan, looked like a Mercedes, following. It periodically accelerated as the road temporarily straightened out, as if preparing to pass, but then would drop back as the straight-a-ways returned to their inevitable curves. Teri checked her speedometer and saw that she was lagging below the speed limit.

She pushed down harder on the gas and upped her speed. "Sorry," she thought, as if the mental apology could somehow reach the impatient driver behind her.

"What kind of trouble?" Chad asked.

"I need a lawyer. A criminal lawyer."

For a moment there was nothing but silence, but Teri could hear Chad's breathing on the other end. Then she also heard familiar sounds, sounds that tugged at her heart and drew her home. Rustling of trees and the steady clip-clop of horse's hooves.

"You riding?" she asked.

"Yeah."

"Then you already know why I'm calling."

"Why do you say that?"

"It's the middle of the day," she said. "You only ride in the middle of the day when you're upset."

"I always thought you should have been a lawyer. Your mind is so logical, you'd be a whiz at putting cases together and drawing conclusions."

"Is it all over the radio and TV out there?" she asked. The reporters had already started to gather at the hospital when she slipped out through the loading dock and hustled to her car. How long before they congregated outside her house? She had to get there first and get inside. Her bunker mentality instincts were kicking into high gear.

"No one knows your connection here, so it's not a big issue," he said. "As far as the good people of Bandera County are concerned, it's just another Hollywood sensation that has nothing to do with them."

"I hope it stays that way. What have you heard?"

"I saw a couple of reports on the national news, but no details," he said. "Just that Mona had been hurt and that you were at the hospital with the police. They made it sound like you might even be a suspect."

"Not for Mona."

Another long pause, as Chad filled in the blanks. "But for something else."

"Like I said, I need a criminal lawyer."

"You know I shut down my law practice a long time ago. Taking care of animals pretty much pays all of my bills these days."

"But you do still have your law license, don't you?"

Chad paused before answering. She heard the clip-clop of hooves fall silent. He had reined his horse in, probably at the river, to let him drink.

"I'd be happy if I never saw the inside of a courtroom again," he said.

"I need someone I can trust."

"That didn't work out so well last time."

"You had a bad client. She wouldn't let you use the truth."

"What about this time?"

Now it was Teri's turn to pause. Let's see, what was the truth this time? She had inherited a screenplay from a man who, it turned out, may not have actually been dead, so she may not actually have owned his screenplay, putting her big comeback movie in jeopardy. Then she had conspired with several others—including a very powerful and very rich man who would have been happy to see the resurrected screenwriter removed—to confront the risen-from-the-dead screenwriter in the middle of the night, who then got into a car exactly like hers and drove up to Big Sur during a period of time she could not account for, and someone put a bullet in his back at the identical spot where he had met his demise in the first place.

That was the truth, and it was a very damning truth. It was a truth that could ruin everything for her, everything she had worked so hard for, to climb up off the trash heap her career had been relegated to. It was a truth that even she had a hard time believing. And yet it was a better truth than the one that she covered up all those years ago.

"Yes," she said at last. "I want you to use the truth."

Chad heaved his shoulders, as if a weight had been lifted. A strange feeling, since he knew Peggy's troubles, whatever they might be, were just beginning. Or, more likely, simply continuing after a two decade long hiatus. But she was promising him *carte blanche* with the one commodity she had withheld from him before: the truth. He knew what a powerful weapon the truth could be. It was every lawyer's dream, to have truth on your side. You could then be Superman, fighting for truth, justice, and the American way. He knew things would have been different last time if Peggy had just relinquished her grip on the truth and let it out into the light of day. He understood why she had not wanted to, the pain it would inflict on people she loved. But no matter how much he had begged, she clutched it to herself even more tightly, as if protecting it from public view with her body.

He never really knew the whole truth, in fact, though he suspected. Peggy's dad suspected, too, as did her mom, but the only person who really knew, who could really say what had actually happened, had been Peggy. And her lips were sealed.

So to hear her now say that she would arm him with the one weapon she had withheld last time was a huge relief. It might not save the day—and given that he didn't even know what the trouble was, well might not—but he vowed to himself that he would reward her trust.

"Okay," he said. "The answer to your question is, yes, I still have my law license. And yes, I'll be your lawyer. But you know I'm not licensed in California."

He could hear relief in her voice, as she said, "Thank you, Chad. Because it's happening all over again. I—"

Her next words were drowned out by a screech of what sounded like tires, followed by a metal-on-metal banging sound.

Then the line went dead.

He looked at the phone and saw that he still had service, albeit weak. He punched the callback button and waited.

A female voice, not Peggy's, answered. "Your call has been forwarded to—"

He jabbed the "off" button, headed Hansel around, and sprinted for the barn.

CHAPTER 32

AS THE TRAILING car rammed into her SUV, Teri's face bounced forward and smashed into the steering wheel. The phone slipped from her fingers, bounced off the passenger seat, and slid into the gap between the seat and door.

Teri shook her head to clear the cobwebs. She looked in the rearview mirror. Two things jumped out at her. The first was the gush of blood down her face, its point of origin a cut on her forehead. She knew that the skin there was thin and notorious for easy blood flow, even with minor cuts, yet the volume of blood frightened her. Glancing at her hand, she saw the culprit. She had apparently slammed her head into her hand that gripped the wheel, and her ruby eternity ring had gouged the skin. Her hand, too, was decorated with her blood.

The second thing she saw, and had to look back to the mirror to confirm, was that she had been rammed by the same sedan that had been following her, the one she originally thought wanted to pass. Now she realized it had been merely stalking her. Its windshield was tinted, and all she could make out was the dim outline of a head, its face and gender unrecognizable.

The sedan disengaged, dropping back about twenty feet. Teri took a deep breath. She looked for a safe haven to turn into—a driveway, a street with traffic, anything. But there was nothing. Up ahead, another curve in the road loomed. She pressed on the accelerator, hoping to widen her lead and clear the curve, then make her escape up the straightaway that she knew was just beyond.

The impact of the second assault staggered her, delivered with far more force than the first. She deduced that the initial impact had merely been a wake-up call; the second was meant for something more sinister, a fact soon confirmed as the sedan not only maintained contact, but also began pushing her forward. She pressed harder on the gas, trying to disengage, but to no avail. Then the sedan pulled back again and followed. Waiting for another chance to attack, no doubt.

Teri formulated her own strategy. She lessened pressure on the accelerator as she entered the curve. Then came the inevitable surge from the trailing car. It closed the gap quickly then, just as impact seemed inevitable, Teri slammed on her brakes. She hoped to surprise her assailant. She almost smiled at the thought of him banging his face on his own steering wheel.

What she hadn't counted on, though, was her own vehicle's reaction. Upon impact, the airbag exploded from the steering wheel. It punched her in the face like a heavyweight's fist and drove her back against the seat. She heard a crackling sound and knew instantly her nose had broken. The airbag deflated nearly as quickly as it opened. She fought at it with both hands, desperately trying to get at least one of them back on the steering wheel.

The sedan maintained contact, pushing now with great force. It obviously had some kind of super-charged engine, and its aggression was powerful. Fighting past the airbag, Teri grabbed the wheel and turned sharply to the left in reaction to what she saw ahead—a sharp turn in the road, with a steep drop-off. She managed to keep her wheels on the pavement as she pushed against the brake pedal with both feet, straightening her legs, her back pressed hard against the seat. The squeal of tires on concrete filled her ears, smoke from burning rubber obscuring her vision much as the fires in the nearby hills had done before.

She looked in the mirror again, hoping to catch some glimpse of the driver's identity. If she was going off a cliff like Leland Crowell, she at least wanted to know who had been responsible. Then she saw a second car, barely visible as the road wiggled in a slight S curve. Another sedan, much older, much larger than her aggressor. Accelerating, gaining on them. Then it appeared to pass as it moved side-by-side with her assailant, between the sedan and the cliffside. Its windows were also tinted, its driver invisible.

A gasp escaped from Teri's lips as the second car swerved sharply and slammed into the attack car. For a few moments, she felt the power of both cars behind her, surging forward, her own vehicle powerless. Then the second car succeeded in driving the first completely to the right. Teri felt freedom as its bumper slid apart from hers. Disengaged, Teri floored it.

She rounded another curve, headed to safety, as her assailant's vehicle slammed through a guardrail, momentarily suspended on air then disappeared down the mountainside. Teri watched in disbelief as her rescuer's car slowed to a near stop, made a Y-turn in the road, and headed back down the mountain.

Teri exhaled, realizing for the first time that she had been holding her breath. Then she limped home, her hands trembling as they tried to hold the wheel and keep her car between the lines.

CHAPTER 33

TERI'S BREATH CAME in ragged gasps. She pulled into her driveway, retrieved her cell phone, then raced for the house and slammed the door behind her. She leaned against it and slid to the floor. She knew she must look like a refugee from a war zone, with blood still streaming down her face from the cut on her forehead. Blood from her nose had already dried and crusted around her nostrils. Her tee-shirt was soaked with dark red splotches, reminiscent of retro tie-dyed clothing from the '60s.

She felt her tender nose, surprised to find a complete lack of feeling. She got to her feet and looked in the mirror on the coat-rack just inside the entryway. Her eyes had already blackened and her nose was a swollen glob in the middle of her face. She wiped blood away from the center of her forehead and looked at her wound, shocked that such a small gash could cause so much blood flow.

She stumbled to a half-bathroom by the utility room, grabbed a hand towel, soaked it with water, and wiped at the blood. The flow had ebbed to a trickle, enough that perhaps she could staunch it completely with a thick bandage. She opened the cabinet door and fumbled around until she found a half-empty tube of antiseptic ointment and an unopened box of bandages. After doctoring her wounds, she stripped out of her shirt and bra and tossed them in the washing machine, then peeled off her bloody jeans and tossed them in as well. Once she had the washer going, she headed, nearly naked, to the kitchen, grabbed the phone, and dialed. After two rings, Mike's voice answered.

"This is Mike. You know what to do at the tone."

She waited for the tone then left her message. "Mike? I need you. Call me on the landline."

She hung up and headed for her bedroom to shower and dress. She stopped long enough to open the curtains over the sliding door, flooding the room with sunlight. Just as she entered the bedroom door, her bedside phone rang. She snatched it up on the third ring.

"Mike?"

"No, it's Chad. Are you all right?"

A wave of dizziness rolled over Teri, accompanied by a churning in her stomach. Before her legs could collapse, she sat on the edge of the bed. She breathed in heaping gasps. A panic attack. She hadn't had one of these in almost twenty years.

"Peggy, are you all right?"

She regained her breath and found her voice, though she knew it sounded weak, as if in a tunnel. "I don't know what to do anymore."

"Peggy, you've got to tell me what's going on. What happened while ago? You got cut off. It sounded like a wreck."

"I—"

The doorbell sounded before she could finish her sentence.

"I think that's Mike at the door. I've got to go."

"First tell me you're all right."

"I'm okay."

"You'll call me later and let me know what's going on?"

"I will. I promise."

She hung up, grabbed a pair of shorts and a replacement tee-shirt, and then ran to the front door. Mike must have already been on his way when she called. She knew that her battered face would be shocking to him, but there was no way to prepare him for it other than to simply let him see it for himself. She just hoped that Doug Bozarth was not in tow. For reasons that she couldn't articulate even to herself, she felt that he had something to do with the car that tried to run her off the road. She also believed that he had something to do with the events of last night, including the attack on Mona, though she had no proof. It was simply a gut feeling, a hunch that she had gone from an asset to a liability as far as he was concerned.

She opened the door without checking through the peep-hole first, shocked to see that her guest was not Mike, but Annemarie Crowell. This time, though, Teri felt as if her own face might top Annemarie's in the bizarre category.

Teri's second shock was seeing the car at the curb: a dark, older model Chevrolet sedan.

With a crumpled fender on the passenger side.

Could it be? Annemarie Crowell was her savior? And if so, why had she been following Teri? There was no other reason she would have been back there. Los Angeles was too big and spread out for this woman to have coincidentally been in the neighborhood when someone tried to run her off the road. She had to have been there by design.

"What are you doing here?" Teri asked, after opening the door.

"May I come inside?"

"I asked why you're here."

"I wanted to see if you were all right."

"You were in the second car."

"Don't you think that entitles me to an invitation inside?"

Teri was torn. On the one hand, she owed this woman her life. On the other, she was just too strange, too bizarre, for Teri to feel comfortable in close quarters with her. Yet Teri had to admit that there was something irresistibly compelling about the woman. She never smiled, not even a smirk. Her eyes betrayed no emotion, yet they locked with Teri's, and Teri found it difficult to avert her glance. It had been barely two years earlier when this same woman sat in her house, following the death of her son, and gave Teri the screenplay that promised to resurrect her career.

And speaking of resurrection, did Annemarie know about the resurrected Leland and his subsequent demise last night? If so, she was part of the scam, whatever it might be. Could she also have been the driver of the SUV that the thin man had gotten in? Surely not. She was odd, but capable of putting a bullet in a man's back? In her own son? If indeed that even was her son.

Teri stepped aside from the doorway. "Please come in."

As soon as Annemarie stepped across the threshold, Teri felt as if the breath had been sucked out of her lungs. Her fingers tingled, and it felt as if a fist squeezed her heart. Obviously she had not completely gotten over the panic attack, but it had lurked in the shadows and now reasserted itself. Or was it simply an alarm going off, alerting her that the fox was in the henhouse.

She closed the door and led Annemarie to the den. Annemarie stood rigid in the middle of the room and stared at the sliding doors.

"My eyes are sensitive to light," she said.

"I'm sorry." Teri pulled the cord to close the curtains, leaving them open about a foot so as not to plunge the room into complete darkness.

Annemarie went to a Queen Anne chair across from the couch, maybe even the same one she had sat in before when she clutched her son's screenplay in her talons. Teri remained standing. To sit might encourage the woman to stay longer, something she didn't want. Her goal was to get her out of the house as quickly as possible.

"You're in pain," Annemarie said. "You've been injured. Please sit."

"I'm fine."

"You're out of breath. The injury to your nose must make breathing difficult. You really must sit."

The words, spoken in a low monotone, seemed to have a hypnotic effect on Teri. Almost unconsciously she sank into a couch cushion. Her breathing eased instantly.

"Please be calm," Annemarie said. "I mean you no harm."

"You were in the second car."

"Yes."

"Why were you following me?"

"Because you are in danger," Annemarie said. She still spoke in a low, hushed tone, with no inflection, no emotion. She pronounced that Teri was in danger as if she were commenting on the weather.

"Danger from who?"

"If something happens to you, who stands to gain?"

Yeah, Teri had been wondering that, herself. The answer was Doug Bozarth. Not only because her death would help skyrocket the box office, even if the movie sucked, but also because the two weak links in the chain of title—the scraggly-haired man and Teri Squire—would have been eliminated. Still, she couldn't bring herself to articulate that fact.

"Nobody," Teri said.

"Are you sure?"

"You tell me."

"Who controls your rights in my boy's screenplay? If something happens to you, that is."

"My partners in the production."

"Including your partner Mona?"

"Yes, but—"

"But she's been injured. I know. Someone tried to get her out of the picture. Who are your other partners in the production?"

"The investors."

Annemarie nodded, the first movement she had made since sitting. She would have made an excellent statue.

"Yes. Your investors. How much do you know about them?"

That was just it: she knew nothing about them. She had reached a dead end in her research. She didn't know what Mona had found, but—

Oh, my God! Had that been what had triggered it? Had someone hacked into their computers to monitor their research? Surely not!

"Are you saying my investors are trying to kill me?"

"I'm saying you should keep all your options open. With you gone, and my boy gone, and Mona gone, who's left to challenge ownership?"

Teri had already connected those dots. "All you do is answer questions with more questions," she said.

"It's a time-honored tradition. Some say it was perfected by Socrates, but I wouldn't know about that."

"Well, I have a question for you," Teri said.

"And I will answer if I can."

"Is Leland really gone this time?"

For the first time in two meetings, Teri saw emotion on Annemarie's face. It was slight, as if any facial movement would crack the thick make-up, but there was an unmistakable smile.

"Leland has always been full of surprises."

"Who went off that cliff two years ago?"

"My son."

"Then who went off that cliff last night?"

"My son."

"That's ridiculous. You're just talking in riddles."

"Am I?"

"You don't seem too upset about losing your son. Twice."

"I grieved over Leland's grave a long time ago. But I have another question for you: If you can't inherit from the victim of your murder, who stands to gain the most to see to it that you are never convicted so that you can inherit?"

"I didn't kill anyone."

"Let's just call it a hypothetical. The way I understand the law, you can't inherit from someone you murder. So, if you go to trial and are found guilty, a murder conviction would invalidate a bequest. But if you never are tried, or are even arrested, there can be no conviction. That means the bequest is not in doubt. Who stands to gain the most from such a circumstance?"

"I do." She paused, as she let her thoughts wander down the Socratic path Annemarie was leading her on. "And my partners."

"And what is the surest way to ensure that you are never so much as charged with the crime?"

Teri remained silent, refusing to state the obvious: A dead person can't be charged or tried.

"So I repeat my question," Annemarie said. "How well do you know these partners of yours?"

A sudden thought hit Teri. "Then again, who benefits if I'm convicted? Who inherits if I can't?" She stood and paced. Annemarie watched her, seemingly without moving her eyes. "The screenwriter's mother, that's who; the alternate beneficiary. Where were you last night, Annemarie? Did you drive Leland up to Big Sur and put a bullet in his back?"

"Don't be absurd. Leland died years ago."

Teri's breath grew labored again. Her head pounded, more than just the pain from a broken nose and a cut. She felt as if her brain were about to explode. Just what in the hell was going on?

"Please, Ms. Squire, sit. Relax."

"I don't understand all this. Who was that in the diner last night? Was that your son or not?"

"You must relax. There is nothing to gain by being agitated. Please, sit."

Teri went back to the couch and sank down. She made eye contact with Annemarie, as if trying to look inside, to see what made her tick. She barely noticed that Annemarie swayed slightly, perched on the edge of the chair. It was very slight at first, but gradually grew more pronounced, both in length and momentum. Teri followed the movement, subconsciously, with her eyes, back and forth.

"You've been under a lot of stress," Annemarie said. "Please relax. Slow your breathing. Take deep breaths, count to ten, and breathe out. Nice and slow."

Teri did as she was told and, surprisingly, the panic ebbed. Her breaths came more easily, her heart rate seemed to decrease. The pounding in her head subsided, and the tingling sensation left her fingers. She felt drowsy, as if on the verge of sleep. Just watching Annemarie sway and listening to her oddly soothing voice.

"Breathe deep," Annemarie said. "Nice and slow. No reason to get upset. You're safe now."

Teri fought to keep her eyes open. Her head nodded, a quick jerk down and up, as if she were falling asleep on an airplane or while driving.

"See?" Annemarie asked. "Isn't that better?"

Teri nodded again, slowly this time, in response to the question.

"You may not believe it, but I'm here as your friend," Annemarie said. "I'm here to warn you. These people you have surrounded yourself with are not your friends. They do not have your best interests at heart. You're a problem to them. But they're a problem to you, as well. And what do you do to problems?"

Teri shook her head, fought to keep her eyelids open. She felt another nod coming on, almost as if in slow motion. She struggled to keep her head straight. She leaned it back against the couch cushion, hoping for support. But to no avail.

It jerked forward, her chin touching her chest.

The crack of a gunshot sounded in the hills outside, followed almost instantly by the shattering of glass in the sliding door. A bullet slammed into the couch cushion where Teri's head had been just an instant before.

The sound snapped Teri from her trance. Instincts kicked in. She had grown up around guns, and she knew their familiar sounds. She dove forward onto the carpet and covered her head with her arms. No second shot followed.

After a moment, she deigned to look up at the sliding door, with shattered glass sparkling on the floor in front of it.

Then at Annemarie, who had not moved. She still sat rigidly perched on the edge of the Queen Anne, her head swiveled to the left so she could see the broken glass in the gap left by the partially open curtains. For just the second time, emotion threatened to break out on her face. It started as a mere look of disgust, but Teri watched it transform into something that bordered on rage, as if darkening clouds had suddenly gathered on Annemarie's personal horizon.

Wordlessly, Annemarie stood, straightened her skirt, and walked to the front door.

After a few seconds, Teri heard the door open and close, and Annemarie was gone.

What the hell?

Staying on her hands and knees, Teri crawled for the phone in the kitchen and hit three digits.

"Nine-one-one," the operator's voice said. "What is your emergency?"

CHAPTER 34

MIKE STOOD BY Teri's side as two crime scene techs processed the scene, not that there was much to process. Broken glass, a bullet hole all the way through the couch, and a slug gouged into the hardwood floor just behind the couch.

Detective Swafford stood at the threshold to the porch and looked through the gap in the curtain, to the hills, then turned back to Teri and Mike. "If we can trace the angle of the shot, we might be able to figure out where it came from. It's a long shot, though." He smiled involuntarily at his pun, as if embarrassed to have said it. "Literally," he added.

"We'll get you a guest spot on Leno," Mike said, his tone harsh and even. "As soon as you finish your comedy act, maybe you can start working on who tried to kill Teri. Look at her face. Who did that to her? And now this."

"It's all right, Mike," Teri said. "I always appreciate a good pun."

Swafford dropped his eyes and nodded, a tacit "thank you" for her defense.

"Let's go through it one more time," Swafford said.

"The answers won't change," Mike said.

"No, I don't expect so. But she might remember something new. Not that you need a lesson in police work, or psychology, for that matter, but repetition seems to fuel memory. You told me to do my job; well, I'm doing it."

"Thank you, Detective," Teri said.

She was growing tired of Mike's posturing and, quite frankly, his unwarranted antagonism. In her experience, cops didn't take kindly to that. In fact, it seemed to confirm suspicions in their minds that, despite protestations of innocence, you were guilty of something, even if not the immediate crime. She also had to admit that there was an awful lot of death and near-death swirling around her, beginning with Leland Crowell's suicide. Swafford would be a poor detective, indeed, if that didn't raise at least some suspicions.

"Now, you and this Annemarie Crowell were sitting here, you on the couch and her on the chair."

"That's right."

"How open were the curtains?"

"Just like they are now. I haven't touched them."

He looked at the one foot opening. "Kind of odd, don't you think? Not really open, but not really closed, either."

"They were open all the way when she got here, but she complained that the sun hurt her eyes," Teri said. "I didn't want it to be too dark, so I closed them most of the way."

"Couldn't you have turned the light on?"

"I suppose."

"Why didn't you?"

"I don't know. I just didn't."

"What the hell has that got to do with anything?" Mike asked. His voice sounded as if he was on the verge of shouting, but fighting the urge. Teri knew from experience that Mike never shouted, but he wasn't above dramatics. He had learned as much about acting from his years in show business as she had.

"Probably nothing," Swafford said. "Just trying to get the details down, that's all."

Their attention was diverted to the entryway by sounds of footsteps and the mutter of male voices. CHP detectives Nichols and Stillman entered almost casually, as if arriving fashionably late to a party.

"Well, the Chippies are on the scene," Mike said. "I'm really confused about jurisdiction with you guys."

Teri cut him a glance that slammed his mouth shut before he could follow up with anything else.

"They're here at my invitation," Swafford said. "I can't help but think that everything relates to their case up at Big Sur."

"Has anything changed at the hospital?" Teri asked the CHP detectives. She suddenly felt guilty at not having checked in on Mona. Not even the fact that she had been distracted by two attempts on her own life assuaged that guilt.

"She's still not awake," Stillman said. "But the doctors say she's stable."

Both of them seemed shocked at the bruising and swelling on her face. Nichols pointed to the bandage on her forehead. "Flying glass do that?" he asked.

"That was from before. The car."

Nichols nodded, as if thinking, *Ah, yes, the car off the cliff.* "Ms. Squire, you do seem to be somewhat of a magnet for trouble these days."

"Not by choice."

The two newcomers swiftly surveyed the site then Nichols asked, "Is this how the curtains were when the shot was fired?"

"Jesus!" Mike exploded. He pointed at Swafford. "You and this guy, and the curtains. Who gives a rat's ass?"

"Just trying to catch up on the details."

"What difference does it make?"

"They're wondering if someone deliberately left the curtains open just enough to create a sight-line to set up a shot," Teri said.

Nichols whistled, soft and low. Admiration, perhaps?

"I may not be a detective, but I play one in the movies," she said, as if parroting a badly-written line plugging an upcoming film.

"Whose idea was it to close the curtains?" Stillman asked.

"That's about where you came in. Annemarie complained about her eyes being sensitive to the sunlight, so I closed them."

"But not all the way?"

"Just like they are now."

"Her idea or your idea to leave them open a bit?"

"Mine. But you're thinking maybe she was setting me up for the shooter."

"The thought had occurred to me."

"If that was the case, why would she have helped me on the road? She would have just let that car run me off the cliff."

Stillman nodded. "That's the fly in the ointment on that theory. Still—"

"Yeah, yeah, yeah," Mike said. "Just getting all the details."

"Did you find the car?" Teri asked.

"Yep," Nichols said. "Right where you said it happened. No one was in it, but lots of blood."

"So the driver survived."

"Maybe. Or someone got a body out of there."

Teri pulled away from Mike and went to the chair Annemarie had sat in. She struggled with her emotions as she stared at the bullet hole in the couch across from her. Her voice quivered as she spoke. "I don't understand what's going on."

"Why was Annemarie Crowell following you?" Swafford asked.

Teri hoped no one noticed the hitch in her breathing before she answered. "I don't know. I guess she was just coming over here to talk to me and saw what was happening."

"Lucky for you," Nichols said.

Teri could tell he didn't believe her. "Yeah, lucky."

"So what did she want to talk to you about?" Swafford asked.

Another hitch. She kept her focus on the bullet hole in the

couch, afraid her eyes would give her away. "She wanted to talk about the movie. I think maybe she wanted to make some kind of connection with her son."

"The son who died twice," Nichols said.

"Is the sarcasm necessary?" Mike asked. He moved over behind Teri and stood with his hands on her shoulders.

"It's one of my few pleasures," Nichols said. "But you can see how strange this all is."

"Mike," Teri said, "they're just doing their jobs."

"Did you tell Ms. Crowell that you met up with her long-lost son last night?" Nichols asked.

Teri looked up and made direct eye contact with him. "I don't know who that was last night, but it wasn't Leland Crowell."

"And you know this, how?"

"I just do. And no, I didn't tell her about last night."

"Where did she go when she left?" Swafford asked.

"I was crawling around on the floor at the time. Sorry if I didn't ask."

"See how much fun sarcasm can be?" Nichols said.

"Especially when you mix it with people trying to kill me."

"Yeah, about that," Stillman said. "Are you sure you couldn't make out anything about the driver who was tailing you?"

"I think he was doing a little more than just tailing her, don't you think?" Mike said.

Nichols looked at him and smiled an insincere smile. "See? Fun."

"This all raises a very interesting question," Swafford said. "Ms. Squire, just who in the hell would want to kill you?"

"And why?" Nichols added.

CHAPTER 35

THE DETECTIVES RECONVENED on Coldwater Canyon Drive, where crews were still working on pulling the Mercedes up the hillside. A wrecker had backed up to the broken railing, with a winch and chain cranking slowly, dragging the car inch by inch through the brush. The detectives watched wordlessly until Swafford broke the silence, expressing what had been on everyone's mind.

"I sure would like to get an advance print of that movie," he said.

"Yeah, me too," Stillman replied. "You read the screenplay?"

"No. I want to see that, too."

"Do you really believe the movie's got anything to do with all this?" Nichols asked.

"I don't know. But what I do know is that it's weird that a screenwriter would will it to an actress, and it's weird that the screenwriter died twice, and it's weird that his mother just happened to save the actress's ass out here, and it's weird that the mother was in the house when someone took a shot at the actress, and it's weird that none of this happened two years ago when the writer died the first time and willed away his script, but it's all happening right before the movie gets released.

"There was a lot of buzz back when they first starting working on this thing, what with the circumstances of the script and all, but now is the money time. For all I know this is about generating heat to fire up the box office. But—and I know this is a big but—what if there's some kind of message in the movie that someone's trying to squash?"

"So how would this squash it?" Stillman asked.

"Well, look at it this way. If you just wanted to legally stop it, you'd try to get an injunction. But if you're worried about the message—or clue or secret or whatever—getting out, you'd have a couple of problems. First, file a lawsuit and you make sure the movie gets analyzed scene by scene, frame by frame, by lawyers and juries and experts and God knows who else. If there's a secret in there, someone's gonna find it."

"Plus, everyone's gonna know who wanted to keep it from getting out," Swafford said. "It'll be the guy who files for the injunction. Not to mention that they're hard to get, so there's a pretty good chance the movie gets released anyway, with a whole buttload of scrutiny around it."

The wrecked Mercedes crested the hill, rear end up, as the winch continued its work. There were paint scrapes on the driver's side, running from the driver's door to just midway through the rear door. Most likely the sideswipe that sent it through the railing.

"But," Swafford continued, "hard as it is to believe, Hollywood sometimes does show a little sensitivity. It wouldn't be the first time that a studio shelved a project because of a tragedy. Or at least delayed it."

"But there are some people who'd stand to lose a whole lot of money if that happened," Stillman said. "How much money did this thing cost to make? Hundred million or something like that?"

"I'm just saying there are a whole lot of questions we don't know the answer to," Swafford said. "And I don't know if there are any answers in the screenplay or the movie, itself, but I'm a big fan of gathering all the information first, then sorting it out later."

"I hear you," Nichols said.

All three detectives walked to the front of the Mercedes, angled down as its rear end hung from the winch. The grill had been smashed, both headlights were out, and dark blue paint was sprinkled across the metal. They knew that the paint would likely match the scratches on the rear of Teri Squire's car.

"But I've got a lot more questions," Nichols added. "Why was Teri Squire meeting with the dead screenwriter last night? And why do our witnesses say he left with her? And what happened to her partner, Mona? And this." He pointed at the battered Mercedes. "Who's trying to kill her? Or is someone really trying to kill her? Awfully convenient that she left the curtains open just enough to create a firing lane, but the shooter just happened to miss her anyway. Maybe it's only supposed to look like someone's trying to kill her."

"My head hurts," Swafford said.

"And here's one more question, because we both know it's inevitable: What the hell weird is going to happen next?"

CHAPTER 36

BOB KEENE SAT at his desk, focused on the computer screen. The bloggers had broken the story first, but now all of the news sites were picking it up, as were the tabloids. No one had enough actual news yet to know what the hell was really going on, but speculation fueled by journalistic imagination lacked the patience to wait on facts. The truth might turn out to be boring, so the media typically kicked early into overdrive to feed on the sensationalism—the "breaking news"—before reality set in. The corrections could be filler on the inside pages or footnotes at a later date.

He clicked from link to link, headline to headline, a faint smile on his lips as he mentally calculated the escalating opening box office. His internal guesstimate had already cranked up to a minimum opening weekend of at least one hundred twenty-five million. "Two time Oscar Winner Questioned in Homicide" was the main theme of the articles, but the subplot included questions about the shooting of Mona Hirsch and where that fit with a murder near Big Sur.

"Love Triangle Ends Badly for Actress." That one was the most far-fetched, although it tried most earnestly to tie the two events together. It had Teri and Mona in a threesome with an unnamed lover that ended with Mona shooting him in the back up at Big Sur, then Teri, in a fit of rage, shooting Mona in the back.

Bob had been fielding phone calls non-stop for the past two

hours before delegating that duty to a squad of younger agents, whose mantra was, "We have no comment at this time about Ms. Squire's involvement in either shooting," thereby implicating her while at the same time spreading gasoline on the rumor wildfires. That had been Bob's idea, one he cleared with Doug Bozarth, who was equally enamored with the idea of upping the hype before the release of the movie, even if it meant sacrificing Teri Squire's reputation. The agency would dump her after all this, anyway, so the goal was to capitalize as much as possible before that happened.

He spun around in his chair and gazed out the window at a layer of smog descending on downtown Los Angeles to the east. God, he was glad he officed in Century City and not downtown. He hearkened back to his younger days, working at a wannabe entertainment law firm on the 28th floor of a bank building in L.A. At least he had been drawing a paycheck while his law school classmates toiled long hours in the mail rooms and at assistant's desks of talent agencies. But they soon moved into agent's offices while he struggled for fifteen years to build his own entertainment clientele.

Then came his big break, a young actress from Texas with no family and no discernible background, shunned by the all the agencies, whom he had befriended at the diner where she waitressed while taking acting classes and going on endless auditions. She brought her first real contract to him—a guest spot on a sitcom—and when she got her big break, a low budget indie film that earned her an Oscar nomination in a supporting role, Bob had ridden her coattails to TAA, where his star skyrocketed. His client list grew exponentially and bore so much fruit that he was now willing to sacrifice his first-born, so to speak, on the altar of show business. He rationalized it by telling himself that she could rise from the ashes again, just as she had a couple of years ago with *The Precipice* script that, ironically, now threatened to take her down. She was still under forty; she had time for another rebound.

And besides, he had a piece of this one. He hadn't told anyone, but he had put in some of his own money with Doug Bozarth's investment group. Not a lot by Hollywood standards, but enough that he could retire and ride off into a tropical sunset with the fountain of income that this project, his final project, was going to create for him.

His cell phone rang. He looked at the read-out: NUMBER BLOCKED. And yet it was someone who had his private number. He answered. "Hello, this is Bob Keene." A pause, then, "Who?" Another pause, then "I'll meet you on the corner across from the mall."

"You've got to tell me what's going on," Mike said.

Teri kept her head down, focused on the glittering glass as she swept the shards into a pile, scooped it up in a dustpan, and dumped it into the trash. It sounded like off-key wind chimes as the pieces clanked against the metal sides of the can, before coming to rest in the bottom. A slight breeze filtered in through the broken frame of the sliding door, carrying with it a hint of plumeria from below the deck, the sweet smell taking Teri back to the north shore of Kauai and her vacation stay in Hanalei, the summer before the box office bomb that sent her career into a tailspin. Oh, to be back on Kauai, hiking to the Alaka'i Swamp or on the Hanakapi'ai Trail along the Na Pali Coast, where her biggest concerns were keeping enough sunblock on her face or avoiding slick spots along the muddy trails, with no worries about cars trying to run her off the road or snipers firing through her windows.

Or intruders shooting her friends in the back.

"You know as much as I do," she said.

"Do I?"

"Do you really need me to answer that?"

"I think I do."

She swept the last of the glass into the dustpan then dropped it into the trash. "Okay, here it is in a nutshell. You and Bob fired me. Then, when I found a good script, you acted like bygones were just bygones. You brought in investors who have no past and untraceable money. A dead screenwriter showed up at my door and demanded a cut of the movie. Your investors told me to meet with the dead guy, who ended up dying all over again. Someone tried to run me off the road. Someone tried to shoot me. Someone nearly killed Mona." She kicked the trashcan over, sending the shards across the floor again. "And now you're here asking stupid questions."

"Teri—"

"What do you want from me, Mike? Do you really think I know why people are trying to kill me?"

"It's just—"

"If I knew, I'd tell you. If I knew, I'd tell the police. Do you think I want to get killed? Do you think I want Mona to get killed? If I knew anything that would prevent that, I'd take out a full-page ad in the trades and announce it to the world."

Mike stayed silent.

"I'll tell you one thing I do know," Teri said. "I don't trust Doug Bozarth."

That loosened Mike's tongue. "Are you telling me you think he's behind all this?"

"I'm just saying he's got a lot to lose here. Maybe more than any of us. My reputation was already trashed, but he's got money on the line. Money that's been put at risk by the resurrection of Leland Crowell, but now that risk has been taken care of. Awfully conveniently, if you ask me."

"Assuming that's true, why would he want to kill you?"

"Because questions about the rightful ownership of the script put the whole project under a microscope. I'm starting to wonder what will show up if that happens. I don't think he can afford that to happen. It's better for him to just get rid of anything or anyone that draws scrutiny, then sit back and rake in his winnings from the box office."

"You don't think the death of the lead actor would draw scrutiny?" he asked.

"Only if it can be connected to the movie. If it's just another unfortunate Hollywood tragedy, it ends up as a segment on cable television, everybody clucks their tongues and says, 'how sad,' but it's over. And, oh, by the way, it beefs up the box office."

"God, when did you get so cynical?"

"When did you not?"

Teri pivoted and walked through the door frame, stepping over the jagged shards at the bottom, onto the deck. She leaned on the rail and gazed at the hills, as if banishing Mike to invisibility.

He watched her for a few seconds, then turned and left.

Teri waited until she heard the opening and closing of the front door before turning back around. Tears glistened in her eyes.

Bob Keene sat rigidly at his desk, cell phone clutched tightly in his right hand, a pose he had maintained since returning just minutes ago from the impromptu meeting down the street. No thoughts troubled his mind. His senses had all but shut down, oblivious to the ringing of phones and hustle of bodies moving by outside the glass doors of his office. His own phone rang. He put it to his ear, listened briefly, then put it in his side coat pocket, pushed his chair back, and stood.

Moving stiffly, almost robotically, he stood. Arms at his side, not swinging, he walked around his desk to the door, opened it, and stepped out into the hallway. The latest addition to the mailroom, an MBA from Stanford, nearly bowled him over with the mail cart as Bob walked directly into his path, before turning sharply ninety degrees and heading toward the elevators.

"Sorry, Mr. Keene," the MBA said, but Bob ignored him. Never even moved his head, as if he had neither seen nor heard the mail cart, even with its squeaky rear wheels.

Bob moved on to the elevators. He pushed the down button, then stood with his feet together, arms at his side, and faced the doors. Several of his colleagues passed behind him, most saying nothing, but a few uttering his name in greeting, accompanied by nods, but getting no response. No one acted as if his lack of cordiality was any kind of aberration. The interactions spoke volumes about Bob's relationship with his fellow workers, most of whom viewed him as the head of the agency—a view he certainly held of himself—while others just considered him the old guy who made too much money and that, as soon as he was out, his share would flow down to them.

A bell sounded, the down light glowed, and the doors opened. Bob stepped on, turned to face the front, and pushed the button for the ground floor even though it was already lit. A young woman carrying her smart phone to her face, as if having difficulty seeing, shuffled to the side to make room for him directly in front of the doors. She never looked up, nor did he acknowledge her presence. The elevator continued its downward descent, an express to the ground floor.

When the doors opened again, the woman with the smart phone stepped toward the door, accustomed to being allowed to proceed ahead of men. Chivalry was apparently not dead, even in Hollywood. It was, however, dormant on this elevator. Bob cut her off, his eyes straight forward, still not acknowledging her presence. She huffed, a disgusted exhale of breath, as he stepped out of the elevator ahead of her. His head never swiveled her way, nor did his eyes track her. He had no idea she was even there.

He turned sharply ninety degrees and headed across the lobby, toward the front door. As he passed the security desk, a blue-jacketed security guard, his close-cropped gray hair testimony to a military career prior to taking a cush position sitting on a padded stool and watching movie stars go by, called to him. "Afternoon, Mr. Keene."

Bob continued on a direct route to the revolving doors, oblivious to the greeting. And oblivious to the next words that escaped in a softer tone under the guard's breath. "You tight-assed sonuvabitch."

He exited the building mechanically, as if marching with a precision drill team. The sun fell on his face and directed his attention skyward. It was the first time he had moved his head, much less re-directed his line of sight in any direction other than straight ahead. He stood for a moment, staring skyward, directly into the sun. But he never blinked.

A couple in shorts and matching aloha shirts, the man clutching a digital camera, passed by in front of him. The man looked skyward. "What's he looking at?"

The woman glanced upward, and then at Bob. "Nothing. Let's just keep moving."

They moved on down the sidewalk, lone pedestrians other than the man in the expensive suit staring at the sun. There were no other walkers, but a steady flow of traffic on Century Park West, just a few feet from where Bob stood. Tourists walked, but Angelenos didn't; they drove. Walking was so…pedestrian.

Bob cranked his head back down, his gaze once again straight ahead, but seeing nothing, his dilated pupils blinded by the sun. He swiveled his head to the right, then farther, looking back at the building. He squinted, as if struggling to regain his vision to focus on something, then he looked forward again.

He stepped forward until he was perched on the edge of the curb. Stood stock still, arms at his side, eyes front. A delivery truck rounded the corner at the edge of the building, accelerated as it hit the straightaway of Century Park West, in the curb lane, approaching the spot where Bob stood.

Just as the truck reached his perch, Bob stepped directly into its path.

The driver blared his horn and slammed on his brakes, but physics dictated the result. Had it been going faster, it might have sent Bob skyward and curbside. Had it been going slower, it might have simply knocked Bob forward and down, then come to a halt before him. But it was going at the perfect decelerating speed to knock Bob upward, to slam into him as he was airborne, smacking his head against the windshield, splattering it with blood, and then ricocheting him onto the pavement where one front wheel rolled over his torso, flipping his body over and askew as the rear curbside wheel crushed his skull before the truck came to a stop.

The driver jumped out of the truck and ran to the rear. He took one look at the body, gray matter oozing from the skull like egg white from a cracked egg. Without warning, he vomited on his shoes.

The male tourist in the aloha shirt ran back up the sidewalk, his female companion trailing him. He pulled up short when he reached the scene. His companion let out a cry, like a dog in pain.

"Holy shit!" he said. Then he did what tourists do: He snapped pictures with his camera.

The security guard from the building rushed to the edge of the curb, cell phone to his ear. He stopped short and stared at Bob's body. "You can still send the ambulance, but I think it's too late."

He snapped his phone shut and tucked it into his side jacket pocket. He shook his head and mumbled to himself. "I guess you got nothing to say now, either, you uptight sonuvabitch."

CHAPTER 37

TERI STOOD IN front of the smaller closet in her bedroom, her mind a blank. She felt as if she had just awakened from a nightmare, not sure what the dream had been about, but only that it had been traumatic. She couldn't even remember what she was doing in front of the closet or how she had gotten there. Although the police had left her with a very movie-like "don't leave town," she knew that she had to get away. She had run from her problems before, but would that work now?

As her thoughts returned, they took a turn for the melodramatic. Phrases like "dark forces" took root. Sure, she was an actress who made her living off of drama, but there was no question that dark forces had been set in motion against her. Just because you're paranoid doesn't mean they're not out to get you, and just because you're melodramatic doesn't mean someone doesn't want you dead.

And speaking of paranoid, Mike hadn't been much support. He had also been a little too quick, a little too glib, in coming to the defense of Doug Bozarth. What did they really know about him, anyway? Nothing, that's what. He was almost a non-entity as far as the Internet was concerned. How was that possible in today's age, where "Google" had become a verb and one's clout was measured by how many "hits" you got when your name was Googled. But not Doug Bozarth. He was just an anonymous billionaire who showed up out of the ether, checkbook in hand,

and begged to foot the bill for the movie.

She wasn't surprised that Bob had tethered himself to Bozarth, and she probably shouldn't have been surprised that Mike had, as well. She knew how important money and success were to him, things she had provided over the years until her fall from grace. She had been naïve enough to think he stuck by her, after a shaky start, because he believed in her and wanted to nurture her back to the top. Now, though, she wasn't so sure. His alliances seemed to run deeper with Bob Keene and Doug Bozarth than with her. So deep, in fact, that his ability to question and to think critically seemed to have vacated the premises, pushed out by blind faith in the promise of wealth and prestige from strangers.

Teri pulled a variety of suitcases from the closet and scattered them across the floor.

God, who needed this many?

Most of them had been gifts from productions she had been on and at least one full set came from an ad for a national brand she had done. They nearly filled this closet, adjacent to her regular closet, added for no other reason than to store things she didn't need, like her suitcase collection. But behind all those bags was the one she was looking for. The battered vinyl bag of faded green, its zipper discolored but still workable, albeit prone to hang-ups. The one that she filled with all her worldly belongings nearly twenty years ago when she had thrown it in the bed of a battered Ford F-150 pick-up truck in the middle of the night, then pushed the truck down the driveway until it was far enough from the house that she thought she could start it without being heard inside. Back when she left Bandera, Texas, behind for a shot at fame and fortune in Tinseltown.

As she had all those years before, she filled the bag with essentials, then lugged it to her SUV and tossed it in the back. With no need for silence, no eyes or ears inside to avoid, she got behind the wheel and turned the key. The Highlander started instantly, unlike the pick-up truck that had required her to pop the clutch as it rolled downhill in the driveway. She pulled out of her driveway and headed for points east.

Police and paramedics dominated the scene outside the Century City office building that housed TAA. A crowd of on-lookers gathered on the sidewalks on both sides of the street, trying to get a glimpse of the body, or at least of some blood. There was curiosity from late arrivals, who wondered whether this was just another scene being shot for a movie.

When Mike Capalletti turned off of Santa Monica Boulevard onto Century Park West, his first thought as he saw the crowd that had gathered was the same as the question from the onlookers. Was someone shooting a movie? Not uncommon in Los Angeles, and certainly not uncommon outside of his office building. He quickly dismissed the thought. If someone was shooting, he would have known it. Permits had to be issued, permissions from building owners obtained, and notices would have been sent to the building's tenants advising them. After all, with the demands of movie-making for controlled silence and orchestrated traffic, it was a standard protocol to advise tenants so they could schedule their comings and goings accordingly. It could be a nuisance at times, but it was one most gladly accommodated. After all, it was the movie industry that put food on the table— and bought luxury cars and summer homes, and provided seven figure incomes.

He pulled into the building's parking garage, descended to his floor, and parked in his assigned spot. Ownership of a coveted parking space was just one more perk of being an up-and-comer at Hollywood's most powerful talent agency. He rode the elevator to the ground floor then punched in Teri's number on his cell phone as he exited. He hadn't liked the way things had been when he left. Teri wasn't thinking straight, not that she could be blamed. No one had ever tried to kill him even once before, much less twice. Still, now was not the time to make waves. The only wave that mattered was the tsunami of publicity that they would all ride to a smash box office weekend. Teri needed to tap the brakes, take a deep breath, and relax.

Straight to voicemail, just like every other call he had made since leaving her house. Well, fine. If that's the way she wanted it, he would wait her out. Sooner or later, she'd call him. She always did. And with Mona in the hospital, she had no one else to call.

As he headed for the bank of elevators that serviced the agency's floor, his attention was drawn outside to the gathering crowd. Just what in the hell was going on out there? He veered to the revolving doors and pushed his way outside. Almost subconsciously, he tried Teri's number again as he forced his way through the crowd, as if he had a God-given right to move to the front. A man wearing a pink polo shirt took offense, refusing to move as Mike pushed on his shoulder. With his elbow, Mike added an extra *oomph* to one last shove that did the trick. The man turned and glared at Mike, who ignored him, just as his call went to voicemail.

"Damn it, Teri," he said as he hung up and tucked the phone in his coat pocket.

Nearly at the front of the crowd now, he got his first glimpse of blood in the street and the body of a man, lying on his back on a gurney. Visible only from the waist down, there was still something oddly familiar about the legs.

And the shoes. Definitely something familiar about those shoes. One shoe still on a foot, the other shoe about four feet away, on its side, as if the man had been knocked clean out of it. It wasn't the maker of the shoe that grabbed Mike's attention. Designer shoes were a dime a dozen in this part of town. There were, however, two significant things about the shoes. One was the extraordinarily small size for a man's shoe. The other was the way the sole, particularly the heel, appeared to be worn on the outside, as if the wearer were unusually bow-legged, putting unnatural stress on the outer edges with each step. Mike knew a man with small feet and bowed legs.

He shouldered his way the final few steps to the front of the crowd, panic rising inside as he got a full view of the body. He dropped to his knees on the curb, afraid he was going to vomit. There was so much blood. And where Bob's head should have been was a flattened lump, covered with a towel or some kind of cloth, as if hiding something horrible from view. He saw bits of bone chips and oozing gray matter around the edges of the cloth.

A cop glanced his way, then started over, obviously prepared to shoo him back into the crowd. But something about Mike's apparent agony—his ashen complexion, the almost inaudible keening sound that emanated from deep in his throat—must have stopped him.

"Sir," the cop said. "I need you to stand back."

Mike heard the jumble of words but couldn't make them out. The cop's voice sounded like so much white noise against the backdrop of the murmuring crowd.

"Sir? Sir?"

Mike felt a hand on his shoulder shake him, gently at first, then rougher. He managed to tear his eyes away from the body in the street and focus on the cop. The man was young, couldn't have been more than twenty-four or twenty-five.

"Sir, do you think you know this man?" the cop asked.

"That's Bob Keene." The words came out in a hoarse whisper.

"You're sure?"

"Those are his glasses," Mike said, as he pointed to the broken frames lying next to the curb. "And I bought that tie for him in Scotland."

"He works here?"

"He's the head of our agency." Mike looked at the body again, as paramedics lifted the gurney and slid it into the back of a waiting ambulance.

"Is he going to be okay?" Mike asked. But even as he asked the question, he knew how stupid it must have sounded. Bob's head had been crushed and covered. You didn't cover the faces of the injured; only of the dead.

The dead! God Almighty!

"What happened?" Mike asked.

"He stepped right out in front of a delivery truck. The witnesses said it looked like he did it on purpose. Do you know why he might have done that?"

"Suicide?"

The cop shrugged.

Suicide didn't make sense. Bob stood to make a lot of money with the release of *The Precipice*. They all did. What made more sense was another murder attempt. Or, in this case, completed murder.

"Mike!"

A familiar voice, yet out of place. Mike turned and scanned the crowd. He could make out faces of fellow workers from TAA, a few assistants, one agent. Even one of the mail room guys. They were all looking at him, but none gave any sign that they had spoken to him, or even cared to.

"Mike!"

He turned to his right. Doug Bozarth stood next to a police cruiser, talking to an officer who took notes on a pad. Bozarth looked directly at Mike as he spoke. He glanced back at the cop and nodded. The cop flipped his notepad shut and excused himself. Bozarth headed toward Mike.

What the hell was Bozarth doing here? And how did he get here so fast?

This couldn't have happened all that long ago. Nobody had even called Mike yet to report the death, which surely would have been done by now if the body had been identified. If the police had checked for ID in Bob's pockets and seen the ubiquitous business cards, they would have contacted the office. But the officer who spoke to Mike hadn't known who the victim was.

Almost as if cued by the thought, Mike felt the buzz of his cell phone vibrate in his pocket. He pulled it out and glanced at the read-out. Sure enough, it was his assistant. Mike answered.

"Yeah."

"Mr. Capalletti, it's about Mr. Keene."

"I know all about it." Then he hung up, just as Bozarth reached him.

"Helluva thing," Bozarth said.

"How'd you get here so fast?"

"You okay? You don't look so good."

"They said it looked like suicide. That doesn't make any sense."

"Maybe it was a conscience attack."

"What the hell does that mean?" Mike asked.

"How's Teri?"

Mike tried to process the *non sequiter*. Bozarth was trying to tell him something, to send a message, but Mike was having trouble connecting the dots of the conversation. Then it kicked in, like a mule's kick.

"Are you saying Bob had something to do with trying to kill Teri?"

Doug Bozarth, the inscrutable man with the textbook case of poise, appeared to blanch. For a brief second, his eyebrows arched and his eyes widened. Mike thought he detected a twitch at the corner of his lips. The reaction might have gone completely unnoticed had Mike not been focusing so intently on Bozarth's face. He tried to process what it was that had caused the reaction. It wasn't the news about Teri. After all, he had asked about her. How he knew, Mike wasn't sure. Mike hadn't called Bozarth to tell him, and he felt sure Teri hadn't. Yet Bozarth knew.

Then it hit Mike: the word that precipitated the response was Mike's use of the word "trying." As in "had something to do with *trying* to kill Teri." Not "had something to do with *killing* Teri." Bozarth had expected Mike to tell him that Teri had been killed, which meant he knew all there was to know about the gunshots from the hills. Which meant he had something to do with putting the shooter on that hill in the first place.

"Is she okay?" Bozarth asked. The tone of his voice indicated uncertainty, which nailed down the certainty for Mike. Teri had been right about Bozarth all along.

"She's fine. Pretty shaken, but otherwise okay."

"Where is she?"

Mike hesitated, unusual for him. Lies usually formed instantly and escaped his lips without delay, without thought. He was, after all, a lawyer and an agent. "She went with the cops."

"Why aren't you with her?"

Mike searched for another lie but couldn't find one.

"She shouldn't be talking to the cops without her lawyer present," Bozarth said. "Why didn't you go with her?"

"I was following them when I got the call about Bob, so I came here."

Bozarth scrutinized Mike's face, as if scanning for truth. Then he abruptly turned and walked into the crowd, pulling his cell phone from his pocket as he walked. When Bozarth put the phone to his ear, Mike dashed through the crowd, back into the building. He had his own phone out and repeatedly hit Teri's speed dial number as he waited for the elevators to the parking garage. It wouldn't take long for Bozarth to find out that he had been lying and that Teri was not with the police. That she was maybe, in fact, still at home. Would he try again? He had to warn her.

"Come on, Teri," he said as the phone rang. "Pick up. Pick up, pick up, pick up."

The bell sounded, the doors opened, and he stepped inside.

CHAPTER 38

BITS OF SHATTERED glass sparkled in the moonlight that peeked in through the narrow gap in the curtains blowing inward with each gust of wind from the hills. No lights were on inside, casting Teri Squire's den in shadows. There was a hint of smoke in the air, thick in the moonbeam, testifying to yet another wildfire kindling in the hills. A gloved hand reached past the shards that rimmed the perimeter of the sliding door. It found the latch and unlocked the door. The frame slid open, the curtains pushed aside, and two ski-masked men stepped inside, both holding guns. There was no sound other than the crunch of glass beneath leather-soled shoes.

The men paused. One breathed heavily, mouth open, each breath ragged. The other made not a sound, as if holding his breath.

The silent one gestured toward the kitchen. The mouth-breather nodded and stepped that way. The silent one headed toward the back of the house.

After a few minutes, they met together in the den. The silent one pulled a cell phone and punched a number on speed dial. "She's not here," he said to the man who answered. "Looks like she dragged luggage out of a closet."

Teri had lost track of time miles ago, about halfway through Arizona. The freeway stretched out before her, illuminated by rows of neon lights lining each side. The moon was still low on the horizon, full and orange and strangely welcoming, as if to say "This way to Texas. This way home."

Nearly twenty years ago that moon had been at her back as she traveled this route in reverse, running from Texas and family, running from a home that no longer welcomed her, that no longer wanted her. But she was a different person then. Now she was Teri Squire, movie star, her face gracing magazine covers and silver screens, attending premieres and high society parties.

But back then she was just a scared teenager. Back then she had been Peggy Tucker, ranch girl, tomboy. She even had a different face then. One that age and a cosmetic surgeon's wizardry had combined to blur into a memory. But other memories remained vivid, unhidden behind the new memories and successes she had built for herself. And now, here she was once again, running from a life she had made for herself. She wondered if she had ever really stopped running, or if she ever would.

Her cell phone rang once again, the blare of *Magnum P.I.* breaking the radio silence. She looked at the read-out, the name MIKE glowing just above the announcement of "21 missed calls." On her right, a green and white sign told her she would be in New Mexico in ten miles. Far enough away now.

She answered. "Mike?"

"Jesus, Teri, where the hell are you?" he asked. "I've been trying to get you for hours."

"It's been a rough day. I just needed some time to myself."

"Bob's dead."

Teri tapped the brakes, as if slowing the car could stem the onslaught of tragedy that had dogged her lately. As quickly as she hit the brakes, she slid her foot back to the accelerator and pressed harder. The speedometer jumped ten miles an hour.

"What happened?" she asked. She clenched the wheel, her

knuckles whitening.

"They said he killed himself. That he walked right out in front of a truck."

Teri tried to process the words. Bob Keene, suicide? Right when he was on the verge of his biggest success? That didn't make sense. She had known Bob for enough years to realize that he worshipped at the altar of the almighty dollar. He was counting on *The Precipice* to be his golden parachute out of the Hollywood craziness and into blissful retirement. He hadn't said anything, but she was pretty sure he had invested a considerable portion of his personal wealth in the project. There was no way he killed himself. Not now. Not this close to the opening.

"Three is too many," she said.

"What?"

"Three is too many."

"Three what is too many?"

"Suicides. Leland Crowell, Spencer West, and now Bob. Three so-called suicides. I know they say tragedies come in threes, but what are the odds? Throw in Mona, the second death of Leland Crowell, and someone trying to kill me—twice. That's too much. And, by the way, if I'd been run off the road, what do you bet that would've been called a suicide, too? Actress, distraught over scandal and the near-death of her friend, takes her own life. Hell, I'd have even been the prime suspect in the shootings up at Big Sur and at Mona's."

There was nothing but silence on Mike's end. Had she lost the connection?

"Mike, are you still there?"

When he spoke, his voice sounded distant. If she didn't know better, she'd have thought it was wracked with emotion. "They said Bob was like a zombie. Like he didn't see anyone around him. He just stood on the curb until a delivery truck was coming, and then he stepped right out in front of it."

"I'm sorry. I know you were close to him."

"That's not it. Don't you see what I'm saying?"

"No."

"Doesn't any of that sound familiar to you?"

"I don't know what you're talking about."

He sighed. "*The Precipice*? Your new movie. Remember?"

Even before he finished speaking, Teri saw his meaning as the frazzled synapses in her brain put two and two together and finally came up with four. "Oh, my God!"

"Yeah. A serial killer who hypnotizes people into killing for her, then they kill themselves."

Teri thought of those two strange visits from Annemarie Crowell, the low monotones, the subtle swaying as she perched on the edge of her chair. And drowsiness.

"Do you think Leland Crowell was writing about his mother?"

"What do we really know about her, anyway?"

"Just what the lawyer told me. That she was his mother."

"I'm going to see what I can find out about her," he said. "In the meantime, you stay out of sight. Maybe even go to Texas."

"I'm one step ahead of you. But you be careful."

"Don't worry about me. You just take care of yourself."

Mike hung up the phone. He sat on the edge of the bed in his darkened bedroom and buried his head in his hands.

My God, what the hell is going on?

A creaking sound drew his attention to the door. He looked up, startled to see the outline of a person standing in the shadows.

"We have to keep her safe," the person said in a low monotone. "Where is she?"

Then the shadow began to sway.

CHAPTER 39

DETECTIVES NICHOLS AND Stillman worked at adjacent desks in a makeshift office the Beverly Hills Police Department had quickly set up for them as a courtesy to the state agency. But even makeshift in Beverly Hills had all the earmarks of elegance, from matching maple desks, cheerful tropical prints on the wall, and cutting edge electronics, including dual monitor computers, high-speed wireless connection to the Internet, and a latte-dispensing coffeemaker.

Nichols worked the old-fashioned way, flipping through pages in manila file folders, while Stillman clicked away at his computer. A copy of the screenplay for *The Precipice* rested on the corner of Nichols's desk. Both men were running on coffee and adrenaline as they puzzled over a series of obviously related deaths and near-deaths. The connections seemed obvious on their face, with a screenplay as the common factor, but the reasons behind the events eluded them both.

They worked their way through the classic motives: passion, power, revenge, and greed. It was that last one that seemed to offer the most promise. After all, a movie based on the screenplay was about to open to what promised to be an unprecedented box office haul. But that fact also appeared to undermine the greed motive. By all accounts, if the box office hit even close to the projections, there would be enough money to go around, Hollywood accounting notwithstanding. How much was too much? If money was involved, maybe the issue was whether there was something that would negatively impact the box office or the distribution of profits, but damned if either one of them could see what that might possibly be.

The key to the whole affair, the detectives concluded, lay with the late Leland Crowell, he of the two-time demise. Choosing to divide and conquer, Nichols took the Hollywood path while Stillman worked backward from Crowell. The result had been a lot of nothing. Until...

"Now here's something interesting," Stillman said.

Nichols looked up from the file folder he had just opened. "What's that?"

"It seems that Annemarie Crowell originally hails from Ludlow, out in the desert, but she got her professional start in Illinois, where she once had a very successful psychiatry practice."

"She seems more like a patient to me than a doctor."

"Nevertheless."

"Would you lie on her couch and tell her your deepest, darkest secrets?" Nichols asked.

"The good news is that at least she wouldn't laugh at you. It would break her face."

Stillman's eye scanned the monitor as he focused on the document on the screen, which bore the letterhead of the State of Illinois Department of Medical Licensing. "Her specialty was hypnotherapy."

Nichols abandoned his file folder and rolled his chair over next to his partner. "Now that is interesting. Especially the way some of those witnesses said Bob Keene looked like he was in a trance. Hypnotized, maybe?"

"But how would she do it? Hypnotize Keene, I mean. We'd need some way to put the two of them together before we can make that leap. Did he even know her? Other than who she is, I mean."

"We know Teri Squire knew her," Nichols said. "Maybe there's a connection there."

Stillman read a few lines more. "Illinois took away her medical license a few years ago. Right about..." He flipped through his notes until he found what he was looking for. "Right about the time she showed up in California."

"What'd they take her license for?"

"Doesn't say." Stillman made a note on the pad beside the computer. "But I'll find out."

"Be interesting if it was for hypnotizing people and making them do stuff for her." He picked up the screenplay and tossed it to his partner. "Like in this screenplay."

"You're kidding, right? Did you read the whole thing?"

"Enough of it to know that Leland Crowell wrote a screenplay about a woman who hypnotizes people and makes them kill for her."

Stillman snorted. "That can't happen. You can't make someone do something they wouldn't normally do, hypnotized or not."

"Maybe, maybe not. Did you ever see *The Manchurian Candidate*? I'm talking about the original, with Frank Sinatra. The actress from *Murder, She Wrote* gets this guy to kill people, including taking a shot at a political candidate, just by calling him and telling him to play solitaire. He goes into this trance then, when he sees this certain card, he goes out and kills people."

"Frank Sinatra does?"

"No, I think it was Laurence Harvey. But the point is, all she had to do was call him on the phone and say the magic word."

"But even if that works, she's still got to have access in the first place, you know, to hypnotize him and plant the suggestion or whatever."

"Then I guess we need to see if we can put the two of them together," Nichols said. "Anything else in that file about

Annemarie?"

Stillman scrolled down and clicked to the next document he had uncovered. "She does have a son, but his name isn't Leland; it's Rodney. Rodney Leroy."

"Not Rodney Leland?"

"Nope. Rodney Leroy."

"Close, though. Maybe he changed his name."

Stillman made another note. The page was filling up fast. A lot of to-do's.

"Anything at all about another son?" Nichols asked.

"Not that I've found so far."

Nichols rolled his chair back to his desk and flipped through the file folders stacked on top. "What we need is a DNA sample from her. Then we try to match it to the corpse in the morgue. Next, we—"

"Exhume the jumper from two years ago and try to get a match to the stiff and to the mom," Stillman said, picking up the phone. "I'll get the warrant started."

The sun was rising, but was still low on the horizon, at eye level. Teri squinted and pulled down the sunshade. She rubbed her face, then grabbed her coffee from the cup holder and downed the last few drops. She looked at the clock on the dash. Accounting for the two-hour time change, that made it still 5:30 a.m. back in Los Angeles. Mike was probably asleep. She wanted to talk to him, to work through some of the crazy thoughts that had engulfed her on her night-time run. He had his problems, but one of his strengths was his ability to think logically, to reason through her craziness, and to keep her grounded. But there would be time for that later. For now, she would let him sleep.

The green and white sign on the side of the road announced that she was 46 miles from El Paso. Forty-six miles from Texas. Forty-six miles from home.

But would Texas still be home when she got there? She didn't know the answer to that question.

She grabbed her cell phone and hit Mike's speed dial number.

Mike's phone sounded on his nightstand, playing *The Rockford Files* theme music, the ringtone he had selected for Teri's calls. Mike lay on his back in the bed, still dressed as he had been the night before, too exhausted to undress. He ignored the phone as it continued to play. Dead to the world.

The bullet hole between his eyes also said dead for good.

CHAPTER 40

STILLMAN AND NICHOLS arrived at TAA's offices with little fanfare, surprised to find a business-as-usual attitude among the employees, as if the death of Bob Keene hadn't even registered on the radar. Men in full suits and women in dressed-to-kill outfits bustled about, crossing the detectives' path like stunt car drivers as they stepped off the elevator and sought the reception desk. The red-haired woman behind the transaction counter wore a headset while she worked her computer keyboard. She stopped and eyed the detectives warily.

"Can I help you gentlemen?" she asked.

"Detectives Stillman and Nichols, California Highway Patrol," Stillman said. "We need to talk to whoever's in charge."

She smiled ever so briefly then almost perceptibly wiped the smile from her face.

"Is that funny?" Nichols asked.

"I'm sorry," she said. "It sounds so—so—television."

"I've got a bad scriptwriter," Nichols said.

"Screenwriter," she said.

"I stand corrected. But we still need to see whoever's in charge."

"Do you have badges?"

Stillman and Nichols exchanged looks. "Are you always this skeptical?" Stillman asked. "Not that it's a bad thing."

He pulled his badge from his coat pocket and showed it to

her. She leaned forward and squinted as she read it. Then she pulled away and looked at him, still smiling.

"It looks real," she said.

"It is real."

"Look," she said. "Do you think you two are the first actors to come in here and try to pull something like this? If you don't have an appointment and if you don't have a demo reel, acting like cops won't get you in to see an agent. And here's another little hint for you: Pretend to be Beverly Hills or Los Angeles cops, not Highway Patrol, unless you're actually on a highway."

"First of all," Stillman said, "we've got jurisdiction statewide, something which I'm getting pretty damn tired of having to explain. And secondly, we need to talk to someone about Bob Keene's death."

She leaned back again, as if making a decision. Maybe it was the set of his jaw or the look in his eye, but her smile slowly disappeared. "You're serious, aren't you?"

"Yes, ma'am."

"Hold on." She dialed an extension then turned her head as she spoke into the headset microphone. "I have two officers here who need to talk to someone about Mr. Keene." She paused, then nodded and turned back to them. "Mr. Hotchkiss will be right here. He's one of our managing shareholders."

The detectives backed away from the counter and stood silently, amused at the pretense of the office. Their amusement was quickly ended by the sounds of leather-soled shoes on marble floors, the staccato beat indicating the walker was a person approaching with a purpose coupled with an air of self-importance.

Marcus Hotchkiss's appearance matched his stride. Barely five feet six inches tall, his hair heavily sprayed into place, graying at the temples, and wearing a silk suit and tie, with European tasseled loafers that made even his small feet look arrogant.

"Can I help you gentlemen?" he asked. There was a hint of the South in his tone, but just a hint, as if he was making a conscious effort to suppress it.

Both detectives showed their badges. "Stillman and Nichols, California Highway Patrol," Nichols said. "And before you say anything, we have jurisdiction both on the highways and off."

"I'm aware of that," Hotchkiss said. "How can I help you?"

"We've got some questions about Bob Keene," Stillman said.

"Why? I thought that was an accident, or at worst a suicide. Hardly something for CHP to get involved with."

"We're not saying it wasn't. We just have some questions."

Hotchkiss glanced at an empty conference room, located through glass walls behind the reception desk. "Let's talk in here," he said, leading the way.

Once inside, he closed the door and sat at the head of the table. "What kinds of questions? And what can any of this have to do with CHP? Jurisdiction or not, I don't understand how a truck running down a pedestrian in Century City would bring Highway Patrol into my offices."

"There's a possibility it may be related to a death on the Coast Highway," Nichols said.

"Is this the one Teri Squire's involved with?" Hotchkiss asked.

"No one said she's involved with it, but yeah, that's the one."

"The person you really need to talk to is Mike Capalletti. That's Teri's agent. And he worked the closest with Bob."

"Is he here?"

Hotchkiss picked up the phone on a credenza behind him and punched an extension. "Get Capalletti down to the conference room at reception."

He hung up and turned back around. "He'll be here in a minute."

"Did Mr. Keene have any visitors yesterday?" Nichols asked.

"Not that I know of."

"How about phone calls?"

"Again, not that I know of. I can check and see if anything came in through the front desk, but if it was on his direct dial or his cell phone, we wouldn't have any way to know."

"Do you know if he ever met with an Annemarie Crowell?" Stillman asked.

"The mother of the dead screenwriter? I don't know."

"Mr. Hotchkiss, do you have security cameras in the office?" Nichols asked.

"We've got them in the reception area and in the halls, and security has them in front of the building. None in the offices or conference rooms. They're digital. Why?"

"We'd like to see whatever you've got from when Bob Keene left the office yesterday."

Hotchkiss leaned back in his chair, his brow wrinkled, as if trying to process what seemed to be an odd request.

"Is there something you're not telling me?" he asked. "Do you have some reason to believe Bob's death wasn't just an accident? Or a suicide?"

"Mr. Hotchkiss," Stillman said, "we—"

The phone rang. Hotchkiss lifted a finger in a "hold that thought" gesture as he answered. "Yeah." He paused, listening, then, "Did he have an appointment?" Listening again, then he hung up and turned back around. All color had drained from his face.

"Mike Capalletti is not here, and no one has heard from him. He's not answering at home, and he's not picking up on his cell. He always answers his cell."

"We'll need his address," Nichols said.

"Gentlemen, just what in the hell is going on here?"

"Mr. Hotchkiss, I wish I knew," Nichols said, as his partner put his cell phone to his ear.

"Swafford? Stillman here. I think you need to get over to

Mike Capalletti's address. Sooner rather than later."

"Mr. Hotchkiss?" the receptionist said as she stuck her head into the conference room. "I have building security on the line. They're sending up a disk with coverage from the front of the building."

Hotchkiss grunted then went to a console in the corner. He punched a button and a large, whiteboard screen at the head of the conference table slowly rose into the ceiling, revealing a massive flat screen television behind it.

"Wish I had one of those," Stillman said.

"We're in the movie business," Hotchkiss said. "All our conference rooms are equipped with them. And we have a screening room upstairs."

"Nice."

Another button or two pushed and the blinds lowered over the outside windows, darkening the room. A few minutes later a blue-jacketed security guard appeared in the lobby with a small envelope. Stillman and Nichols watched as the receptionist took the envelope, removed a disk, and held it up for Hotchkiss to see. He nodded, then she walked away from them toward the hallway.

"Where's she going?" Nichols asked.

"The media room is next door. She'll—"

Before he could finish his sentence, the screen flickered to life. A black and white image of the front sidewalk outside the building filled the screen. Nothing unusual, just the comings and goings of office workers to and from the front door, with pedestrians passing by on the sidewalk. The time was stamped in the lower right hand of the screen.

Hotchkiss picked up a remote control. "Want me to fast forward?"

"Let's see the impact for starters. After that, we can go back and study the earlier footage." Nichols looked at his notepad.

"Start about four p.m."

Hotchkiss sped up the scene then suddenly hit the pause button. "There's Bob. Grey hair, dark suit."

Sure enough, Bob Keene was just exiting the building.

"That's the wrong time," Stillman said. "It's more than twenty minutes too early."

"Let it run," Nichols said.

Hotchkiss hit play; Bob turned and walked away from the building.

"Now fast forward," Nichols said.

Hotchkiss complied. Less than fifteen elapsed minutes later, Bob returned to the building, cell phone held to his ear.

"Any idea where he might have gone?" Stillman asked.

"Not a clue."

They watched for a while longer then Hotchkiss hit the pause button again. "There's Bob coming out again."

"Okay, timing's right this time," Nichols said. "Run it forward in real time and then we'll go back and look at it in slow motion."

Hotchkiss nodded then hit "play." Keene moved forward mechanically a few steps, then stopped and turned his head to the right. Slowly, again mechanically, almost robotically. Then eyes front again.

"He doesn't look right," Hotchkiss said. "I thought so before, when he came back to the building, but since he was on the phone, probably preoccupied, I thought that explained it."

"What do you mean?" Nichols asked.

"Bob played a lot of tennis. I know he walked a little funny, with his bowed legs and all, but he still moved like an athlete. Smooth, you know?"

But that didn't match the description of the man they were watching on the screen.

"Run it back to what we saw while ago," Stillman said.

Hotchkiss complied, and they saw what he was talking about. Keene did, in fact, move smoothly when he left the building the first time, but walked much more stiffly upon his return, almost as if his legs had straightened. Talking on the phone probably didn't explain it. The two detectives exchanged a glance, the same unspoken question on both their lips: Had Bob Keene just met with his hypnotist?

Bob continued to the curb, where he stopped. Rigid, as if standing at attention on a military parade ground. He was barely in the video picture, which was designed to take in the front of the building and its immediate environs, but not the street. Mercifully, when Bob stepped off the curb, he disappeared from the screen before being slammed into by the delivery truck. A pedestrian opened her mouth, as if to scream, then others rushed over. The image soon filled with bystanders.

"Okay," Stillman said, "run it back and then go forward real slow."

Hotchkiss again complied and the men watched the final minutes of Bob Keene's life in slow motion. As Bob swiveled his head to the right, Stillman said, "Freeze it there."

The images stopped moving, Bob's head turned.

"What's he looking at?" Stillman asked.

Nobody answered.

"Any way to widen the image?"

Hotchkiss pressed a button on the remote, and the area on the screen broadened, but revealed nothing new, other than to take in a bit more of the front of the building, away from the entrance. At the far edge of the screen, a portion of a column was visible, but nothing more.

"Okay, go forward."

The images jumped into motion again. The men watched closely until Bob Keene stepped off the curb and disappeared from sight.

"There!" Stillman said. "Back it up again. Slow."

Hotchkiss reran the footage until Stillman stopped him. "Now forward, slower."

Another button push and the images moved forward at a glacier's pace.

"What are you looking for?" Hotchkiss asked.

"Watch that column," Stillman said. "Where Keene was looking when he turned his head."

Seconds seemed like minutes as Bob Keene mechanically swung his head around, eyes front, and moved forward. The men kept their eyes glued to the column as Bob walked toward the curb. Hotchkiss saw it first.

"There's a shadow."

Sure enough, darkness fell on the sidewalk, as if someone standing behind or beside the column had stepped out, allowing the sun to hit his or her frame and create a silhouette.

"Good eye," Stillman said. "Keep watching."

Bob kept moving toward the curb, but now no one was watching him. All eyes were on the shadow by the column. As Bob drew nearer to the curb, it wavered, almost a wiggle. Just as Bob stepped off the curb, a figure came into view, briefly silhouetted, then turned abruptly and disappeared from the frame.

"Who is that?" Hotchkiss asked.

"Can you zoom in?" Stillman asked.

"Sure." Hotchkiss backed the image up then moved it forward again. He zoomed, which cut out the column.

"No, no, no," Stillman said. "Any way to zoom on that column?"

"Not on this," Hotchkiss said. He stopped the picture just as Bob turned his head. "You'll probably need some kind of software program to do that. All this can do is zoom in on the main picture."

"Can you widen the picture?" Nichols asked.

"A little bit." Hotchkiss pushed a button, and the scope of the picture's image opened up, taking in more of the column. The outline of a person's body at the column's edge was vaguely visible.

"Can't see the face," Hotchkiss said.

"Okay, forward," Stillman said.

Hotchkiss advanced the picture, but Bob Keene was again just a footnote. All attention was riveted to the column. The shadow appeared again, but this time the outline of the person's body was more distinct, although the face was still hidden in shadow. Then the person spun and walked away as Bob stepped off the curb.

Hotchkiss froze the picture then looked at the detectives.

"Who the hell is she?"

CHAPTER 41

DETECTIVE SWAFFORD PULLED to a stop in front of a two-story stucco house on Bedford Drive in Beverly Hills, not far from the Los Angeles Country Club. A hedge of hibiscus framed the yard like a fence, blood red blossoms polka-dotting rich green leaves. A chain link gate was closed across the sidewalk to the front porch that split the hedge into halves. An elderly Hispanic man clipped stray tentacles that threatened to mar the perfect face of the hedge. A second, younger man, a leaf blower strapped to his back, came along behind him, blasting the trimmings into the street.

The younger man stopped the blower as Swafford exited his car and watched him with the kind of wary eye typically triggered by cop-detector radar that some people naturally maintained. People who have reason to be wary.

"Is Mr. Capalletti home?" Swafford asked.

The elderly man stopped his trimming to observe the conversation. His radar hadn't gone off at all, but his curiosity had.

"His car is in the garage, but I haven't seen him," the leaf blower said with remarkably precise diction.

Swafford immediately felt guilty for his assumption that, if you had a leaf blower strapped to your back, you must be an illegal.

"Is that normal?"

"He's generally already gone to work when we show up, so yes, it's unusual for his car to be here in the middle of the day."

Swafford nodded, swung open the gate, and walked to the front porch. He pressed the door bell and, satisfied that he heard the sound of a ring inside the house, pulled out his cell phone. He rang the bell again while he waited for Stillman to pick up on the other end of his call.

"So what have you got?" Stillman said.

"What? No hello? See, that's the problem with caller I.D. No one says hello anymore."

"Hello," Stillman said. "So what have you got?"

Still no answer at the door. Swafford tried the handle, but found it locked, so he stepped off the porch and walked around the house, looking in windows.

"I've got workers here who say Capalletti's car is in the garage, but they haven't seen hide nor hair of him since they've been here. He's not answering the door, and I'm not seeing any movement inside. They say it's unusual for his car to be here in the middle of the day."

"Do you see a phone in any of the windows?"

Swafford cupped one side of his face with his free hand and pressed close to a window on the side of the house. The room was dark, the narrow gap in mini-blinds barely wide enough to permit sunlight inside. Still, it was enough that Swafford could make out a table and chairs, a counter and, beyond the counter, cupboards and a stove.

He squinted and surveyed the walls in the room. "Yeah, got one on the wall in the kitchen," he said.

"Okay, hang on a sec."

After a few beats, the phone on the wall began to ring.

And ring. And ring. And ring.

"It's ringing," Swafford said.

"No one's picking up. And we've been trying his cell for the past fifteen minutes with no luck."

"It got a GPS in it?"

"If it does, he's turned it off or disabled it. We can't pick up a location."

"Call the cell again and let it ring."

"It goes to voicemail after about ten seconds or so."

"Then keep calling it," Swafford said. "I'm going to move around the house and see if I can hear it."

"Why don't you just pick the lock or kick the door in and go inside?"

"This is Beverly Hills. We do things different here. I can't go busting inside unless I think a crime is in process or someone's in danger—"

"Yeah, yeah, yeah. The irony is that, even though you're in a movie city, you'd never make it as a movie cop. In the movies they just—"

"I know; I've seen 'em. This would be the part where I say, 'Do you hear that? Sounds like a cry for help.' *Then* I kick the door in."

"All right, put your ears on," Stillman said. "We're gonna start calling."

Swafford hung up and put the phone in his coat pocket. He leaned close to the kitchen window, waited, then moved on to the next window upon hearing nothing. He had just made it around the back corner of the house when he heard faint strands of music coming from above his head. He looked up and saw a patio extending from the rear of the house. At the far end, a stairway led down and spilled onto a flagstone sitting area, with outdoor furniture centered around an exterior fireplace. As if anyone needed an outdoor fireplace in southern California. Still, the wealthy had a need to spend their dollars in ways that might seem impractical to working stiffs, like police detectives.

Swafford pulled out his phone and punched re-dial. "Keep

calling that number," he said when Stillman answered. "I think we're on to something. I'll keep this line open."

"Will do."

Swafford held the phone at his side as he took the stairs two at a time. At the top, the music was louder and clearer.

"Rolling Stones?" he asked into his phone.

He heard muffled voices in the background and then Stillman said, "That's his normal ringtone."

Swafford crossed the second-story patio to a sliding glass door. Heavy drapes had been drawn, blotting out any view of the interior, but the door was open just slightly, enough to allow the music to be heard. Swafford grabbed the door handle and slid it open. Slowly. Silently.

The musical strains played louder.

Swafford pulled his gun from his holster and used the barrel to push the drapes aside. He stepped across the threshold then paused momentarily to allow his eyes to adjust to the dimness. He found himself in a small alcove, a sitting area of sorts, with a floor lamp and love seat across from a three-shelf bookcase.

He stepped out of the alcove into the full bedroom area. The room was dark as night, only faint outlines of furniture visible. The drapes were thick, obviously designed for day-sleeping. He stepped back to the alcove and pulled the drapes open all the way. Light streamed inside, made its way across a hardwood floor, to a Persian rug that outlined a king-sized bed, in which—

Mike Capalletti lay still as death, a bullet hole between his eyes.

"Time to kick the doors down," Swafford said.

PART THREE:

THE HILL COUNTRY

CHAPTER 42

CLAD IN A long-sleeve denim work shirt, jeans, and heavy work boots, Chad Palmer slipped safety goggles over his head and adjusted them around his eyes. He fitted plastic ear muffs over his sweat-stained Texas Rangers baseball cap, tugged up his work gloves, then flipped the chainsaw switch to on. Kneeling on one knee, he grasped the starter cord and gave it a sharp yank. On cue, the saw went from zero to sixty almost instantaneously, the sound just a faint buzz thanks to the ear muffs.

He lifted the saw and scanned his target: a copse of cedar trees clogging an ancient stand of giant Post Oaks at the far edge of a meadow that separated the entry road to his ranch house from a thick stand of woods that covered the east thousand acres of the ranch. In the semi-arid Texas Hill Country, water was scant, and conventional wisdom had it that one adult cedar tree consumed up to thirty-five gallons of the precious liquid per day. Better to eliminate trash trees that were as plentiful as cockroaches in order to protect the more desirable oaks and, in some areas of his 4,760 acre ranch, rare maples.

That's right; maples. Although most commonly associated with northern climes, such as New England, these trees also called the Texas Hill Country home. In fact, not thirty minutes away, as Chad often liked to point out, one of Texas's most popular parks, Lost Maples State Natural Area, fostered a stand of maples on its 2,200 acres that annually drew nearly 200,000 visitors from across the country.

Chad bent, turned the chainsaw sideways and placed the bar nearly flush with the dirt. Because a felled cedar won't re-grow, the goal was to sever it right at ground level so as not to leave any stump. He squeezed the trigger, the chain whirred, and he pressed against the trunk. The teeth bit instantly, spewing chips of wood and unleashing the aroma of fresh-cut cedar. He loved the smell, which for him ranked right up there with burning wood in a fireplace and charcoal-grilled steaks.

When the saw cleared the trunk, he pulled it clear, pressed the sole of his boot against the tree, and pushed. As it started its fall, he stepped back and applied his saw to the next, larger, tree in line. Just as he pulled the trigger, he caught a glimpse of movement in his peripheral vision on the dirt road that led to his ranch house. A vehicle was approaching, plumes of dust trailing behind.

Chad pressed harder, forcing the chain deeper into the cedar, now halfway through the eight-inch diameter. He tried to keep his focus on the saw, despite the approaching vehicle. He wasn't expecting anyone, but country veterinarians often had unexpected visitors, which was why he typically left his front gate open during the day. It was just one of the hazards, if you could call it that, of the job in rural ranch and farm areas, especially when you were a large-animal vet. Cows and horses didn't keep track of time or days; when they needed a vet, they needed a vet now.

The chainsaw cleared the far side of the trunk. Chad extracted the bar and pushed the tree with his foot. As it started its fall away from him, he turned and sought out the vehicle, which had now stopped at the edge of the field where he was working, maybe five first downs away. It pulled in through an opening in the fence that he had created by removing a stretch of barbed wire and stopped beside his old Ford pick-up truck. It was a newer model SUV, looked like a Toyota; not a car he recognized. He held the chainsaw at his side, finger off the trigger so as to still the spinning chain. He removed his goggles and waited to see who his visitor might be.

The driver's door opened and a young woman stepped out.

He flipped the switch to kill the saw, ripped off his goggles and ear muffs, dropped the saw, and raced to the SUV.

Teri met him in the middle of the meadow in a strong, sweaty hug.

Teri paced while Chad perched on the edge of an un-reclined recliner in the den of his ranch house. Through sliding glass doors, a view beckoned that was not unlike that from Teri's house in California, but instead of the smog of Los Angeles and the low-hanging smoke that lingered from the recent fires, this was pure, unspoiled Texas Hill Country. The house perched on the edge of a low bluff, overlooking a valley below that featured the Medina River. Water rippled effortlessly down a small waterfall, no more than a foot or two high, but just enough to create the kind of natural sounds that "sleep machines" and "white noise" makers replicated and that sold like wildfire to city dwellers.

Chad held a coffee mug with both hands, the liquid long since cooled. Teri looked as if she had aged thirty years since the last time he had seen her, though it had been but twenty. But while the stress that settled on her face robbed her of youthfulness, it had no impact on her beauty. Not even the broken nose and black eyes. At least not as far as he was concerned. He waited without interrupting for her to finish her story—a tale that he struggled to grasp and, quite frankly, to believe.

At last she finished her recitation and turned to face him. "I had to come home," she said. "I just got in the car and kept driving until I got here."

"I like hearing you use that word: home."

"It hasn't felt like it in a long time. But now..." Her voice trailed off. "Tell me what to do, Chad."

He thought for a moment, any number of thoughts, admonitions, and advice struggling for prominence.

Stay here, turn back the clock...Marry me.

He shook off that last one as he found his voice. "Have you eaten?"

"I've just been running on coffee."

"When was the last time you had any sleep?"

"I don't know. Before I left Los Angeles. Twenty-four hours ago, maybe?"

"The first thing you do is get something to eat and some sleep. Then we'll figure it out from there."

"A shower and a nap do sound nice. Any chance I can get some of those famous *huevos rancheros* of yours?"

"I'll fire 'em up while you shower. Take my bedroom. There should be fresh towels in the bathroom. I'll bring in your bag from the car."

As Teri started toward the hallway that led to the bedrooms, Chad watched her walk away. Her gait had a new spring in it since she arrived, and her face had brightened, as if the mere act of unloading her story lifted the burden that weighed her down during her drive from California. Or maybe it was because he was shouldering that burden with her.

She stopped and looked back at Chad.

He met her eyes and waited for her to speak.

"You're the only one who always believed in me, no matter what," she said.

Then she turned and disappeared down the hall.

CHAPTER 43

SWAFFORD SAT AT a rear booth of Nate'n Al's Deli on Beverly Drive, pancakes half-eaten on the plate before him, his coffee mug nearly empty. The two CHP detectives entered and looked around for a moment. Swafford waved to get their attention then gestured at the waitress as they headed his way. They slid into the booth across from him as the waitress brought menus.

Nichols looked at Swafford's plate. "Breakfast? You know what time it is?"

"It's never too late or too early for pancakes."

"Point taken."

"So what happened to Capalletti?" Stillman asked.

"One between the eyes, contact entry, and the gun in his hand," Swafford said. "And blowback on his wrist."

"No one does it that way," Nichols said. "You either eat the gun or put it to the side of your head."

"I know all we usually get here in Beverly Hills is littering, loitering, and parking violations—except as of late—but even I figured that one out," Swafford said.

"So the scene was staged by someone who doesn't have much experience at it."

"Or someone who wants to confuse us," Stillman said. "You think Capalletti really pulled the trigger himself?"

"Somebody could have put it in his hand and then fired it.

We're gonna run a tox screen and see if he was knocked out first. But either way, I'm betting someone else was in that room with him."

"Somehow this has all got to be tied to whoever tried to take out the actress, right?" Stillman asked. "And her friend?"

"Contrary to movie dialogue, sometimes there are such things as coincidences."

"You and me eating at the same In-N-Out last weekend, that's a coincidence. Identical screenwriters taking headers off cliffs, people shooting at actresses and their BFFs, then the actress's boyfriend getting his ticket punched and the boyfriend's boss eating a truck grill—that's not a coincidence; that's a pattern."

The waitress returned and took their orders: two coffees, two short stacks, and eggs over easy for both of them—another coincidence a vindicated Swafford noted as the detectives followed his lead and ordered breakfast in the middle of the day.

"Here's something else to throw into the mix," Nichols said after the waitress left. "We got Bob Keene acting like he was in a trance; we got Annemarie Crowell with a license to do hypnotherapy back in her home state; and guess who we've got on camera lurking around Keene's building the same time he buys it?"

"Do tell."

"You get one guess, so make it a good one."

"I think I know the answer to this one: Annemarie Crowell."

"Give that man a cigar," Nichols said. "She's our next stop. You want to come with us?"

"I don't want to be a third wheel, but just try and stop me."

"It's out of your jurisdiction. Don't want you to stretch your leash too far from BH."

"It's not a leash; it's a bungee cord. I think I'll survive both the fall and the rebound."

* * *

Swafford thought the apartment complex where Annemarie Crowell lived was equally as drab as Mike Capalletti's house was elegant. Though exactly how elegant did any house look with a dead guy in the master bedroom?

He wheeled into the parking lot and found a space directly in front of the apartment that also bore an "Office" sign on its door. He got out and stood next to his car while waiting on the CHP officers. He scanned the complex, the parking lot in bad need of re-paving, the stucco in bad need of updating, the doors in bad need of paint, and the whole thing in bad need of a wrecking ball.

The CHP guys came along a few minutes later. They parked next to Swafford's car then got out.

"You boys get lost?" Swafford asked.

"And I guess you got here like a homing pigeon," Nichols said.

"GPS."

"They check your passport at the border?"

"No, but they told me I had to switch to polyester. You got an extra suit I can borrow?"

"Trade you for an Armani," Nichols said.

"Okay, now that we've all sufficiently insulted each other, let's go talk to this mesmerizing witch. You got an apartment number?"

"Just the street address."

Swafford pointed toward the "Office" sign. "Then let's see what we can find out here."

He pushed open the door and led the way in.

Rondell, the apartment manager, stopped with a bean and cheese burrito halfway to his mouth, feet propped on a small coffee table, black-and-white western reruns on the television.

"Damn it," he said. "Doesn't anybody knock anymore?"

"It says 'office,'" Swafford said. "I never knock at a place of business."

"It's also where I live."

"Then may I make a modest suggestion. Add a sign under 'office' that says 'please knock.'"

"Yeah, maybe I'll do that," Rondell said. "You're the second person to make that suggestion this week." He took a big bite of the burrito then spoke while he chewed. "You po-lice?"

"The bad haircut give it away?" Stillman asked.

"Something like that," Rondell said. "But you ain't from this part of the city. Clothes are too fine."

"Beverly Hills," Swafford said, flashing his badge.

"You know you in Los Angeles, right? Don't got no jurisdiction outside of Camelot."

Swafford stepped aside and, with a sweeping gesture of his hand, ushered Stillman and Nichols to the front. "Ahh, but these gentlemen are state cops, and they have jurisdiction all over this fine city and beyond."

Rondell squinted, swallowed the mouthful of burrito, and took his feet off the coffee table. "So what business you got here?"

"Annemarie Crowell."

"The crazy lady." Not a question; a statement of fact.

"So you know her?"

"Yeah. What'd she do?"

"She live here?"

"Not no more. Like I told that actress, she moved out."

"What actress?" Swafford asked, though he felt like he already knew what the answer would be.

"Teri Squire. Annemarie said she'd be around, and she left me an envelope to give her. And I'm like, yeah, right, Ms. Oscar gonna come slumming around here. Then damned if she don't show up. She's the one who told me about the 'please knock' sign, by the way. So, anyway, I gave her the envelope and she left without so much as a thank you."

"What was in the envelope?" Swafford asked.

"Don't know. Never looked. It just had a name on the outside."

"What name?"

"Peggy Tucker."

"Who is Peggy Tucker?"

"Hell if I know," Rondell said as he took another bite of burrito. "Shook up that actress, though, when she saw it."

"Shook her up, how?"

"You know, she looked kinda surprised and she got all red in the face."

"She open the envelope?"

"Not in front of me. Just took it and skedaddled out the door."

"We need to see Annemarie Crowell's apartment," Swafford said.

Rondell took a key from a hook on the wall behind his head. "Like I said, she done moved out a few days ago, but the apartment's empty. Just follow me."

He led the way out of the office, then up a flight of stairs to a concrete walkway that looked to be hanging on for dear life. Swafford walked beside Rondell, the two state cops behind.

"How long you been managing this place?" Swafford asked.

"Hell, must be better'n five years now. It ain't much, but it's rent-free."

"You know all the tenants?"

"Most of 'em. Course, most of 'em come and go, so by the time I learn their names, they done split." He pointed to a door badly in need of a fresh coat of paint, which hardly distinguished it from any other door along the way. "Here it is."

He inserted the key and pushed the door open, then stepped aside. Nichols and Stillman went in first, followed by Rondell, then Swafford. The bare apartment consisted of a cramped living area that combined with a kitchenette to create one long, but narrow, room. On one side of the kitchenette, a doorway led to a bedroom, with a matcher on the other side. Threadbare brown carpet covered part of the floor, with linoleum the base for the kitchenette. Early American Depressing-as-Hell.

"How long did Ms. Crowell live here?"

"Longer'n most. Few years, I guess," Rondell said. "Maybe a little more. Her and her loser son moved in with Leland a little bit before he offed himself."

Any distractions created by the rundown apartment disappeared in an instant as all three men suddenly found themselves riveted by what Rondell was saying.

"She lived here with Leland?" Nichols asked.

"Yeah. Her and Leland's brother Rodney moved in at the same time. Rodney and Leland was twins, I think. Damn sure looked like each other, if they weren't."

"Did you know Rodney?" Swafford asked.

"Not too good. Not like I did Leland. Leland was a good dude. Pretty much kept to himself. Writing on that computer of his. Always writing. Kept saying he was gonna be a famous writer some day."

"Where's the bathroom?" Nichols asked.

"In the bedroom over there," Rondell said, pointing to the left of the kitchenette. "Ain't but one. Don't know whose idea it was to put only one bathroom in this place, then stick it inside one of the bedrooms."

"Okay, we got it from here," Nichols said. "We'll lock up before we leave."

"I should stay here with you," Rondell said. "It's my ass if—"

"If what?" Stillman asked. "If the Beverly Hills cop takes out his pocket knife and helps himself to a hunk of this fine carpet?"

Nichols snorted.

"We're cops, man," Stillman said. "What are we going to do?"

"I seen cops search places before," Rondell said. "I've seen how they trash 'em."

"We'll put everything back like we found it," Stillman said. He looked around then raised his eyebrows in mock surprise. "Oh, that's right. There's nothing here to put back."

"All right, I got ya," Rondell said. "You the funny cops. Just let me know when you leave."

With that, he exited the apartment. The three detectives stood in a triangle and exchanged glances. "So," Nichols said at last. "Anyone else interested by this little turn of events? Our dead screenwriter has himself a look-alike brother. What do you want to bet he was our latest cliff diver?"

"I think we need to get moving on an exhumation order, do a little DNA comparison," Swafford said. "We—"

His cell phone interrupted him. "Swafford," he answered.

"Detective," a voice on the other end said, "we got the phone records for Capalletti. The last call he made was to Teri Squire's cell phone."

Swafford tucked the phone between his ear and shoulder then extracted a pen and notepad from his coat pocket. "Give me the number. Then I need you to check out a name for me: Peggy Tucker." A pause, then, "I don't know who that is, but she's got something to do with Teri Squire."

While Swafford talked on the phone, Nichols wandered into the bathroom, which was hardly more than an indoor outhouse. A small sink supported by aluminum props, a mirror that doubled as a medicine cabinet, a toilet with no lid, and a porcelain bathtub with shower curtain. All in all, no more than five by five—twenty-five square feet for the hygienic needs of three people.

And from the looks of the facilities, not much hygiene was

involved. Orange rust stains marred the sink and tub, and other stains marred the toilet, which looked like it hadn't been flushed in a couple of days. The reflective surface of the mirror had flaked away right in the center, as if designed to prevent anyone using the sink from actually looking himself in the eye. Nichols wondered if there was something psychological involved, like a guilty conscience at work, at least metaphorically.

He pulled a pair of rubber gloves from his pocket along with a plastic bag, tools he always carried with him. You never knew when you might run across evidence during the day. From his pants pocket, he extracted a pocketknife. He paused for a second as he considered whether to cut loose a hunk of carpet just to prick the apartment manager around.

He sat on the edge of the tub, opened the knife to expose a blade about an inch-and-a-half long, and probed around the perimeter of the shower drain. The pop-up plug was loose, so he pulled it all the way out and put it aside. He inserted the blade into the drain, scraped it around the sides, and pulled it out. Several clumps of hair stuck to the side of the blade. A single long gray strand, at least ten inches long, dangled beneath it. He lifted the blade and pulled the single strand all the way out, then inserted the entire clump in the plastic bag, sealed it, and tucked it in his pocket.

Swafford was dialing his cell phone under the watchful eye of Stillman when Nichols returned to the main living area.

"Got enough for a DNA match for someone," Nichols said. "Got at least one belonging to a female."

"Annemarie Crowell," Stillman said. His partner nodded.

"All right, here goes," Swafford said as he punched the speaker button on the cell and held it out so all three men could hear.

Rather than going straight to voicemail, the phone rang. And rang and rang.

Then the ring tone abruptly ceased as someone answered on the other end, but said nothing.

"Hello?" Swafford said. "Hello? Ms. Squire?"

CHAPTER 44

TERI DIDN'T KNOW when a shower had felt so good. The events of the past forty-eight hours had wearied her like nothing she had ever experienced since...well, not since the events that drove her from Texas to California twenty years earlier. The big difference was that, back then, she understood what was happening. She didn't understand *why* it had happened, but she certainly understood the *what*. But now, she didn't understand either the *what* or the *why*—or the who or the how or the what-the-hell-was-going-to-happen-next.

Hot water came out in a muscular stream, the kind that massaged as well as cleaned. She turned her back to the showerhead and let pinpricks of water pulsate against the base of her neck. She had never tried acupuncture, but if it was anything like this, she might be willing to give it a shot. She struggled to clear her mind, to chase away extraneous thoughts and emotions, to crystallize the events that brought her back to Texas.

Everything started with the screenplay.

That damn screenplay! That damn, brilliant screenplay!

The screenplay that had left a stream of victims in its wake. Leland One—dead. Leland Two—dead. Bob Keene—dead. Mona—in critical condition. And Teri, herself—nearly dead twice, and now on the run.

She adjusted the showerhead to aim it at a tile bench in the corner of the oversized shower stall. She sat and let the shower spray beat against her face, hot water mixing with tears.

Chad paced in front of the sliding glass door, which he had opened to let a breeze float in. Even with hundred degree summertime temperatures, there was nothing quite like a Hill Country breeze. It was good to have Peggy home again. Check that—to have Teri home again. She seemed to have aged far more than the years that had elapsed, but he had seen that before. She had undergone a similar aging years ago, though she bounced back fairly quickly, as if someone had turned back the clock on the portrait of Dorian Gray. But now, it appeared as if the aging process had been accelerated even more than the time before.

His pacing was interrupted by the muffled sound of music. Sounded like the theme music to *Magnum, P.I.* He located the source in Teri's purse. Her cell phone. He hesitated for a moment, unsure whether to invade her privacy, then made a decision. He grabbed the phone and hit the "answer" button, but said nothing.

A male voice spoke on the other end. "Hello? Hello? Ms. Squire?"

A pause, then, "This is Detective Swafford from the Beverly Hills Police Department. If you're there, please answer. I'm afraid I have some bad news."

Chad made another decision. "Hello?" he said.

"Who's speaking?"

"I'm Ms. Squire's attorney."

Now a pause from the other end, then, "You got a name?"

"I do," Chad said.

A long pause. "But it's a secret, right?"

"You said you had some bad news for Ms. Squire?"

"How do I know you're her attorney? And why would she need one?"

"You'll just have to take my word on the first question, and none of your business on the second. Now, you said you had some bad news."

"It's about her agent, Mike Capalletti. I need to ask her some questions."

Chad heard rustling in the bedroom. Teri was out of the shower, probably dressing. She would be there momentarily. Should he put her on the phone or not?

"Ask me the questions, and I'll pass them along."

The voice on the other end of the line exhaled loudly, as if the speaker was exasperated. Chad smiled. Unless you frustrated the police, you weren't doing your job as an attorney. Even though he hadn't practiced law in nearly two decades, it still brought back familiar feelings. A rush of adrenaline that he now experienced with the birth of calves and foals.

"Detective, the bad news?"

"Capalletti's dead."

The words slammed into Chad. The next words pummeled him into near submission.

"He was killed with the same caliber gun that Ms. Squire alleges someone stole from her house," Swafford said. "The last phone number he called before he was killed was to this number. Now, counselor, I think you can figure out the questions on your own."

Chad sat on the edge of the couch and stared out at his beloved Hill Country. He grasped back into his memory for the training he had long since forgotten, the rules of law on privilege and procedure and protecting your client.

"Who is that?"

The voice was Teri's. She stood at the end of the hall, hair wet and glistening, clad in jeans and an oversized tee-shirt. She looked refreshed, maybe a bit younger—by months, not years, and still much older than her age—but grim-faced. He could only imagine that every call brought more bad news for her. And this one surely did. Her boyfriend, the guy Chad had never met but was almost murderously jealous of, was dead. Did he really want to be the guy to stack that burden on top of the others that already saddled her?

"Is that her?" Swafford asked, obviously able to hear her voice.

Chad lowered the phone and covered the speaker. "It's a Detective Swafford from Beverly Hills."

Teri held out her hand. "Let me talk to him."

"I don't think that's such a good idea."

"My call, Chad. My decision. Remember that from before? The client gets to make the choice."

"Peggy—"

"There is no Peggy. It's Teri."

"I don't think it's a good idea."

"You'll be right here, Chad. You can hear everything I say."

Chad made another decision.

He handed Teri the phone and she raised it to her ear. She opened her mouth to speak, but Chad silenced her with an upraised hand. She pulled the phone down and held the speaker against her thigh so Swafford couldn't hear.

"He's going to tell you that your agent was killed last night," Chad said.

"I thought it was suicide."

Chad stood in surprise, unable to stay still. He began pacing again.

"You mean you already know about it?" he asked.

"It happened before I left L.A. I told you about it. He was killed by a truck. But I thought it was suicide."

"The detective said he was shot with your gun. Or at least a gun like it."

"Shot? A truck hit him."

Confusion set in on both of them.

241

"The guy said he was shot," Chad said.

"Bob was shot?"

"I thought his name was Mike."

"No, Bob. Bob Keene."

"No, Mike. Mike Capalletti."

Teri felt the breath suck out of her chest. "Oh, my God!"

She sat on the couch, as if her legs had just melted from beneath her. Blood drained from her face and she gasped for air.

"Peggy, you okay?" Chad asked. He sat next to her and put his arm around her.

She nodded, took one last deep breath, and lifted the phone to her ear. Her voice came out in a hoarse whisper, clogged with emotion. Chad leaned close so he could hear what was being said on the other end.

"Detective? I need to hear your voice."

"Excuse me?"

"Say something. Anything. Enough for me to recognize your voice."

"How about the one about the lazy fox jumping over the brown dog, or however that goes? Or maybe the one about all good Americans coming to the aid of their country."

No mistaking that voice. She had heard it before, and the circumstances had seared everything about that day into her memory.

"Is Mike really dead?" she asked.

"I'm afraid so."

"What happened?"

"That's what we're trying to find out. That's why we need to ask you some questions."

"But I don't know anything about it. I just found out about it, just now."

Chad nodded, as if to confirm she hadn't said anything stupid yet; nothing that could implicate herself. She instinctively knew that there was no possibility that she could implicate herself. After all, she *truly didn't know* anything about Mike's death. She didn't know a single thing about the whole damn maelstrom that had overtaken her life and thrown her into what surely was a bottomless abyss. An abyss she had fallen into once before. An abyss she had managed to bounce back from. An abyss she was beginning to believe would offer no second chances this time.

"You're the last person he called," Swafford said. "You want to tell me what that was all about?"

"I was in Arizona when he called."

"Arizona?"

"On my way to Texas. That's where I am now. Check the time he called me, when you know he was still alive, and ask yourself how fast I would have to drive to kill Mike and then get all the way from L.A. to Texas by now."

"How do I know you're in Texas?"

Chad turned the phone toward himself. "I can vouch for that, detective."

"Where in Texas?"

"It's safer for her if nobody knows that."

"You know we can trace the signal on her cell."

"So be it. She can be long gone by then."

"Why would she do that?"

Chad gave an exaggerated sigh. "Somebody wants her dead."

"Maybe more than one somebodies."

Teri exchanged a look with Chad. She hadn't thought about that. She had just assumed one person was behind everything.

"Detective, what makes you think it's more than one?" Teri asked.

"Well, for starters, we've got some real questions about Annemarie Crowell."

"But she saved my life."

"I'd start by asking myself why she did that," Swafford said.

"And something else you ought to know about her: she's into hypnotism. I hate to sound paranoid, but I wouldn't want to find myself in a locked room with her."

Mike's voice echoed in Teri's head: "Your new movie, remember?...A serial killer who hypnotizes people into killing for her, then they kill themselves."

"Who else, detective?" Chad asked. "You said you thought maybe there was more than one person after her."

"We're looking into a guy named Bozarth. One of the investors in her movie."

"Doug Bozarth?" Teri said. "What makes you think he's got anything to do with it?"

"I didn't say we did. I just said we're looking into it. It's an old law enforcement adage: follow the money, and he's the money guy. He's got the most to lose if things go south on your new movie, and the most to gain if you become the next Marilyn Monroe or Heath Ledger."

"I don't understand," Teri said.

"Your last movie turns into gold if you die tragically."

The suggestion raised new suspicions in Teri's mind. She didn't like Bozarth, didn't trust him, but she had never thought he was dangerous—at least not to her. But it made sense. She suspected him of having something to do with Leland Crowell's death—or Leland Two or whoever that was. And she knew Swafford's theory was sound, but for reasons even he wasn't aware of. The only people who knew that she might not legally own the screenplay, that she was the weak link in the chain of title, were Mike—dead; Bob—dead; Leland Two—dead; and herself—and someone wanted her dead.

And maybe Annemarie. Probably Annemarie. If Bozarth was behind everything, then Annemarie was actually on the victim list.

"Ms. Squire, I need you to trust me," Swafford said. "Tell me where you are."

"Right now, I don't trust anyone," she said.

She hung up before he could say anything more.

Swafford tucked his phone back in his pocket then looked from Stillman to Nichols, who stood silently in Annemarie's former apartment.

"What do you think?" Swafford asked.

"I believe her," Stillman said. "She's scared. You could hear it in her voice."

"And she really sounded freaked when you mentioned Bozarth," Nichols said. "It kinda freaked me, too, since that's the first time I knew we were even looking at him."

"Yeah, I kinda surprised myself with that one, too," Swafford said. "I just threw it out there without really thinking about it, just to see what she'd say."

"Well, she didn't say much," Stillman said.

"But it was the way she didn't say what she didn't say," Swafford said. "She's buying it as a possibility. And that means she knows something we don't know."

"Then maybe we better find out what that is," Nichols said. "And we need to find out everything we can about Doug Bozarth."

CHAPTER 45

TERI STARED AT herself in the mirror as she pulled up her jeans, then slipped a tee-shirt over her head, put her cross-training shoes back on, and laced them up. She had figured out a couple of years ago—back when she inherited the screenplay, in fact—that Mike Capalletti was not the man she thought he was. He had his moments, though. He could be funny and charming and, when no one else was around, sweet, but he could also be cold, calculated, and conniving. The three Cs he had learned from Bob Keene. She had loved him for a time and even once thought he would be the man she would marry. That all came tumbling down two years ago when he decided to join forces with Bob Keene to fire her. He had been given the choice of his career or her, and he had made his choice.

Even after that, he helped to shepherd her through the movie that seemed destined to provide her the comeback she needed. He still seemed to care about her, but she knew, intellectually, that he was driven solely by self-interest. The movie would make his career, too; that it would help her was secondary to him. If the time ever came again that Mike needed to jettison the ballast from his ambition, though she might be the last to go overboard, she nevertheless had no doubt that she would go. But the last thing she wanted at this stage of her life was to be alone, so she had turned a blind eye to Mike's ambition, even though she knew it was just a matter of time until they separated again. She knew that the next time would be for good.

As it turned out, she was a prophet, and now they were permanently separated. Not by greed, not by ambition, and not even by betrayal, but by a bullet. Not the first time a bullet had done that to a relationship for her.

She opened the door and went back to the den, where Chad waited.

Chad. The man who was everything Mike had turned out not to be. The man who had put her interests in front of his, even at the ultimate cost of his career.

"You gonna be okay?" he asked.

"I thought things couldn't get any worse, but now I know they always can."

"I thought we might go for a ride. That always seemed to help in the old days."

An involuntary smile crossed her lips, just for a moment, but then it was gone. "I'd like that," she said. "But I don't have any riding boots."

"I've got some at the barn that'll fit you. Grab your sunglasses. I've also got a hat you can borrow."

Clad in straw cowboy hats and wearing sunglasses, Teri and Chad walked in silence from the house to the barn. Though it was hot, with the sun beating down through a canopy of trees that stood between the two structures, Teri felt a sense of coolness wash over her. She left Texas under a cloud; now she had returned to Texas under a cloud, but no matter how long she had been gone, Texas was still home—and there was just something about home that made problems seem a little smaller and burdens a little lighter.

Inside the barn, Chad led two quarter horses, both chestnut in color, one with black stockings and the other white, out of their stalls. The gelding was already saddled.

"This is Hansel and Gretel," he said. He handed the reins of the mare to Teri. "Saddles are in the tack room. So are the boots."

The tack room was on the south wall of the barn, next to a gun cabinet that held but one weapon, a rifle that Teri knew well. She brushed past the cabinet with scarcely a glance. Inside the tack room, she found a pair of women's cowboy boots that had the worn look of years of rough use, their leather cracked and soft. She knew those boots, just as she knew the rifle, even though it had been two decades since she had last worn them. She picked up the left boot and blew off a layer of dust. Memories flooded through her as she kicked off her cross training shoes and pulled on the boots. They were a bit stiff, yet still fit like a glove. She guessed that hers had been the last feet to wear them.

She walked to the saddles and, like a pro, selected one best suited for her mount. She also knew that saddle, having ridden in it for hours at a time during her teen years. She grabbed it with one hand and lugged it over her shoulder to where Gretel awaited. In a matter of seconds, she had the saddle situated, balanced, and strapped tight. After she finished tightening the cinch, she stepped back and noticed, for the first time, that Chad had been watching her.

"What?" she asked.

"How long has it been since you've done that?"

"Saddled a horse? Not since I left."

"Doesn't look like you've missed a beat."

"Like riding a bicycle," she said.

She put her left foot in the stirrup, then threw her right leg over the horse and settled easily into the saddle. The smoothness of the leather felt right beneath her butt, just as the boots felt as if they belonged on her feet. If it was the little things that made a home, these two might top the list. She fitted her right foot into the right stirrup, then stood up and settled back into the saddle again.

"Or riding a horse," she said. "It feels good to be back in the saddle."

"Gretel's no Bingo, but she's a good horse," Chad said.

At the mention of the name, Teri sombered.

"I'm sorry I had to put her down," Chad said. "I didn't want to but—"

"I know you had to. She was old. She had a good life."

"You two won a lot of barrel races together. She made a pretty good mount for shooting contests, too."

He went to the gun cabinet and moved a pitchfork that leaned against the front glass, then took out the rifle, a Winchester Model 70 bolt-action. A bronze plaque on the stock proclaimed: "First Place, Open Division: Peggy Tucker."

He carried it to Teri and handed it to her. She gripped the reins in both hands and refused to take the weapon.

"Given what you've told me, and what the police said, it's not a bad idea for you to be armed," Chad said.

"Why don't you take it then?"

"I wouldn't know what to do with it, but you would." He tucked it into the scabbard on her saddle. "No man in Bandera County ever shot better than you."

As Chad mounted Hansel, Teri pulled the rifle partway out of the scabbard and studied the plaque on the stock. "I haven't seen that since…"

Her voice trailed off as a bad memory surfaced. The last time she had seen the rifle was the last time she had used it.

"Your mom gave it to me," Chad said. "I always knew that, some day, I'd give it back to you."

"My shooting days are over."

"Just do me a favor and keep it close."

"I won't use it."

"I hope you don't have to."

Without another word, they turned their horses and headed outside, with Chad leading the way. As they passed a bed of hay just inside the door, Teri pulled the rifle from the scabbard and tossed it aside. It landed soundlessly in the hay as they left the barn. While the saddle and boots brought good memories, the rifle was simply one more bad memory she didn't need.

Teri caught up to Chad at the top of a ridgeline that ran north and south through the ranch. To the east, flat range land stretched to the next hill, nearly two miles away. On the west side, the ridge sloped down sharply to a stand of cypress trees that lined a creek cutting across the property. Spanish moss hung from the cypress branches, blowing in the hot breeze.

"I miss it," Teri said.

"Miss what?"

"All of it. The hills, the trees, the smells, even the heat."

"You sorry you left?"

"I'm sorry I had to."

"You didn't have to."

"You know as well as anybody that I had no choice. It was time to grow up and be on my own."

"You did us proud. The only problem was, we couldn't acknowledge it. We always worried that some reporter would come snooping around, looking for deep background on Teri Squire. Thank God it never happened."

"I know," Teri said. "I was always afraid someone would figure it out. Every now and then, a reporter would trace me back to Texas, but the trail always ended there, as if it disappeared at the New Mexico line. I never knew how you did that."

"It's the advantage of living in a small town and having an aunt who does all the computer work for the county."

"I hope she didn't do anything illegal," Teri said.

"She didn't do anything she didn't want to do."

"I'm sorry I wasn't here for her funeral."

"Uh huh."

They lapsed into silence again. The only sounds were the

hooves of their horses picking their way along the ridgeline. When the ridge turned east, Chad turned west and headed down the slope on the other side, which had flattened over the past quarter mile or so. At the bottom of the slope, they merged onto a dirt road and turned north again. Teri felt a sense of familiarity, as if she had been here before, but she couldn't quite figure out where she was. A prickly sensation ran up the back of her neck.

"We're off your property, aren't we?" she asked.

"We left it about a mile back."

"Where are we going?"

He said nothing, but just kept riding. About two hundred yards down the road, he turned west again, through an opening in a barbed wire fence where the wire had been cut, and onto a flat pasture. In the near distance, a copse of trees shaded a structure. As they drew nearer, the structure became clearer: a country church with a bell tower. Nearby, small blips on the landscape indicted headstones. A solitary figure stood by one of the headstones.

She did know this place. "Chad, why are we here?"

Still he remained silent. They reached the cemetery, which stood free and unfettered by any gate or fence. The solitary figure was a woman in a denim skirt, her back to the riders, gray hair draped across her shoulders.

Chad and Teri headed toward the figure, who turned to watch their approach for the last ten yards. The woman smiled but remained silent.

Teri dismounted and ran to her. "Mama."

Mary Tucker embraced her daughter in a hug, and the two women wept.

Chad clucked the reins and turned Hansel's head, then returned back the way he had come.

Mary held her daughter at arm's length and brushed tears away with her fingers. She allowed tears to run unchecked down her own cheeks.

"Baby, you came home," Mary said.

"I didn't know where else to go."

"You came to the right place. Chad told me you were in trouble." Then she focused on Teri's swollen nose and blackened eyes. "What kind of trouble? Are you hurt?"

Teri rubbed her nose gingerly. "It's nothing I can't get over."

For the first time, Teri looked at the headstone where her mother had been standing. In bold letters, chiseled into granite, was the inscription: FREDERICK ADAM TUCKER, NOV. 19, 1969—JULY 6, 1993.

Teri bowed her head; her tears beat out a steady pit-a-pat on the toes of her shoes.

"I come here every week," Mary said. "He's still my little boy."

"I'm so sorry, Mama."

"It wasn't your fault, Baby. I know that."

"It wasn't yours either, Mama."

"I keep wishing I could have done something different. Then it never would have happened."

"You didn't know."

"I think I did. I think I always knew." Mary paused, and then added, "I think your daddy did, too. But we didn't do anything about it until it was too late."

"Does he know I'm here?"

"No. He thinks this is just my weekly visit."

"Does he still hate me?"

"Oh, Baby, he never hated you. He just couldn't make his mind understand it, that's all."

"It sure seems like hate to me."

Mary gestured to a wooden bench under a nearby oak. "Let's sit over there."

She took Teri by the hand and led her to the bench, where

they both sat. "Something you've got to understand about your daddy is that he comes from a long line of Texas ranchers," Mary said. "He was raised to believe in God, land, and family. He believes it's his God-given duty to be a good steward of the land and to protect his family. He's always been good at the first one. He's taken real good care of the land. But he feels like he failed at the other. He couldn't protect his family. First he couldn't protect you, and then he couldn't protect Adam. Then he lost both of you."

"He didn't lose me, Mama. He kicked me out. I may be the Prodigal Daughter, but I didn't leave on my own. He abandoned me when I needed him the most."

"It was just too much for him. He thought you would be better off without him."

"Mama, I know he's your husband and you love him. He's my father, and I love him, too. But that's just bullshit. He made a decision, and then I made a decision. And now I have no father."

Mary got up and walked back to the tombstone. "He's hurting. He has been for twenty years. He lost his son. No parent should have to bury a child."

"And I lost my brother." Teri stood and went to Gretel. She grabbed the pommel of the saddle and mounted up. With the reins in her hands, she headed the horse toward the place where her mother stood. "Daddy buried two children. The problem is that the second one he buried is still alive."

Mary didn't look up but kept her eyes on the tombstone.

"Did you bury me, too, Mama?" Teri asked.

The question spun Mary's head around. "No, Baby, of course not. But don't make me choose between my daughter and my husband."

Teri's voice softened, thick with emotion. "It seems like you already chose, a long time ago." She brushed away a tear. "I love you, Mama."

Mary looked back at the tombstone. "I love you, too, Baby. I always will."

A buzz of uncertainty swirled in Mary's head as she stared at the gravesite of her only son. Had Adam's death been her fault? Could she have stopped it if she hadn't turned a blind eye and a deaf ear? The uncertainties, the questions, the doubts of the last twenty years swarmed like a Texas twister, the buzz increasing to a dull roar and then to a full-blown roar. The chasm the shooting had dug between Peggy and her father had driven Peggy away all those years ago. Now she was finally home again, and still Mary had no words of comfort to offer her daughter.

Words of comfort.

Words of comfort? Of course.

Chad had said Peggy was in trouble. That was why he had called and told her to meet Peggy here. But Mary had been so wrapped up in thoughts of Adam that she hadn't even bothered to ask.

"Chad said you were in trouble," Mary said, as she turned to face her daughter. "What—"

There was no one there. Mary hadn't heard Peggy leave, hadn't heard the horse's hooves on the hard earth. Had she been so oblivious, once again, to her daughter's pain? Was it the same lack of concern that had chased Peggy off all those years ago? An adage settled on the forefront of her mind: Those who don't learn from history are doomed to repeat it.

She hung her head and sobbed.

CHAPTER 46

SWAFFORD LEFT A message on Stillman's cell for a call-back, then pulled his car into a parking slot at an In-N-Out Burger, got out, and went inside. He hadn't finished his pancakes at Nate'n Al's, so he felt like a little something to eat was in order, though, if she knew, his wife would kill him over his diet today. After leaving Stillman and Nichols, he made a few calls for some updates—at least one of which was extremely surprising to him—then took a little detour to his favorite fast food restaurant while waiting to hear back from the CHP detectives. He requested his double-double "animal style," then filled his cup with iced tea and found a booth. As soon as he sat down, his cell phone rang. He glanced at the read-out: Stillman.

"You got something on the DNA yet?" he said as he answered.

"Always be good to the computer geeks and they'll be good to you," Stillman said. "But no."

"Do tell."

"We found out that Leland's buried in Ludlow, out in the desert. We're working on an exhumation order right now. We also got the hair from that tub to the lab. We're front of the line, but still don't know how long that's gonna take. I hope we'll have something to match it up against at least by the time we dig Leland up."

"I got my people looking for Annemarie, but no luck yet,"

Swafford said. "Looks like she's fallen off the face of the earth."

An In-N-Out worker approached Swafford's table with his order. Swafford accepted it with a nod then dismissed the kid with a wave of his hand.

"So here's the scenario I've been putting together in my head for this," Swafford said. "It assumes, of course, that the DNA's all going to match up."

"Your elevator pitch, huh?"

"Leland writes a script and wills it to our actress, Miss Squire. Then Mommy Dearest sends him off a cliff. She knows the story of a suicidal screenwriter just about guarantees a blockbuster. She knows just enough about the business to know it really doesn't matter if the screenplay's any good. All that matters is how it ended up in the hands of Teri Squire. Then, just when the blockbuster is about to hit—"

"Brother Rodney shows up, pretending to be Leland, and he tries to horn his way in on the back end."

"The problem with that is planning that far ahead," Stillman said.

"What do you mean?"

"Nichols and I have been thinking the same way. The problem is this: How can Annemarie know the screenplay is worth a damn? I mean, how can she be so sure it's going to be a hit, that she offs her kid just hoping that the screenplay is good enough? Most screenplays suck."

"Like I said, she knows it's the hype that'll blow up the box office, not the actual script."

"But that still takes a lot of luck. How do you factor that into an actual plan?"

"You got a theory?" Swafford asked.

"Our theory is she's just taking advantage of happenstance. She may or may not have gotten her kid to take a header off a cliff, but when he did, she figures out an angle for it. Then, when the blockbuster special's about ready to roll, she decides it's time to get on board before the train leaves the station. She pulls Rodney into the deal to pretend to be Leland and throw a monkey wrench into the whole deal."

Swafford grabbed his burger in one hand—not an easy task with a double-double—and took a big bite. Sometimes he thought better when he ate. "The rest of the story still plays out the same way," he said. "Along comes Doug Bozarth and his hedge fund, but all of a sudden he finds out Teri Squire may not really have owned the screenplay all along. Not if the screenwriter is still alive."

"So the screenwriter needs to be dead to clear title. That means bye-bye Rodney."

"It's still a leap to tie that to Bozarth," Swafford said. "What if it's the actress? She's the one who needs him dead."

"You really think she's capable of killing someone?"

Swafford swallowed then brought the hamburger up for a second bite. Just before biting, he put it down on the table. "Well, see, that's why I called. We've got some pretty good computer geeks of our own. It took some doing, including calling in some favors from the FBI, but I found out a little something about Miss Teri Squire."

"My turn," Stillman said. "Do tell."

"She's killed before."

There was silence on the other end of the line for a few seconds. Swafford smiled as he realized he had finally struck the smartass state cop speechless.

"Her real name is Peggy Tucker, and about twenty years ago, she shot and killed her brother Adam back in Bandera, Texas. They said it was a hunting accident, but it doesn't pass the smell test. She spent a year in a state youth home for it."

"So is that where she's from? Bandera, Texas?" Stillman asked.

"Yep. I'm betting that's where she's gone. She had a lawyer named Chad Palmer, who's now a veterinarian full-time. He was pretty much fresh out of law school when he handled the hunting accident case, then shut down his practice after Peggy Tucker went to the youth home. My money says that's who we were talking to earlier."

"Where's Bandera?"

"About an hour, give or take, from San Antonio."

"Shit!" Stillman said.

Swafford set his hamburger down and perked up in his seat. "What?"

"That fits nicely with a piece of information we learned about Doug Bozarth. His private Gulfstream filed a flight plan today for San Antonio. He should be getting there right about four-thirty Central Time." He glanced at his watch. "That's about a half-hour from now."

Swafford glanced at his watch then said, "You guys ever flown on a private jet? I got another favor I can call in."

Mark Dolan and Will Morgan waited at one of the hangars at San Antonio International Airport that serviced private jets. They looked like typical Texans, clad in jeans, denim workshirts, and cowboy boots. The differences between them were readily discernable, though it would take a slight bit of analysis to actually articulate them. Dolan wore calfskin boots, while Morgan wore alligator; Dolan's jeans were worn, the cuffs frayed from years of being stepped on by the heels of his boots, while Morgan's were true blue, creased as if professionally ironed; Dolan's workshirt was wrinkled, as if he'd slept in it, while Morgan's was starched and pressed. By all appearances, Morgan was the boss, Dolan the hired hand.

Appearances could be deceiving.

Morgan looked at this watch. "Jet should be here by now."

"It'll get here when it gets here."

"I'm just saying."

"You usually are. But saying doesn't change anything."

A Gulfstream taxied to the structure and pulled inside the air conditioned hangar. As the engines shut down, the door opened and stairs descended. Doug Bozarth exited, clad in a silk suit straight from Europe, every hair groomed and slicked back, a leather briefcase clutched in one hand. He didn't smile or even look from side to side, just moved straight forward as if with a purpose. He eyed the two men in jeans and boots, who fell in beside him, one on each side. They veered across the hangar and toward the exit that led outside to the parking lot.

"What have we learned?" Bozarth asked.

"She hasn't been to her parents' ranch," Dolan said. "We've had eyes on it since we first heard from you."

"She came to Texas for a reason," Bozarth said. "If not so see her parents, then what?"

Dolan opened the door and the men stepped outside into a hot Texas sun that heated the wind, blasting their faces like a furnace. Sweat immediately leaked from Bozarth's brow, his perfect hair mussing.

"It always this hot here?" he asked.

"It's Texas in the summer," Dolan said. He pointed toward the private parking area. "This way."

"Where else would she go?" Bozarth asked.

"She's got an old boyfriend here. A lawyer turned vet."

"Interesting career change."

Dolan led the way to a newer model, oversized Dodge pick-up truck. He pressed the remote control on his key ring, unlocking the doors. Dolan got in on the driver's side and Morgan squeezed into the back while Bozarth got in on the passenger side. Dolan cranked the engine, turned the air conditioner as high as it would go, and backed out of the parking spot.

"Talk to me about this old boyfriend," Bozarth said. "The former lawyer."

"He was her lawyer on a manslaughter charge."

Bozarth snapped his head around, a momentary lapse of composure. The news obviously took him by surprise. "Manslaughter!" he said.

"They said it was a hunting accident, but she still got a year for it. A plea deal."

"Who'd she kill?"

"Her brother."

Dolan pulled a folded page from his pocket and handed it to Bozarth, who studied the page, then smiled. What a delectable piece of information. Little Miss Teri Squire, who seemed to take offense at the unspoken threats of violence that accompanied their meetings to discuss the screenwriter problem, with a holier-than-thou attitude that she lorded over him—that same Teri Squire had killed her own brother.

"How come no one knows about this?" Bozarth asked.

"She was sixteen when it happened. When her year was up, her record was sealed, since she was a juvenile. Her father disowned her, so she changed her name when she moved to California, maybe even had a little work done, and started acting. Anyone trying to track down her background would have run into a dead end."

"You said her lawyer was an old boyfriend. But if he was her lawyer at the time and she was sixteen—"

"Yeah, the math is funny. The way I figure it, they probably had a fling during her case. He was about a year out of law school, and he took it personally when she decided to plead guilty, so he stopped practicing law and went back to vet school."

"What makes you think they had a fling?"

"It just figures. Good-looking girl like that, he gets all broken up that she went to a prison for kids so he quits law practice.

Sounds like he took it awfully hard if it was just business."

"Where do we find this vet?" Bozarth asked.

"In Bandera County," Morgan said from the back seat. "About an hour from here, give or take. He's got a ranch there."

"Then gentlemen," Bozarth said, "let's go to Bandera County."

CHAPTER 47

TERI HAD NEVER felt so alone as she meandered to Chad's ranch. She needed time to think, so she chose a long, roundabout route rather than going directly back. Just as Chad liked to ride when he needed to clear his head, that had once been her pattern, as well. Being alone in the Hill Country, astride a horse, was as close to heaven as she had ever been, but that was a long time ago. She wondered if she would ever regain that feeling of closeness to God.

As good as it had been to see Mama again, it hurt doubly to be reminded of old wounds and to have the scabs ripped off anew. Teri knew it wasn't fair to put her mother in the middle of things, to draw a line in the dirt about Daddy, but at some point, choices had to be made. Adam had done what he had done; he had made his choices. Teri had done what she had done; she had made her choices. Then Mama and Daddy made theirs, and Teri had left. Twenty years was a long time not to see your parents. Likewise, it was a long time not to see your daughter.

But then there was Adam, and she understood that a lifetime was a long time not to see your son.

She shook her head and flicked the reins, turning Gretel back up the slope to the ridgeline that led to Chad's ranch.

Chad.

The only person who had always believed in her, who had always stood beside her. The only person she could trust and depend on. She had dragged him into the middle of her problems years ago, and now she had dragged him into her current spate of problems. But unlike before, her current problems could bite him if he stood too close to her. He was still her friend, and she had put him in harm's way. If whoever was trying to kill her—and had already killed two people close to her and tried to kill another—found Chad, he, too, might be in danger.

She checked her watch; it was nearly six. She was shocked to realize she had been riding for nearly three hours. She dug her heels into Gretel's side and turned the horse toward the barn.

Chad pressed the trigger on the chainsaw and started on the next row of cedars, right where he had left off this morning when Peggy arrived. Riding horses cleared his head, but so did manual labor in the Texas sun. There was just something about sweat and dirt that made a Texan feel really alive and on top of his game. He'd had a lot to think about ever since Peggy showed up. He was having a hard time putting all the pieces together, but one thing he did know: Peggy was in far worse trouble than before.

He wondered, and worried, how things might have gone with her mom. He felt a little guilty about calling Mary behind Peggy's back, but he knew Peggy never would have agreed if he had suggested it. At the same time, he knew that Peggy *needed* to see and talk to her, just as much as Mary needed to see and talk to Peggy. Sometimes you had to make decisions for other people, even if it might make them mad. This was one of those times. His biggest worry, though, was that Tom might have found out about the meeting, or simply shown up by accident. Mary had told him that Tom rarely went to Adam's gravesite, but it would just be Peggy's continued misfortune if Tom decided that today was the day for a visit.

In his peripheral vision, he saw movement on the dirt road that ran along the fence line. He felt an odd sense of déjà vu. It was just like when he had seen Peggy arrive this morning, and, just as then, he wasn't expecting company. He killed the chainsaw, removed his ear muffs and goggles, wiped sweat from his eyes, and squinted. It looked like a pick-up truck, a newer model, kicking up dust. Clearly heading his way.

He crossed the meadow to his truck, grabbed a cup from the front seat, a rifle from the back, and retreated to the truck bed. He laid the rifle inside—the same rifle he had given Teri before their ride, who had apparently just tossed it into the hay behind his back as they rode from the barn. He poured himself a cup of water from a large jug on the edge of the tailgate and waited.

The pickup turned into the opening in the fence and pulled to a stop about twenty feet away. Brand new, oversized Dodge, midnight blue in color, covered in dust. Three doors opened, three men stepped out. One looked local—faded jeans and worn boots; one looked like a drugstore cowboy—new duds sharply creased and alligator boots; and one looked like he was on his way to a formal dinner. He had loosened his tie, but even the pre-planned casual look couldn't disguise the cut of the cloth of his suit or the aura of entitlement that engulfed him.

One more thing stood out about him: absolutely dead eyes.

"Can I help you fellows?" Chad asked.

"I think we're lost," the well-dressed one said.

"That goes without saying. You're on private property, and you had to drive through two gates just to get here."

The three men spread out, creating a triangle around Chad's truck. The well-dressed man faced him across the bed of the truck; the drugstore cowboy flanked to the rear, the local to the front. Chad longed for a wall at his back.

"Where you headed?" Chad asked.

"See, that's just it," the well-dressed one said. "We're not real sure where we're headed. We're looking for someone."

"And who might that be?" But Chad thought he already

knew.

"We're looking for a lawyer turned veterinarian named..." He turned to the local. "What was his name again?"

"Chad Palmer," the local said.

"Yeah, Chad Palmer. You wouldn't happen to know where he is, would you?"

Chad reached over and put his right hand on the stock of the rifle, hopefully hidden behind the water jug. "Don't know where Mr. Palmer is."

"This is his ranch, isn't it?"

"I'm his foreman."

"Strange," the well-dressed one said. He reached inside his coat pocket and extracted a folded sheet of paper. He unfolded it and held it up: a photocopy of a newspaper article, with a photo under the headline. Chad knew who was in the photo. After all, he had been there at the time. It was the one photo that made it into the local paper before he had been able to kill the story.

"You look an awful lot like the man in this picture," the well-dressed man said. "A picture from Peggy Tucker's manslaughter trial."

Chad picked up the rifle from the truck bed and held it across his folded arms. "Like I said, this is private property. You're trespassing."

"Not if you invite us to stay."

"I'm not feeling very neighborly. I need to ask you to leave."

"I've always heard that Texans were supposed to be friendly." The well-dressed man smiled, but it stopped short of his cold eyes.

"Have you also heard, 'Don't mess with Texas'?" Chad pulled his lips back and bared his teeth in an attempt to mirror the well-dressed man's mirthless smile.

"So we seem to have reached a stalemate," the well-dressed man said.

In his peripheral vision, Chad saw the other two men slowly moving wider, an obvious flanking maneuver. He raised the rifle, still holding it across his folded arm, barrel now pointed directly at the drugstore cowboy.

"Not another step," he said. The two men stopped then looked to the well-dressed man, as if awaiting instructions. He was clearly the alpha dog.

"You're good where you are," the well-dressed man said.

Chad saw that both of them stood in exactly the same position, with their feet shoulder-width apart, hands at their side. He'd seen enough TV westerns and cowboy movies to recognize the quick draw stance. But they had no gun belts hanging low at their hips or guns visible by their hands. That could only mean that the guns were tucked into the backs of their jeans. He did a quick calculation. If he shot first, it would likely take at least two seconds for the other to swing a hand around back, grab the weapon, and bring it around front. Lee Harvey Oswald got off three shots in about eight seconds with a bolt action rifle from the schoolbook depository in Dallas. Surely Chad could get off two, including chambering a second round as he swung the barrel of his rifle from one gunman to the other, in two to three seconds, especially since he'd have the element of surprise with the first shot.

Assuming, of course, his opponents didn't shoot first. If that happened, he could still get off his first shot, provided he could see the exact moment of hand movement. Even a fraction of a second delay could make the difference. But whether he could hit both targets under those circumstances was another question altogether.

The real wild card, of course, was the well-dressed man. Was he armed? Chad couldn't tell. He wasn't in the gunfighter stance, and there was no detectable bulge under his coat. But he was "the guy." No question about that. Chad needed to keep that man occupied, but he didn't need to focus on him so much as to miss movement by his cronies.

"What do you want?" Chad asked.

"I need to talk to Teri Squire," the well-dressed man said.

"The actress?"

"None other than." The well-dressed man held up the photocopy of the article again. "I think she used to go by Peggy Tucker."

"Maybe you haven't noticed, but this is Texas. I think you've wandered about thirteen hundred miles too far east. There are no movie stars here."

"If she's not here, she will be soon enough."

"Then leave me your card, and I'll have my people call your people when she shows up. We'll do lunch."

There was that smile again from the well-dressed man. "I think maybe we'll wait."

Teri held the reins loosely, giving Gretel her head. The horse knew exactly where to go, hoping a bag of oats awaited her in the barn. Teri hoped a sandwich and cold lemonade awaited her, as well.

She dismounted and led Gretel into the barn, where Hansel stared at her while he munched on oats. Gretel whinnied, almost as if to say, "Where's mine?"

Teri glanced toward the haystack where she had tossed the rifle earlier, but it wasn't there. She looked at the gun cabinet; not there, either. Chad must have it. She had just reached beneath Gretel's belly to loosen the cinch on the saddle when she heard the first gunshot.

The man to Chad's right, the local, seemed to be moving, continuing the flanking motion. Chad swung the rifle around to point it at him.

"Tell your boy to stop."

It was just a brief moment of inattention, but the flanking movement diverted Chad. The rhinestone cowboy took that lapse as an opportunity to pull his gun from the back of his belt and fire.

"No!" the well-dressed man shouted.

Chad felt a searing pain as the bullet tore into his left shoulder. He spun, staggered to regain his footing, and pulled the trigger on the rifle. The local dove to his right, hit the ground, and rolled. The bullet whizzed harmlessly by. Chad swung the rifle around, jacked in another round, and squeezed off another shot.

The drugstore cowboy hadn't moved, as if proud of himself for his first shot, and feeling bulletproof as a result of his prowess. Chad's second shot caught him in the throat. His head snapped back and he threw his arms out to the side, the gun flying from his hand as he staggered backward two steps and then crumpled to the ground.

The three survivors moved at once, as if in a synchronized choreography team. The well-dressed man lunged for the gun the drugstore cowboy tossed his way. The local scrambled for cover behind the Dodge, and Chad dove into the driver's side of his own truck. His left arm was useless, blood spilling from his shoulder and streaming down his side. The keys were still in the ignition. He cranked the engine, ducked beneath the dash as he shifted into reverse, and floored the accelerator. The truck jumped backward as a hail of gunfire erupted from the front.

The trunk lurched down a slight slope toward the trees where Chad had been felling cedars just before the arrival of the gunmen. He could hear, and even feel, the bullets slamming into the grill of his truck. The windshield shattered and glass rained on his head. He stayed low, hoping the engine block would provide enough of a shield to last until he could reach the trees.

Suddenly the truck slammed to a stop, its bed crunched

against a large oak tree. End of the line. Chad grabbed the rifle and a nearly-empty box of bullets, slid across the seat to the passenger side, then opened the door and rolled out. He got to his feet and ran into the trees.

Teri whipped the reins, her heels clutching Gretel's side, and rode full force up the dirt road to the meadow, then suddenly pulled up short at the sight. Chad's truck was butted up against a tree at the edge of the woods. A second pickup, a newer model, pulled up next to Chad's and two men got out. She didn't recognize the man who emerged from the driver's side, but even at this distance she recognized the passenger: Doug Bozarth.

Both men appeared to be carrying guns. They ran into the trees.

They hadn't seen her, their attention riveted on the woods beyond Chad's truck. Chad had obviously escaped, at least momentarily, and ducked into the woods. She hoped it was he who had retrieved her rifle from the hay and that he had it with him. She debated whether to return to the house for another weapon, but she didn't know if he had any other guns there. With his love of animals, he never hunted so, as far as she knew, he had no reason to own any weapons. After all, the lone occupant of his gun cabinet in the barn had been her rifle, and he hadn't even kept that in the house.

She pulled her cell phone from her pocket and pushed 9-1-1. She held it to her ear and listened, but heard nothing. Not surprising, given the relative isolation of the ranch. She knew there was a signal at the house; after all, Detective Swafford had called her there. Again, she debated whether to head back to the house to call for help and to search for a gun, but she didn't know how much time she had. She had no idea how much of a lead Chad had on his pursuers, but he knew his property intimately, including a few creek beds, bluffs, and even a dry cave. He could probably evade his pursuers, one of whom was a city slicker, without too much trouble. That meant she probably had time to go call for help.

It seemed like minutes, but in actuality she knew all these thoughts had coursed through her mind in a matter of seconds. But still, time was of the essence. She started to turn Gretel to return to the house when, up ahead, she saw a lump on the ground near the spot where Chad's truck had been parked that morning when she arrived. She figured he had likely done so again, so whatever had happened, it had started there. She headed that way.

Blood pounded in her ears as she drew nearer. The lump took on a distinct shape. It was a man lying on his back, arms outstretched. Up close, she could clearly see that he was dead, blood streaming from his throat. So Chad was definitely armed.

She looked downhill toward the spot where Chad's truck had been parked. The chainsaw lay on its side, silent. Next to it, tire tracks, and a dark splotch on the grass and dirt nearby. She dismounted and ran to the spot. Her heart seemed to stop as she looked down. Blood.

She rushed back to Gretel and jumped on her back. She held Gretel in a sprint across the meadow to the two trucks at the edge of the woods.

She jumped off and landed on her feet in a dead run. She rushed to Chad's truck, its engine quiet. Blood pooled on the floorboard on the driver's side and was smeared along the inside of the door. It stained the seat in a swiping motion toward the passenger door, which was open. Looked like a lot of blood to her, but at least Chad was on the move. The question was how fast and how far he could move in the condition he was in. And how far ahead of his pursuers was he?

She checked the interior of the other truck, not knowing what she might find. A gun, maybe. The dead man wasn't armed, but the two who had entered the woods were. If they had each been armed initially, then one gun was unaccounted for. Or maybe Bozarth now had the dead guy's gun.

She checked the glove compartment, under the seat, in the rear seat. The only thing of interest was the keys in the ignition. She pocketed those. If nothing else, it might hinder their escape.

She went back to Chad's truck and checked it again. Nothing but tools in the back. Spare chains for the chainsaw, a socket set, screwdrivers, a pair of work gloves—but there was one item that might be of some help, a pruning saw with a retractable blade about six inches long. Ideal for trimming small limbs or branches.

Or fingers or arms. God forbid that matters should end up in close quarters fighting, but by now Teri had learned to always think worst-case-scenario. The bar had been set pretty high for her in that regard, yet these past days had already cleared it by a wide margin.

She gripped the saw tightly with her right hand and tried the retractable blade. It fit snugly into a slot in the handle, but opened easily, the blade clean and unrusted. She folded the blade back and held the saw at her side.

Last chance to decide: into the woods or back to the house to call for help.

A gunshot rang out from deep in the shadows.

She plunged into the trees.

CHAPTER 48

CHAD LEANED HIS rifle against a tree trunk and pulled his tee-shirt over his head. With his teeth and one good arm, he ripped free a ribbon of cloth. Working as best he could with one hand and his mouth, he strapped it around his shoulder, tied an awkward knot, and pulled it tight. The cotton strip turned red in just a matter of seconds, soaked with blood. The pain throbbed, running down his arm to his hand, and pulsed across the back of his shoulder, up his neck, and right into his brain, pounding, pounding, pounding.

Veterinarians knew a little bit about human anatomy; large animal vets knew even more than small animal vets. Chad knew that his wound was bad but not fatal. At least not instantly fatal. The bullet was still inside, probably lodged in his chest after passing through his shoulder. No organs had been hit, but there was blood. Not so much that blood was gushing, but enough that there was a steady flow. The bullet must have nicked an artery. If he could keep that in check, he could buy time. But if not, or if the pressure widened the nick and he lost too much blood...well, he didn't really want to think about that.

He heard the *zzzipp* of an angry projectile whizz by his head almost before he heard the echo of a gunshot. Instinctively he ducked, though it would have been too late had the shot been more accurate. He grabbed the rifle and ran deeper into the trees.

The ground sloped upward, heading toward a ridgeline.

Chad knew every inch of his land, which had been in his family for four generations. As a boy, he had roamed these woods with his cousins, playing boy-games like cowboys and Indians, pirates, cops and robbers, and hide-and-seek. He knew where the ridges were, where the valleys were, where the bluffs were, and where the caves were. Should he hide in one of the caves or seek higher ground to gain an advantage on his pursuers? He felt sure that if he got to one of the caves, he could conceal himself as long as it took. The sun would be down in a couple of hours, but darkness always preceded the actual sunset in these thick woods as the sun drooped in the western sky. When that happened, the two men would give up and leave, defeated by lack of light.

Wouldn't they?

The problem, though, was how long it would take for them to leave, even once it grew dark. And how would he know if and when they did? Especially if he were hiding in a cave. If it took too long, and if he couldn't slow the flow of blood enough to stay conscious, then maybe he would simply stay hidden until someday a future spelunker in the caves found his dry bones.

And what about Peggy? The armed men only cared about Chad Palmer as a conduit to Peggy. Or Teri Squire, or whatever the hell her name was these days. When the men stopped looking for him, they would go looking for her. He knew that, after talking to her mom, she would ride for a while, to clear her head, but sooner or later, she would return to the ranch house, if she hadn't already. If the men were still on the ranch...well, he couldn't let that happen.

He kept moving deeper into the woods, but at the same time higher, to a ridgeline about two miles in that bisected the ranch. From there, he would make his stand.

Teri barely felt the branches that scraped at her cheeks and grabbed at her arms, their tips like fingernails, clawing at her flesh. The ground was uneven, threatening at any moment to upend her. The biggest hazards were small stumps of cedar trees that had been chain-sawed nearly, but not quite, flush to the ground. Every step was an adventure, but she willed her feet to almost float above the surface, to avoid the obstacles, to keep her body upright.

The trees got thicker the deeper into the woods she ran. The ground sloped gradually downward, but she knew it would soon start to rise. It had been a lot of years since she had been here, but the Palmers and Tuckers had been close ever since she was a little girl, and the Palmer kids and Tucker kids had spent hours playing in these woods. Adam and Chad, especially, neither of whom seemed to care if little sister Peggy tagged along. She knew the hiding places, she knew the observation sites, and the caves. And she knew Chad. He wouldn't hide; he would protect her. She knew where Chad would go.

She crossed a dry creekbed, planted her left foot, and cut right, headed uphill.

Doug Bozarth paused and leaned back against a tree. They had lost sight of the veterinarian shortly after the last shot. He wiped his sleeve across his face, soaking up perspiration that bathed his temples. It pissed him off that Dolan seemed immune to the heat. Though sweat had soaked through his shirt, turning the denim dark blue, the man barely seemed out of breath. If anything, he seemed bothered that they had to pause even momentarily to rest. Goddamn Texans.

"Looks like an upslope that way," Dolan said, pointing with his gun. "My money says he's headed for high ground. He'll try to get an angle on us."

"He's shot. He's bleeding. He's just looking for a place to lay low." Bozarth paused, painfully aware of the uplilt in his voice as he said it, as if the sentence ended in a question mark instead of a period. An expression of wishful thinking instead of a statement of confidence.

"If you say so, Chief," Dolan said. "But I'd keep my head down if I were you."

Bozarth looked at this watch. The shadows were already starting to lengthen in the trees. "How long 'til the others get here?"

"Hour, give or take."

Bozarth pushed away from the tree. "Let's keep moving. Maybe we can finish this before they get here."

Chad crested the ridgeline and knelt behind a deadfall, a large oak that had been uprooted years ago following a thunderstorm that generated near-hurricane strength winds. The roots stretched like tentacles at one end, the massive trunk extending parallel to the edge of the ridgeline for a good fifty feet.

Down below, at the start of the ridge, was a cluster of prickly pear cactus, with a narrow opening in the middle. A parallel row of cedars climbed the slope from the cactus, almost as if forming a fenceline on either side of a path to the top. It would be nearly impossible for someone down below to see through the cactus and over the tree, but with the right perch behind the trunk, and at just the right angle, a person would have a perfect funnel of vision from above to below.

Just perfect for a sniper. Assuming, of course, that the target entered the field of vision at the bottom end of that funnel. Chad was counting on it. The opening in the prickly pear virtually beckoned entry, as if it were the gate to the easiest route to the top.

Chad rested the barrel of the rifle across the trunk, gripped the stock tightly, and sighted down the funnel. He would have one shot, at the first man who appeared. After that, the element of surprise would be gone. Besides, his ability to work the bolt would be virtually non-existent for a second shot.

He took the box of shells from his pocket and set it on the ground. Eight bullets. He wasn't sure how many were in the rifle. One-handed, he put two into the magazine, but the effort of even that exhausted him. He put the other six in his pocket.

He curled his index finger around the trigger, took a deep breath.

And waited.

Teri continued what she hoped was a flanking movement, of a sort that would have made any military field commander proud. She wasn't sure where the armed men were, but she knew why they were here. If it had just been two unidentified men with weapons, she would have assumed, but couldn't be sure, that they were after her; after all, it seemed like everyone was these days. But Doug Bozarth was the dead giveaway. He must perceive her as some kind of threat, although she couldn't be sure exactly what that threat was. Was he behind the murder of Leland Two? She only had suspicions on that front, but maybe he viewed her as a weak link in the chain of silence that would lead to him.

Or was it simply because the questions about ownership of the screenplay would be brushed aside if she were to turn up missing? And she had no doubt that, if Bozarth and his cohort found her, it would be the last time anyone found her. She would end up buried somewhere on Chad's land, and the mystery of the missing two-time Oscar winner would be the subject of future documentaries and sensational stories on the Entertainment Channel or other tabloid shows on television. In the meantime, he would count his back-end profits all the way to the bank.

Common sense told her to turn, get back on Gretel, and ride for help. But Gretel had probably already run off by now, probably back to Hansel at the barn. Besides, Chad needed her. He was bleeding and he was hurt, and it was all because of her.

276

Now it was time for her to stand beside him as he had done for her all those years ago.

She increased her speed, the ground flying beneath her feet. Dodging trees and rocks as if she were a running back covering a broken field, she moved gradually higher, aiming for a ridgeline that she knew would give her a vantage point even in the thickness of the woods, but maybe a half mile beyond the track she believed the gunmen were taking. If she was right, she would end up ahead of them, not behind, giving her the element of surprise she desperately needed.

In San Antonio, California Highway Patrol detectives Nichols and Stillman exited a Gulfstream III private jet that had been provided, at Swafford's request, courtesy of the chairman of Cinema USA, the studio set to release Teri Squire's new movie. An airport employee drove them in a golf cart to the car rental counters, where they picked up a pearl-colored Toyota Camry. Stillman plugged in the coordinates for Chad Palmer's Bandera ranch on the GPS device as Nichols got on his cell phone to call the Bandera County Sheriff's Department and announce their arrival.

"My guys have eyes on the Tucker place, but no sign of Ms. Squire or anyone else, for that matter," Sheriff Trey Waggoner said.

"We think she may have gone to Chad Palmer's ranch," Nichols said. "Do you know where that is?"

"Sure do."

"That's where we're headed."

"I'll meet you at the gate."

"I'd appreciate it if you'd stay out of sight," Nichols said. "We don't want him to know we're coming until we get there."

"If he hasn't done anything wrong, why's it matter?"

"If Ms. Squire's there, we don't want to spook her."

"You really think she had something to do with your killings out there?" Waggoner asked.

"Our concern is that she's the next victim. If she's at the ranch, we don't want her running off before we can get there. Especially if the bad guys already have boots on the ground."

"Okay. I'll meet you out on the state highway leading to the place, and we'll go in together. It'll probably take you an hour, hour and fifteen minutes to get there. I don't figure anything much will happen before then."

An ancient Ford pick-up chugged across the meadow, kicking up dust in its wake. It slowed briefly by the body spread-eagled on the ground, blood soaking the dirt around it. The driver, a bearded man in his late thirties, glanced at the body.

"That's Morgan," he said. "Poor bastard."

The clean-shaven passenger, a .38 resting on the seat beside him, looked past the driver and shook his head. "Happy birthday, Morgan."

"Today his birthday?"

"Yeah. Me and him was going down to the Riverwalk tonight to celebrate."

"Looks like you got your evening back."

The clean-shaven man laughed. "Life sucks, and then you die."

The driver eased down the slope and stopped next to the Dodge. Both men got out, the clean-shaven man tucking the .38 in his belt while the bearded man retrieved a rifle and a box of bullets from behind the seat. He also wore a holster, just like an old west cowboy, a Colt .45 New Frontier revolver riding low on his hip.

While the bearded man loaded the rifle, the clean-shaven man checked the interiors of both trucks. "Got blood here," he said, looking in the window of Chad's pickup. He scanned the ground around both trucks. "Also got some prints. Looks like a horse." He looked around, peered into the trees, then back toward a ranch house in the distance. "Horse went that way, but I got boot prints, too. Looks like the rider went into the trees."

The bearded man pulled a cell phone from his pocket and hit a speed dial number as he approached. When he heard nothing, he tucked it back in his pocket. "No signal." He noted the prints on the ground, the blood in the truck, and nodded his consensus with the clean-shaven man's assessment. "Boot prints are small. A woman."

"The actress?"

"Let's find out."

The clean-shaven man pulled his gun from his belt while the bearded man gripped the rifle in both hands. They disappeared into the trees.

CHAPTER 49

CHAD WIPED SWEAT from his eyes. The salt stung and momentarily blurred his vision. He didn't know if it was the heat getting to him or the blood loss. He had never been a hunter. How did they do it? How did they stay on alert long enough to spot prey and get off that one perfect shot? He knew he would get but one shot before giving himself away, and he had to make it count. But even that was largely out of his hands. His target had to walk into the right spot, at the end of the funnel, and had to be still long enough for Chad to squeeze the trigger. It was all going to be about luck and split second timing. He hoped God was on his side.

He lowered his left arm, letting the barrel of the gun rest solely on the fallen tree. The pain in his shoulder continued to throb but felt duller. It left him with mixed emotions; less pain was less pain, but less feeling was a harbinger of bigger problems. A wave of nausea steamrolled across his body. Bile rose into his throat, burning as he swallowed hard to force it back down. Tiny wiggles of white swam through his vision. He shook his head. Warmth settled across his being. All he wanted to do was to lie down on the leaves, close his eyes, and sleep. But he knew that if he did, he might never wake up.

A sound below snapped him to attention. The crack of a broken twig, the rustle of movement on fallen leaves. Using his right hand, he raised his left arm, which felt like dead weight, as if it had fallen asleep. He positioned his left hand on the barrel of the rifle, like placing ballast on top, to hold it in place. He gripped the stock with his right hand, his finger along the trigger, and sighted down the barrel.

And waited.

The rustling grew louder, closer. He tensed, fighting an urge to vomit. His vision blurred, obscured by sweat and impending unconsciousness. He had to stay alert, just a minute or two more. His life might depend on it. Peggy's life might depend on it, too.

A shadow appeared in the opening at the end of the tunnel. Chad shifted his weight, lifted higher on his bended knee. He tightened his finger on the trigger, squeezing. It moved slightly, just a hair's breadth away from firing. The shadow moved closer, now filling the target area. It was followed a beat later by a figure.

Chad squeezed the trigger.

Blackness overwhelmed him. He slumped to the ground behind the deadfall, his finger still curled around the trigger of the rifle.

Teri picked up her pace at the sound of the gunshot. Her hunting instincts, honed as a little girl raised on a ranch, had been dulled by years in the Hollywood limelight, but they were merely dormant, not extinguished. She knew instantly the source of the sound. High, along the ridgeline. That meant the shot had been Chad's; that was good news. There was no return shot, at least not yet, and that was more good news.

But the ensuing silence was also worrisome. It was a total sensory blackout that allowed her imagination to run rampant, and given the nightmarish events of late, her thoughts instinctively took a dark turn.

She reached the foot of a steep bluff along the edge of the ridgeline. She veered to her right, where the face of the drop-off transformed to more of a slope than a cliff. She drove hard off of her right foot and leaped. She scrabbled for purchase with both hands. With the grace of a mountain goat, she skittered up the hill until she reached the crest. Once again on level ground, she turned left and sprinted toward the source of the gunshot.

Dodging tree branches, leaping over rocks and low stands of prickly pear cactus, she weaved her way along the ridge. The shadows were already darkening as the evening sun descended in the west, making it hard to see more than ten or fifteen feet in front of her. But the same dimming of the light that hindered her vision would also help provide cover from the assailants. Provided she could get to Chad in time.

Her toe kicked a stump, throwing her off balance. She stumbled forward, waving her arms in front in a swimming motion, free-styling her way forward as she struggled for balance. Her upper body outdistanced her feet. With one last stroke, she dove forward. Her knees hit the ground first, followed by the heels of her hands as she sought to avoid a face-plant. Pain screamed in her body as her right hand slammed down on a rock. Its sharp edges didn't break the skin but bruised the heel of her hand deeply.

She rolled sideways then scrambled back to her knees. As she gripped her hands together, a hint of color in her peripheral vision drew her attention away from her own pain.

"Oh, my God," she said under her breath. "Chad."

Staying low, on her hands and feet, she skittered toward his crumpled body lying behind a fallen tree. Blood soaked his left side, running down his arm to his hand. The blood had also soaked his shirt, which sopped it up like a sponge. She felt for his pulse. Nothing at first, then she shifted her fingers and found it. Weak, but steady.

She rolled him onto his back. He moaned, but his eyes stayed closed. She leaned close and listened for his breath sounds. Shallow, but as with his pulse, steady.

"Veterinarian!"

The voice came from below, down from the fallen tree. Loud and strong.

And familiar. Doug Bozarth's voice.

"I hope you've got your hunting license, veterinarian," another man's voice said. "You done killed a deer."

Teri moved close to the fallen tree, lifted her head as much as she dared, and looked through a dark funnel that telescoped downward to an opening where a bleeding deer lay on its side.

She pried the rifle from Chad's hand, laid the barrel along the tree trunk, and sighted toward the deer. Then she waited.

"Bad news, veterinarian," the strange voice said. "You gave yourself away with that shot."

And you gave yourself away with your big mouth, Teri thought. She shifted her aim subtly to the right, into the branches that obscured her view, but which she now also knew concealed her target. Open your mouth one more time, she thought, and I'll be able to get a final fix.

She closed her eyes and listened. Silence at first, then a rustling. Footsteps. Were they moving? She squeezed her eyes and strained to decipher the sounds. Multiple footsteps, then the sounds of muffled voices. A conversation but there were too many voices. Not just Bozarth and the other man. Reinforcements.

"Veterinarian," Bozarth called out.

She shifted her aim in his direction, working on a blind bead.

"Veterinarian," the other man called. He hadn't moved.

"Veterinarian," a third voice called. This one came from up ahead, but still below. The speaker was working his way up the slope to the ridgeline.

"Veterinarian," a fourth man called. This voice came from her left as the speaker tried to flank her position.

She waited. No more voices. It was four against one. Time to lessen the odds.

She shifted her aim back toward the second man. She thought she had him in her sights before, but couldn't be positive. She needed to hear him one more time, to insure he hadn't moved.

"Veterinarian," Bozarth said.

"Veterinarian," the second man said.

She squeezed the trigger. She heard the sound of impact over the echo of the gunshot, followed by a male scream. "Goddamn!"

Then the *thump* of a body falling.

Followed by more *thumps* as three men dove for cover all around her.

She worked the bolt and chambered another round, then fired a shot in the direction of Bozarth's voice. She worked the bolt again, squeezed the trigger one more time for good measure, but nothing happened. She hoped the men below hadn't heard the clicking sound. If they knew she was out of ammunition, they might take this moment to attack.

She turned back to Chad, who was still breathing raggedly, but a bit more strongly than before. Rolling him on his back had opened his airwaves. She felt his pockets and found six bullets. A full box would have been nice, but she was grateful for small favors. Six shots, four assailants—maybe three, now—with two or three bullets left over.

She almost laughed at the thought. If there had ever been any place where she felt full confidence, it had been shooting a gun. Medals and trophies from years of competition had done that for her, much as two Oscars had boosted her confidence as an actress. But while shooting at targets was one thing, shooting at men was another. That was a lesson she had learned the hard way. The thought sobered her. But now, just like then, necessity demanded a human target, even if the ultimate result was another grieving mother standing over her son's grave.

She put the first bullet in the rifle and listened for movement below.

Chad groaned. She glanced at him. His eyelids fluttered for a beat then he opened his eyes. He blinked them a few times, as if clearing his vision. Then he looked squarely at her.

She loaded a second bullet into the rifle.

Chad smiled. He opened his lips to speak. The words came out in a hoarse whisper, but she heard them clearly enough. "Howdy, Annie Oakley."

She leaned down and kissed him on the forehead.

She loaded three more bullets and, with the magazine full, she laid the barrel of the rifle over the trunk of the tree and listened for her targets.

Dolan sprawled on a bed of leaves, his eyes glassy. Blood trickled from the side of his mouth, pink and frothy. He gasped for breath, but all that escaped was a hollow sucking sound from the wound in his chest. Doug Bozarth stood next to him, staring down. There was no compassion on his face, but merely curiosity. How long until Dolan was dead? He picked up Dolan's gun; he didn't need it anymore.

Dolan opened his mouth and mumbled something. Bozarth bent over, not wanting to dirty his suit pants by kneeling on the ground, and certainly not wanting to get blood on them. Dolan mumbled again, the words more distinguishable this time.

"It hurts."

Of course it does, you fool, Bozarth thought.

You've been shot. It's supposed to hurt.

He stood and held his gun at his side. "I'll make it stop," he said. He aimed between Dolan's eyes and fired.

"What the hell?" The voice belonged to the bearded man, who emerged from the bushes to the right of Dolan's body.

"I told you to get up that hill in front," Bozarth said.

"There's no cover."

"Ain't it the truth," the clean-shaven man said, rejoining them as well.

"It's one guy with a rifle," Dolan said. "And he's hurt."

"Tell that to Dolan," the clean-shaven man said. He glanced at the body. "Holy shit! Right between the eyes."

"It's an easy shot at close range," the bearded man said. "And when your prey ain't moving."

"You did this?" the clean-shaven man asked Bozarth.

"He was already dead; he just hadn't quit breathing. Now, let's get on both sides of that bastard and shut him down before this gets out of hand."

"You going with us?" the bearded man asked. He cast a glance at his clean-shaven compadre, which was not missed by Bozarth, who rarely missed anything.

"You're being paid well to do a job."

"Not well enough."

"You didn't complain before."

"That was two dead guys ago."

Bozarth stood silently and fumed.

Goddamn Texans!

Unfortunately he needed them. At least for now. "All right," he said. "Double for the vet, triple for the actress."

The men exchanged glances again. The bearded man nodded.

"Okay," Bozarth said. "Now move out."

CHAPTER 50

TERI KNEW SHE had hit someone. She also knew that the second shot had not come from her weapon, nor had it been aimed at her. It was a close shot, a handgun. That meant that someone had been put out of his misery. She didn't feel sorry for him, or for the dead man back in the meadow. And even with another one gone, that still meant three were left. If they flanked her, there was no way she could cover three directions all at once. She needed to find a better spot. The real question, though, was Chad. He was in no shape to walk, but she couldn't carry him, or stay here once they reached the ridge and surrounded her.

She looked down the other side to the valley that sloped away from the ridge. If ever there was a time when she needed Chad awake and coherent, it was now. She needed his input on the lay of the land, the nooks, crannies, escape routes, and ambush spots. While she knew the land to some degree, that knowledge was decades old. She refused to entrust his life, and hers, to a faded memory.

She heard movement on opposite sides as her assailants made their way up the hill to the ridge. Once they reached the top, they would have her in a pincer movement. She could slow them down with gunshots, but each would eliminate precious ammunition. By her reckoning, she had three shots to waste, but only if she were dead bang perfect with the remaining three.

Her mind kicked into overdrive. If she were playing an

action hero in a thriller on the big screen, what possible escape would the screenwriters write for her? She thought of the story, apocryphal though it might be, of the old Saturday morning serial in which one episode ended with the hero trapped in a locked room with no possible exit, only to open the following Saturday with the hero free and clear, and a narrator who intoned, "After our hero escaped from the locked room..." If only she could narrate herself and Chad off of this ridgeline, far, far away from Doug Bozarth and his armed sidekicks.

She had, at best, minutes if not seconds before the final showdown began. If she were the screenwriter, how would she write the escape? She knew the rules: (1) you had to be fair to your audience, no cheating; (2) no *deus ex machina*—no miracle of God to make your escape; (3) no timely arrival of the cavalry; the hero had to make her own escape; and (4) you had to make extraordinary use of the ordinary.

And in that last rule lay the answer. The rootball of the downed tree had been ripped from the ground, creating a hole, now filled with leaves. To the west, the edge of the ridge sloped downward to a shallow valley with a dry creekbed that meandered through it. In the spring, during the April rains, it ran with water, but in the drought of summer, it was merely a dusty path—a roadway, in effect, that led away from her current spot. It was by that path that she could make her escape; it was by the rootball's depression that she could save Chad.

She knelt beside Chad, who was struggling to retain consciousness. She slapped him lightly. His eyelids fluttered and then opened. His eyes rolled back in his head. She slapped him again and his eyes focused on her.

"Are you awake?" she asked in a hoarse whisper.

"Barely."

"I'm going to bury you in the leaves, and you can't move. Not a muscle. Understand?"

288

He nodded.

"They don't know I'm here, so if they hear someone trampling down the other side of this ridge, they'll assume it's you. When they follow, you get out of there and go the other way. There are three of them. Wait for all three to get by first."

"What if they don't all follow?" he asked.

"They will." She left unspoken her real thoughts: They have to.

She heard voices from below. A murmur or two, then silence. Then rustling as footsteps began their flanking movement before ascending the slope.

"Now," she whispered.

She grabbed Chad by his good arm as he struggled to his knees, then she helped him crawl to the end of the tree. He slid into the depression, as if sliding into a pool of water. Teri took the small folding saw from her belt and gave it to him. She opened the blade and put the handle in his right hand.

"Just in case," she said.

Moving quietly, she scooped leaves over Chad until he was completely hidden from sight. She felt as if she were burying him and hoped to God that this was not the last time she would see him alive.

She knew her assailants had ascended the hill to the ridgeline, and two of them now stood on either side of her, to her north and to her south. How far away, she didn't know, as they were blocked from sight by trees and shadows.

And where was Bozarth? It would be just like the coward to stay below, to leave the dirty work to others. How would Chad get down if he was still there?

"Veterinarian!" a voice called from the north.

"Veterinarian!" another voice echoed from the south.

They were here.

She popped to her feet, leveled the rifle and fired north, in the direction of the first voice, then spun and fired to the south. As the shots reverberated, she heard both men scramble for cover. It sounded as if each of them had made the same move, sliding down the slope in the direction from which they had come.

She turned and ran down the other side, deliberately making as much noise as she could, kicking up leaves, snapping branches, starting a small landslide. She lost her footing, hit on her butt, and slid for about fifteen feet, before popping back up at the bottom. She made it to the dry creekbed, turned south and sprinted.

From behind and above her, she heard a voice call out, "He's gone down the other side."

She smiled and inserted the last bullet.

Chad lay as still as he could, but pain ravaged his left side. He yearned to move about, to twist and flop, as if the release of energy would lessen his pain. But he remembered the command from Teri. He lay still.

A gunshot rang out beside him, followed by a second, then he heard sounds of Teri scrabbling down the slope. After a brief moment, he heard footsteps trample the ground nearby, then follow her downhill. He held his breath and forced himself to concentrate. He had heard two sets of footsteps. How many had Peggy said there were? Three? That didn't make sense. There had been three at the start, but he was pretty sure one of them was dead in the meadow. And he was pretty sure Peggy had shot one down below. His head hurt, his shoulder hurt, his whole body hurt, but he could still do basic arithmetic: three minus one equals two, minus one equals one.

But he had distinctly heard two sets of footsteps, one to the south and one to the north, go by. That meant that the one Peggy shot down below wasn't hurt bad, or was at least not disabled. But with both of his pursuers accounted for, that meant he was safe.

He cupped his right hand to brush away leaves, but something stopped him. A rustling sound, very slight, down below. Another deer, perhaps? A fawn looking for its dead mother? A dead mother that he had killed? Or just the injured animal thrashing around in the leaves. He suddenly felt overwhelmed by remorse. He was a veterinarian, for God's sake. He took care of animals. He *healed* animals. Medical doctors may have their Hippocratic Oath, and their adage *primum non nocere*, Latin for "first, do no harm," but veterinarians had their own oath, dedicating themselves to the "protection of animal health, the relief of animal suffering..."

If the deer was merely injured, if it was in pain, he had a duty to tend to it, to relieve its suffering. Shame pulsed through his body like a blast of thermal heat. He pushed aside a handful of leaves from his face, then stilled. Even that small movement sent pain to every nerve.

Then he heard something else down below again. The distinct *beeps* and *boops* of keys being pressed on a cell phone. Then a muttered "damn." That meant two things. One, no cell service. But two, there was a third man.

He extended his hand, cupped a batch of leaves, and pulled them back over his face. The man below began to move, ascending the incline, heading his way. After a few seconds, the man reached the top of the ridge and stood not more than ten feet away. Feet shuffled through leaves, drawing closer as the man walked around the deadfall to Chad's side, then wood creaked as weight was placed on the fallen tree. The man had sat down right next to the rootball.

Time to play the waiting game. Chad closed his eyes and tried to will unconsciousness to settle in. He thought it was the only way to guarantee that his pain-wracked body would remain deathly still. His very life depended on it.

* * *

Although Teri regularly worked out, running three miles a day in the hills around her house and pumping iron two or three times a week, artificial workouts in gyms and neighborhoods didn't really prepare you for sprinting through trees, running for your life. Similarly, staged shootouts on movie sets were no practice for real gunfights with real bullets with people who wanted you dead. She was running on adrenaline now, and she knew that exhaustion would soon kick in. She didn't how much of a lead she had nor was she inclined to check. As legendary Negro Leagues pitcher Satchel Paige once said, "Don't look back. Something might be gaining on you."

She thought she was far enough away now for Chad to unearth himself and go for help. Sooner or later, she needed to find a spot to take a stand. Short of a chair at a bar table in a corner, with her back to the wall, facing the swinging doors, she needed a bluff or rise where she could obtain a height and visual advantage, and where the men chasing her couldn't circle around behind.

She heard the *zzzzp* of a bullet whiz by her ear. It disappeared into the deepening shadows in the trees ahead of her. She hadn't heard the shot. She didn't know if that meant silencers or if it meant she simply hadn't been paying attention. It did mean, though, that her pursuers were close enough to see her darting through the trees, even in the deepening gloom. She hoped she was still far enough ahead that they couldn't distinguish her female form. It was important that they think she was Chad, because that would give Chad the advantage he needed to seek help before one or more of them returned to hunt for him. In his weakened condition, he needed as big a lead as she could give him.

Up ahead, the creekbed seemed to elevate. She couldn't tell how high it sloped, but it appeared to be a fairly steep rise, a perfect vantage point to target her pursuers. As soon as they felt the upswing in the topography, they would assume Chad had gone that way, and would likely slow and regroup at the foot of the slope, assess their options, and scout out a plan of attack. They would be standing in the perfect place for an ambush—particularly if she chose *not* to go uphill.

She dropped to her knees, hopefully removing herself from any glimpse the pursuers might have of her. Then she crawled off to the side, into the thickest stand of trees, a cluster of oaks nearly choked by cedars. It was barely passable, even that low to the ground. She had to lie on her stomach at one point and pull herself beneath the lowest cedar branches. Once she felt she was safely out of sight, she turned back the way she had come, circling back to the creekbed, but downstream. And hopefully behind her pursuers.

Staying in a crouch, she duck-walked to an oblong boulder in the midst of two bushes that bordered the creekbed, angled away from it. It was about the height of a bedroom nightstand and the length of a coffee table, an excellent spot to hide behind and rest the barrel of her rifle. The only question was whether the bad guys had passed by this spot yet.

She got her answer soon enough, ducking just in time to avoid being seen. From the sounds of it, there was more than one man, but not enough noise to account for all three. She raised her head and saw two men jogging away from her.

And neither one of them was Doug Bozarth!

Where the hell was he? Had he stayed behind because he was a coward, or had he already found Chad? She was betting on the former—he seemed like the type to hire his dirty work done instead of doing it himself. But if it was the latter, she might already be too late.

She laid the rifle across the boulder and sighted down the barrel. One man lagged behind the other, who was already around a small bend and out of sight. She drew a bead right between his shoulder blades. She had learned long ago that some people simply needed killing. That was an old Texas tradition that had allowed many a killer to walk free. It hadn't worked for her before, and it might not work for her now. But when men with guns were searching for you, with murder on their minds, they need killing, even if it meant shooting them in the back. No time for remorse.

Teri pulled the trigger. The man at the rear dropped.

A fusillade of shots rang out. The survivor apparently decided a spray of gunfire would help him avoid the fate of his compadre. And it might have, had there been any reason to the shots. Instead they sprayed wildly, none of them even coming close to her location. The only purpose they served was to allow her to home in on the source.

She cocked her head, listening. Aimed carefully. And squeezed the trigger again.

The shooting stopped.

CHAPTER 51

CHAD HAD NOT covered his face as thickly as he should have. Sky peeked through the leaves and, when he opened his eyes again, he had a clear view with one eye of the man who sat on the tree trunk. Perspiration had plastered his shirt to his chest, but his heavily groomed hair remained in place, notwithstanding the rivulets of sweat that ran down his temples.

Chad could see him, but could he see Chad? That was the question. Chad was tempted to brush a few more leaves over his face, but he knew that moving, with the accompanying rustle of dried leaves, was the absolute worst thing to do right now. He had to lie perfectly still and hope that his eye, if that's all that was exposed, would simply be invisible against the bed of leaves.

From a distance, a gunshot split the stillness, followed a brief second later by a flurry of shots. Then a second shot like the first, followed by silence again. Chad recognized the sound of the rifle; Peggy had taken the first and last shots, spurring and then ending the intervening gunfire. He listened hard for any answering shots after Peggy's second. Nothing but silence. That meant that the gunmen had been rendered incapable of returning fire.

The man on the tree jumped to his feet at the sound. He, too, seemed to be listening, anticipating even. At the ensuing silence, he frowned, his countenance visibly darkening. He pulled his cell phone from his pocket, held it high, and stared at it, as if willing a connection. He turned slowly in a complete circle, phone held aloft. Chad knew his endeavor was doomed to failure. If ever you wanted to retreat to the good old days of the non-existence of technology, ninety percent of this ranch in Bandera County, Texas, was just the place to be.

The man punched buttons on the phone, the ineffectual *beeps* and *boops* infuriating him.

"Goddamnit!" he said as he flung the phone to the ground— right on top of Chad's chest. It skittered slightly, then slid under the leaves and came to rest at Chad's throat.

Chad held his breath. Could the man tell the difference in sound from throwing a cell phone into a pile of leaves as opposed to hitting something solid? He hoped not. And God forbid that he should seek to retrieve it.

The man looked north, as if trying to see what had transpired where the shots had been fired. He stood statue-still for a good five seconds then cocked his head, as if he had heard something.

Or as if there had been a delayed reaction in his brain to something that happened earlier. Five seconds earlier.

He looked at the pile of leaves where he had thrown his phone. A blank expression replaced the frown. He took a step toward the depression and looked down. At the edge, he flexed his knees slightly, bent, and stared. It seemed as if he was staring directly into Chad's eye. He squinted, leaned closer.

Chad willed himself not to blink, hoping the darkness of his eye was obscured by the leaves. Or, if worse came to worst, an unblinking eye might convince the man that a dead animal lay beneath the leaves.

The man dropped to one knee and reached forward. Chad watched in horror as the hand reached the leaves on his chest, then disappeared beneath the surface, feeling for the cell phone. Fingers touched Chad's shirt.

"What the hell?" The man's eyes widened, his brows lifting damn near to his hair-line. He raised his gunhand and pointed the weapon directly at Chad—

Who grabbed the hand touching his chest and yanked with all the strength he had remaining in his one good arm. It was enough to pull the man off-balance and into the depression, directly on top of Chad. The gun went off, and Chad felt a sting of pain along the side of his head, then a deafening *thud* as the bullet embedded itself in the earth beneath him.

His left arm useless, Chad struggled to force the man's body off to the other side, and then he scrambled to his knees. He reached into the morass of leaves while the other man got to his feet. Chad homed in almost instantly on the small saw Peggy had left with him. His vision blurred as he straightened and tried to focus on his enemy. It was more than just dizziness and pain that obscured the view. Blood gushed from his scalp, pouring into his left eye. Between that and the wound in his shoulder, the left side of his body was virtually worthless.

The man pointed his gun at Chad, while Chad struggled to raise the saw, wielding it like a sword.

"Goddamn, veterinarian, you think that's a match for a gun?" Bozarth asked. He laughed. "I think you've been spending too much time with animals."

"I'll take animals any day over the likes of you."

The excitement of the moment must have frayed the man's thoughts. He adopted the same pose he had earlier, when thinking about the sound of the cell phone hitting Chad's chest. Then he asked the question that Chad knew was coming.

"If you're here, who are my men chasing? Teri Squire?"

Chad smiled.

"I don't know what you're so happy about, veterinarian," Bozarth said. "Did you hear those gunshots?"

"I did." Chad's smile broadened.

"Then what the hell are you so happy about?"

"You don't spend much time around guns, do you?"

"I leave that for others."

"It's a shame. If you did, you'd know that the first and last shots came from a rifle."

The impact of the words hit Bozarth like a punch in the face. "Bullshit."

"Two shots, two men. The next bullet will be for you."

"Again, bullshit. She's an actress, for God's sake."

"She's a ranch girl. She's been hunting in these woods around here since she was a little girl. And she's been shooting competitively since she was ten. She won that rifle at the county fair when she was fifteen. She's the best—"

A shot rang out. Bozarth spun in a half-circle and dropped to his knees. The gun flew from his hand and landed a few yards away. Blood painted a broad swatch down his wilted white shirt, starting just above his right breast.

"—shot in Bandera County."

Bozarth slumped to his side and pitched down the slope from the ridgeline. He flipped head over heels then sprawled onto his side, continuing to roll until he came to rest against the dead deer.

Chad looked back along the ridgeline. Peggy ran toward him, carrying the rifle in front of her with both hands.

Blackness washed over him, and he toppled back into the depression of leaves.

Teri knelt beside Chad and felt for his pulse. Weak, thready, but there.

She crawled to the edge of the ridge and peered down, careful not to show too much of herself. She knew she had shot Bozarth, but she didn't know if the shot had been fatal or even disabling. Was he still armed? Was he waiting for her down there? She had to make sure.

It was hard to see in the dark, but all she could make out down below was the deer.

She crawled south along the ridgeline, endeavoring to get a better line of sight around the cedars on the slope. Still nothing. How long had it been? Surely no more a minute from the shot until she reached Chad, checked his pulse, and then looked down the hill. He couldn't have gotten far. But what if she had missed him? What if this was just a trick, designed to lure her closer and get her to drop her guard.

No, that was impossible. She didn't miss. She *didn't* miss. She knew, because she never missed.

She backed up until she was beside Chad again. He was still out, but breathing. She slid into the depression beside him.

And waited for Bozarth's next move.

CHAPTER 52

NICHOLS AND STILLMAN followed in their rental car as Bandera County Sheriff Waggoner led them in his squad car along the state highway that bordered Chad Palmer's ranch. The speed limit signs said "65," but Stillman viewed that as more of a dare than limit. No way you could hit that speed, much less maintain it, on this road that serpentined its way through rough, craggy hills on both sides, with constant elevation rises and drops. A blue haze hung over the valleys, adding to the 3D effect as you looked in the distance.

Waggoner spoke on his cell phone. Nichols, in the passenger seat, held his phone between his partner and himself, the speaker on.

"This land has been in Chad's family for a hundred years. They used to run cattle and horses on it. His folks died in a car wreck about ten years ago and left it to him. He still runs horses, but not so much cattle anymore."

"How do you do any kind of ranching in these hills?" Stillman asked.

"We're about to level out and hit the meadows and pastures," Waggoner said. "Most of the hills are just for show. The ranching takes place in the valley up ahead."

"How many acres?"

"I don't know exactly. Five thousand, maybe. Main gate's up ahead."

Sure enough, they descended a hill and reached a broad expanse of flat land, an anomaly in the area. Horses roamed a pasture on one side of the road, while the other was just an open meadow.

"Beautiful," Stillman said.

The main entry consisted of white rock pillars on either side, with a wrought iron archway that proclaimed "Palmer Acres." The gate was open, so the sheriff slowed and entered, followed by the detectives.

"Don't be surprised if you lose cell service in here. It's spotty, at best."

"That gate always open?" Stillman asked.

"Chad generally keeps it that way during the day. In case anyone needs to bring an animal to see him."

"So this is where his vet office is?"

"Most large animal vets are pretty much just visiting doctors, so not much need for an office. But Chad takes on all comers. Dogs, cats, squirrels—"

"Squirrels?" Nichols asked.

"More than once, someone hit a squirrel crossing the road, but didn't kill it, so the driver or someone coming along later picked it up and took it to Chad."

"You're kidding me."

"Nope. Chad's an animal lover, and everyone—"

Waggoner cut out in mid-sentence. Nichols pocketed the phone. "Guess we're out of service."

They rode silently for just over another mile before Waggoner slammed on his brakes, threw open his door and got out. Nichols pulled up and stopped behind him, and he and Stillman joined Waggoner by the fenceline. They saw instantly what had grabbed his attention: a body, with blood covering his throat, splatters on his face.

All three men pulled guns from holsters as Waggoner led the

way through an opening in the fence. "Been some traffic through here recently," he said. "Tire tracks look fresh."

He pointed across the meadow toward three pick-up trucks, barely visible in the shadows next to the trees about a half a football field away that marked the beginning of dense woods. "That's Chad's truck. Don't know who the others belong to."

They reached the body. Waggoner checked for a pulse then shook his head.

"You know him?" Stillman asked.

"Never seen him before."

The report of a gunshot echoed across the valley. The two CHP detectives instinctively ducked, but Waggoner remained standing.

"Could just be hunters," Waggoner said. "Gunfire's not uncommon out here."

"And could be whoever's in those other two trucks," Stillman said.

Waggoner nodded. "I'll call for back-up."

He hustled back to his vehicle, spoke into the radio, then motioned for the detectives to follow. They retreated to their rental, got in, and followed Waggoner as he slowly drove across the meadow to the three trucks. A quick once-over of the newer model vehicle and the one next to it revealed nothing interesting, but Chad Palmer's truck was a different story.

"That's a lot of blood," Stillman said.

"I just hope it's not Chad's," Waggoner said.

"I think we better find out," Nichols said.

Waggoner nodded. The radio chirped in his car. He slid into the front seat, spoke briefly, and then returned. "Back-up's on the way. And Chad's not answering his landline at the house."

"Let's move out," Stillman said. He led the way into the trees.

* * *

Bozarth ran through the woods as if his life depended on it. And given that a dead-eye Texas bitch with a rifle, who had already put one bullet in him, was after him, there was a good chance it did. The whole thing was unraveling faster than he dreamed possible. With the screenwriter gone—both the real one and the fake one, whichever was which—and then the agents gone, the hype over *The Precipice* was building to a crescendo, and he and his investors stood to make their entire investment back in the first weekend. The only nagging loose end was Teri Squire. It appeared that she might have a conscience, and consciences were troubling, especially when there were skeletons to keep in closets, secrets to keep buried, and money to keep untraceable.

Add to that the additional hype that might accompany her death or disappearance—who knew how many box office dollars might be attributable to folks jumping on the "See Teri Squire's last movie" bandwagon?—and the obscure contractual provision that would make him, as the sole survivor of the production team, the big winner of the profits, and she had to go. It was simple: Profits divided by three were less than profits divided by two, which were less than undivided profits. All that had to happen was for Teri Squire to simply disappear. She didn't even have to die, at least as far as the world was concerned; just disappear.

Now it looked like he might be the one to disappear.

His foot hit a tree stump. He staggered, his legs weakened by loss of blood from his chest, but strengthened by adrenaline. When he grabbed a tree branch to steady himself and catch his breath, he heard rustling sounds of leaves.

Hell!

She was chasing him.

He looked back and cocked his head to listen. It was already too dark to see anything in these damn trees, but the sounds seemed close. And, strangely, they seemed to come from in front of him instead of behind him. Close. Very close.

He spun around and found himself staring down the barrel of a gun.

"Douglas Bozarth," the man holding the gun said. "I'm California Highway Patrol Detective Stillman."

"A little out of your jurisdiction, aren't you?"

"I get that a lot."

"They're with me," a second man said. This one wore the uniform of a Texas sheriff. A third man stood beside the sheriff. All three had guns pointed at him.

"You've got two options," Stillman said. "You can decide to test your luck in court, or you can be carried out in a body-bag. Which is it going to be?"

Bozarth raised his hands over his head and dropped to his knees.

"Where's Teri Squire?" Stillman asked, while Waggoner handcuffed Bozarth.

"And Chad Palmer?" the sheriff asked.

"Behind me, on a ridge," Bozarth said. "I'd be careful if I were you. She's deadly with a rifle."

Waggoner jerked Bozarth to his feet and led him out of the woods. Stillman and Nichols went in search of the girl with the gun.

Teri lay silently on the ridge, rifle aimed below. She listened for sounds to tell her where Bozarth might be and from what direction his attack might come.

Minutes passed. Maybe even thirty minutes; she couldn't tell—she had lost all sense of time. Then she heard movement. She leaned forward on her elbows, vision virtually nonexistent. Multiple footsteps, coming closer.

Then a man's voice. "Ms. Squire? It's Detectives Nichols and Stillman. CHP."

She remained quiet. It could be a trick, though the voice certainly sounded familiar, and it wasn't Bozarth's.

"We've got Bozarth. We need to know if you're all right. And Dr. Palmer."

She'd only heard the detective a time or two, but that was definitely his voice.

Still...

"Ms. Squire? This is Detective Stillman. We're going to step forward slowly. We understand you've got a rifle and are a pretty good shot with it."

"She's goddamn Annie Oakley!" Chad yelled from behind her.

That drew laughs from the two men below. Even Teri had to smile.

"You're out of your jurisdiction," she said.

"Damned if we're not."

She stood. "We're up here. Chad needs a doctor."

"Okay," Stillman said. "We're coming up. Don't shoot. We're the good guys."

"I know that," she said in a soft voice.

CHAPTER 53

TERI RODE WITH Stillman and Nichols to the hospital, while Sheriff Waggoner carted Doug Bozarth to the Bandera County Jail. Teri sat in the back seat, her eyes glued to the night sky, watching the helicopter heading toward San Antonio, forty-five miles southeast of Bandera. Although Bandera had several good medical doctors in town, and a good emergency clinic, Chad's wound, especially with the blood loss, was deemed too severe for the town's limited facilities, so the helicopter was summoned to deliver him to the closest hospital with the kind of trauma care facility that his injury demanded.

"I'm sure he's going to be okay," Nichols said. He sat in the passenger seat while his partner drove.

"He was just trying to protect me," Teri said.

"I know."

"I should have protected him. Just like I should have protected Mona." She fought back a sob, but made no effort to check the tears that ran down her cheeks. "And Mike."

"There's nothing you could have done for Mike. And it looks like you protected Dr. Palmer just fine."

"Did Bozarth kill Mike?"

"We don't know yet. We do think he was behind the attack on Ms. Hirsch, though."

"Why?"

"It's just a guess at this point, but we noticed her laptop was on and she was logged into the Internet, so Beverly Hills PD put their tech guy on it. She'd been doing research on Doug Bozarth."

"I asked her to," Teri said. "But how would anybody know?"

"Who knows. Spyware? Some kind of virus? Maybe just a straight-out hack job. Like I said, it's just a guess, but Mr. Bozarth apparently likes his privacy."

Teri lapsed into silence. It wasn't until they got on I-10 heading south to San Antonio from the small town of Boerne that she spoke again.

"Why did he try to kill me?"

Stillman looked at her in the rearview mirror. "How much do you know about him?"

"Not much. Mike and Bob said they vetted him, so I never saw the need to look any deeper for myself."

Nichols put his arm on the seat and turned to face the back. "Then why did you have Ms. Hirsch doing Internet research on him?"

Teri started to answer, then bit back her reply. She didn't know how much they already knew. They knew enough to come to Texas, presumably after her, though, and not after Bozarth. It had just been her good fortune—in a very strange way, of course—that they happened upon a murder attempt that clearly painted her as a victim, not a perpetrator. Assuming, of course, that Chad regained consciousness and corroborated her story. But as far as she knew, they were looking for her. Because of Mike? Did they think she had anything to do with that? The timing of the calls would clear her of that, once they followed the technology trail and placed her in Arizona or New Mexico, or maybe even Texas, at the time of his death.

But what about Bob's bizarre suicide? Or the demise of Leland Number Two? Was she still a suspect in those deaths? She couldn't tell them of the late night meetings where she, Bozarth, Mike, and Bob strategized and schemed—a prosecutor might say "conspired"—about how to deal with the extortion effort by Leland Crowell. Even though she never really knew what Bozarth had in mind, and even though she voiced some concerns, she had closed her eyes and her mind to the possibilities, content to let Doug Bozarth run free so long as it benefitted her.

"Ms. Squire?" Stillman said. "Something on your mind?"

"I'm sorry. I'm just worried about Chad."

"You were about to say why you asked Ms. Hirsch to research Doug Bozarth."

"I guess it was too little, too late, but I started wondering where the money came from. Back when this all started, I was so desperate for a comeback, I was just glad Bob and Mike found investors. I didn't ask where the money came from, and I didn't care. Like I said, Mike told me they had vetted the investors and that the source of the funds was cleared through the Patriot Act."

"So what made you start worrying?"

"I wish I knew. But now I wish I hadn't. If that's what set this all in motion, if it's what put Mona and Chad in the hospital, and Mike..." She choked up, and her voice trailed off.

"We're just getting started on it," Nichols said. "But it looks like you were right to worry about where the money came from."

"What have you found?" she asked.

"Nothing concrete. But we do know he made his money in the oil and gas business, primarily in the Middle East. At least his legitimate money. But there's plenty of illegitimate money to be made in that part of the world for a man with his contacts. We're still trying to run that down."

"And you wouldn't tell me if you had found anything, would you?"

He smiled and turned back around. "Here's all you need to know: You started checking him out, and he tried to kill you. I think you can draw your own conclusions from that."

"Am I a suspect for anything?" she asked.

"If you were, we'd have to Mirandize you," Stillman said. "And we haven't, so again, draw your own conclusions."

They rode in silence the rest of the way to University Hospital, just off of Interstate 10, northwest of Loop 410 in San Antonio. They pulled up to the emergency entrance and parked. Stillman opened the rear door to let Teri out, and the two detectives escorted her inside. Nichols approached the front desk, made his inquiry, and then returned to Stillman and Teri.

"He's still in surgery," he said. "Looks like we'll have to wait."

Teri nodded. She found a seat in the half-empty waiting area and sat. Exhaustion overwhelmed her. She slumped in the chair and closed her eyes. The throbbing behind them kept pounding as she tried to force the pain away.

"Ms. Squire?"

She opened her eyes and looked up at Nichols, who handed her a bottle of water and two aspirins. It was a small kindness but a welcome one.

"Thank you, Detective," she said. She put the pills in her mouth, took a swig of water, and swallowed. She leaned her head back and closed her eyes. She had no idea how much time had passed when she felt a nudge at her shoulder and a woman's voice.

"Baby?"

She opened her eyes and looked into the face of her mother. "Oh, Mama," she said.

She broke into sobs as Mary put her arms around her and held tight. "That's okay, Baby. It's all gonna be okay. Shhh shhh shhh."

Nichols and Stillman stood across the waiting room and watched, almost embarrassed to be intruding on such a private moment.

A gray-haired doctor clad in green scrubs entered the room. The detectives both snapped to attention, as did Teri, pulling away from her mother's embrace. She and Mary stood and approached him.

"Are you Dr. Palmer's family?" the doctor asked.

He scrutinized Teri, as if he knew who she was—or at least as if he thought he was supposed to know who she was. Teri guessed her appearance, the product of a broken nose, driving all night, a chase through the woods, and a gunfight, left her looking a whole lot less like the famous actress Teri Squire than she appeared on the big screen.

"We're the closest thing he has to it," Mary said.

"So you must be Peggy," he said to Teri. "I'm Dr. Owens, his surgeon."

Out of the corner of her eye, Teri noticed a glance pass between Stillman and Nichols at the name "Peggy." Let them be curious, she thought. They'd probably figure it out sooner or later, anyway, if they haven't already.

"How is he?" Teri asked.

"He's going to be just fine. The bullet didn't hit any organs, but it nicked an artery. We got that taken care of, but he lost a lot of blood. We're getting it pumped back in him as fast as we can, and he should be up and about in just a matter of days."

Teri let out a big sigh. She hadn't been aware that she was holding her breath until she let it go.

"Can I see him?" she asked.

"He's asleep, and probably will be overnight. He just had one instruction for you before we put him under: Take care of the horses."

She smiled. "That sounds like him."

The doctor looked around the room, his eyes finally coming to rest on Stillman and Nichols. "Are y'all the police?"

"In a manner of speaking," Stillman said.

"He just had one instruction for you, too: Don't talk to his client without him being there. I assume you know which client he is referring to."

Now Stillman smiled. "I think he sometimes refers to her as Annie Oakley."

"Yes, well, I've delivered my messages, so I'll leave you to sort them out."

The surgeon left without another word, clearly annoyed that a man as talented as he had been reduced to being a messenger boy.

"What did he mean about talking to his client?" Mary asked Terri. "I don't understand."

"He was talking about me, Mama." Then something suddenly struck her. Actually it was more of something that wasn't there that struck her. "Where's Daddy?"

Mary dropped her head and looked at the floor. "He said he had work to do. He said tending to the folks laid up in the hospital was woman's work."

"So he knows I'm here."

"He knows you weren't hurt. Just Chad."

"Does he know what happened out there?"

"Honey, I don't even know what happened out there. I just know that Chad got hurt."

"That he got shot."

"Yes."

"Does Daddy think I did it?"

"Of course not, Baby." She paused then looked up. "Did you?"

"Oh, Mama, how can you ask that?"

Teri looked away. She saw the detectives studiously ignoring the conversation, which meant they were listening to every word.

She walked over to them. "Are you going to wait here until Chad wakes up?"

"Yes, ma'am," Stillman said. "We need to talk to him about what happened out there."

"Am I free to go?"

"Yes, ma'am. Just don't go too far."

She turned, then stopped and looked back. "Am I safe now?"

The detectives exchanged glances again. By now she was pretty well clued in on their little signals.

"Why am I not safe? Sheriff Waggoner's got Bozarth. Who else is out there?"

"Annemarie Crowell," Nichols said.

"Annemarie? I know she's a bit creepy but—"

"Did you know she was a hypnotist?"

That made sense, as Teri thought about it. Mike had first brought it up, but now she remembered the way Annemarie had sat in her house, speaking in a low monotone and swaying.

Had Annemarie been trying to hypnotize her? And if so, why?

"We think she may have killed her sons," Nichols said. "And maybe Bob Keene."

"Sons?"

"Leland and Rodney. Twins. You may have met Rodney recently."

Teri felt her knees go weak. Her head spun. She felt for a chair and sat, lest she pass out and take a nose-dive on the floor. "What makes you think she killed Bob? I thought it was a suicide. He walked out in front of a truck."

Then it hit her: Annemarie was a hypnotist! The parallels to *The Precipice* were unmistakable. In her foggy state, she was slow putting the pieces together, but that had been exactly what Mike had suggested in her last conversation with him. Had Leland Crowell's screenplay been a true story, about a murderer who hypnotized others into doing her dirty work? Is that why he had gone off the cliff—because his knowledge was a threat to his mother? But that didn't make sense. After all, it was Annemarie who had hand-delivered the screenplay to her. If she had been covering up, she would have buried it.

"We're just guessing about all this right now," Nichols said, "so I'd prefer not to say anything. Just suffice it to say we have good reason to think so."

"And to make things worse," Stillman said, "we've lost track of her."

"Do you think she's coming after me, too?" Teri asked. This was all too much to process.

"But we have no reason to think she even knows you're in Texas," Nichols said. "We lost track of her before you left town."

Teri looked at her mother, whose face registered confusion. Teri had left her completely in the dark on most of what had transpired over the past few days. All Mary knew before was that her daughter was in trouble; now she knew that she was also in danger. She had already lost one child. From the look on her face, the possibility that she might lose another seemed too much to bear.

"Take me back to Chad's, Mama, so I can take care of the horses. I'll tell you everything on the way."

CHAPTER 54

WHEN TERI AND Mary arrived back at Chad's ranch, they found Gretel standing forlornly in the moonlight in the middle of the meadow. The sight was a great relief to Teri, who had simply dismounted and rushed into the trees earlier without tying her off. When they emerged from the woods later, Gretel was nowhere to be seen. She assumed—or maybe the correct word was hoped—that Gretel had found her way back to the barn. She prayed that Gretel had not found her way to the opening in the fence and wandered off. So seeing her standing proudly in the meadow lifted the blanket of guilt that had draped itself around her shoulders, replacing another guilt blanket that had been lifted by unburdening herself to Mary. She wondered how many blankets were still left.

Mary turned her truck into the opening in the fence. In the beam of the headlights, Teri scanned the area then looked toward the woods. The body she had seen close to the fence was gone, as were the trucks that brought Doug Bozarth and his minions to the ranch, no doubt now being scrutinized by Bandera County's forensics personnel, or maybe even Texas Rangers. Only Chad's truck remained at the far edge of the meadow. There were no other signs that a crime, or crimes, had been committed here.

"Tell Daddy I want to talk to him," Teri said as she opened the door to get out. "He can either come to me, or I can come to him. But it's time we talked."

"It's long past time," Mary said. She leaned over and kissed her daughter on the cheek. "I love you, Baby. Your daddy does, too. You have to believe that."

"I want to." She paused, one foot on the ground. "I've gotta go get Gretel. But you tell Daddy. I'll wait to hear from you."

Without looking back at Mary's departure, she walked across the meadow to where Gretel waited patiently, munching on grass and looking at her.

"Hey, girl," Teri said. "Sorry I left you, but I'm back now."

Teri ran her hand along Gretel's side then stroked her nose. Gretel snorted, pressed against Teri, and nuzzled her.

"That's a good girl. Let's get you back to the barn and get that saddle off you. I know how a lady hates to wear the same outfit too long."

She grabbed the reins, put one boot in a stirrup, and pulled herself up and into the saddle. She shifted her weight, getting comfortable, then eyed the woods. Part of her wanted to scout out the battlefield, to guarantee herself that no more men with guns lurked in the trees, but she knew Sheriff Waggoner and his deputies had already scoured the area. Besides, with Doug Bozarth in custody, his minions, if any had been left, would long since have scattered. She knew they had no quarrel with her. For them, she was just a job with a paycheck, but with the man who held the checkbook behind bars, it would take only the most idealistic of villains to keep the faith.

She headed Gretel in the direction of the barn, alone in her thoughts as she rode. What the detectives had said made sense. The source of Bozarth's money likely would not hold up to scrutiny, but since she had been the only person raising questions, she had become a liability. As had Mona.

Mona.

Teri pulled her cell phone from her pocket and checked for a signal. She had programmed the hospital's number into speed-dial before leaving Los Angeles, and had, in fact, gotten constant updates during her drive across the desert to Texas. Still critical, but holding on, had been the constant refrain.

No signal. She would try again when she got back to Chad's house.

But what was all that about Annemarie Crowell? At least part of it made sense, the part about twin sons. It explained the resurrection of Leland, showing up at her doorstep demanding his cut of the movie's proceeds. That must have been...Rodney, was it? An opportunistic mother and her conniving son. Brilliant, really, when you thought about it. Almost diabolical.

She tried to come to grips, though, with why, if Annemarie was a hypnotizing killer, she did away with Leland, yet delivered the screenplay for production. Unless she simply never thought anything would come of it. But it had been mentioned, by name, in Leland Crowell's will, which had been in the hands of Stuart West, attorney-at-aw. And it had been registered with the Writer's Guild of America, which meant there was at least one copy of it in existence that was beyond Annemarie's reach. Maybe she figured that, if others already knew about the script, destroying it might simply raise questions once it was actually retrieved from the WGA.

But why all the ceremony about personally bringing the script to Teri? Unless, and this meant having a great deal of foresight, Annemarie was savvy enough in the world of Hollywood to understand that the sensational story of a despondent screenwriter taking his own life and willing his script to an Oscar-winning actress had some cachet to it. Enough appeal to maybe turn even a bad script into a money-maker. If not, then no harm, no foul. But if so, then she and Rodney would be on stand-by to capitalize when the moment called for it.

Incredible!

And yet here she was on the brink of the blockbuster

opening of a movie with a compelling behind-the-scenes story, a trail of bodies that led from California to Texas, and a missing hypnotist.

She rode Gretel into the darkened barn, dismounted, and turned the light on, though it barely lit up the center of the barn. She removed the empty scabbard from the saddle and tossed it to the floor. The sheriff had her rifle, but with a promise to return it as soon as they confirmed her story of the events on the ranch— not that she ever wanted to see that damn thing again. She took the saddle off and carried it to the tack room, where she grabbed a curry brush and then scrubbed Gretel down. When she finished, she led her to the stall next to Hansel, who whinnied a greeting. The hay on the floor of the stall had been scattered and beaten down, so she retrieved a pitchfork from beside the gun cabinet, scooped hay, and tossed it into the stall.

As she worked, she heard a sound behind her, a scuffling noise, like footsteps. She looked over her shoulder, but saw no one. It must be her imagination playing tricks. After all, it was past midnight, and no one was here other than the horses and her.

She hoped.

She continued to scatter hay then paused as she heard the sound again. A shadow fell across the floor of the barn. She spun quickly.

Annemarie Crowell stood at the entry to the barn, a .22 in her right hand, her face just as clownishly made-up as always.

"Well done, Ms. Squire," she said.

Teri held the pitchfork upright beside her, in an American Gothic pose. "Is that my gun?"

"Does it matter?"

"I suppose not. What are you doing here?"

"I was concerned about your safety."

"So you came all the way here from California?"

"So it would appear."

"How did you know I was here?"

"It's like your question about the gun. Does it matter?"

"Just curious."

"It's a common story," Annemarie said. "Children usually run to their mothers when they're in trouble." She attempted what Teri assumed was meant to be a smile, but more closely resembled a grimace. "And sometimes they run to their lawyers. At least that's what your Mr. Capalletti told me."

"And so you're here." Teri spoke with a calmness that she didn't feel upon hearing Annemarie essentially confess to killing Mike. Unless she managed to close the distance between them, the .22 trumped the pitchfork. But she also knew that Annemarie would only shoot her as a last resort. It was more likely that she had some sort of staged scene in mind that, she believed, would exempt her from scrutiny. What she didn't know was that the detectives were already on to her and that if anything untoward happened to Teri, Annemarie Crowell would be their prime suspect. Of course, if Annemarie simply disappeared again, it wouldn't matter if she was a suspect. She definitely held the upper hand here, even if she didn't fully recognize it.

"We need to reach a…business arrangement," Annemarie said.

"So you're here to pick up where Leland or Rodney—or whatever his name was—left off."

"Leland really did write that script. He was always very creative, even as a boy. He just didn't have a business head."

"Who went off that cliff two years ago?"

"Leland. He couldn't cope with rejection. He'd had too much of it in his life."

"Then Rodney played the resurrected Leland. Was that your idea?"

"Maybe I should think about a career in show business. I have lots of story ideas. And Rodney is a natural actor, don't you think?

Perhaps you should think about putting him in one of your movies."

Hansel and Gretel both whinnied, almost in unison. Hansel sniffed the air, as if aware of the aroma of impending doom.

Or maybe someone was approaching. The CHP detectives, maybe?

No, they were still at the hospital in San Antonio.

Then who?

She had to keep Annemarie talking, keep her distracted until whoever was out there was close enough to see what was happening, and more particularly, see the gun in Annemarie's hand.

"It's a little late for Rodney's movie debut, isn't it?" Teri asked.

"Oh, that's right. I nearly forgot."

"I have a feeling you never forget anything."

"I'm going to miss Rodney, more so than Leland. He knew things that Leland either didn't know or was unwilling to share with his mother." She paused, as if for dramatic effect. "Sexual things."

Teri recoiled a step. For the briefest of seconds, her grip relaxed on the pitchfork then she snagged it again before it fell to the floor.

"You're even sicker than I thought," Teri said.

"Mothers and sons are not really all that different from brothers and sisters when it comes to sexual things, are they?" She paused again, but this time Teri didn't give her the satisfaction of a reaction. "But then you know all about that, don't you?"

"Go to hell."

Annemarie laughed, an emotionless cackle suited for the barn in which they stood. Teri shifted her focus from Annemarie's face to the gun. Annemarie raised it, as if to allow them both to admire it in her hand.

"It's amazing how easy it is to get into someone's house

when they're overconfident in their security system," Annemarie said.

"And of course you had a chance to scout it out from the inside."

"You were most gracious to allow me into your house. It must have been the Texas hospitality in you."

"All right, enough of the bullshit," Teri said, a curt tone to her voice. She intended to sound confident, but worried that she came across as shrill, because that would make her seem desperate. Which, of course, she was. "How much do you want?"

"Is it always about money with you Hollywood types? Box office and production bonuses and back end and gross points, and all that?"

"It's what Rodney had in mind when he paid me a visit. I have no reason to believe it died with him."

"That was certainly my original plan," Annemarie said. "To get my fair share."

"By blackmailing me."

"Such a terrible word."

"Such an accurate word. And now, with Rodney dead—with a bullet in his back from my gun, I assume—if the police ever found it—"

"And they would."

"—it would all lead back to me."

"Yes, poor Leland. When he showed up alive on your doorstep, you killed him to guarantee your bequest."

"But you and I both know that the most recent son to die was Rodney, which means that Leland really did die two years ago. And that means I have owned the script all along."

"An argument to be made. Of course, that assumes those facts are discovered."

Teri flinched, involuntarily. She hoped Annemarie hadn't noticed the movement. After all, Annemarie had just confirmed that she was unaware that the cops were already on to the existence of her twins. Good. Teri needed to keep her in the dark.

"But even so..." Annemarie paused. "Do you know what a codicil is?"

"It's a change to a will."

"It turns out that there was a codicil to Leland's will that no one knew about. Prepared by his attorney, Mr. West."

"Who conveniently committed suicide."

"Yes, an unfortunate man. I only recently found the codicil, myself. It seems that, instead of an outright bequest of his script to you, Leland only gave you a life estate. Upon your death, it and any proceeds from it go to the secondary beneficiary."

"His beloved mother."

"A predictable storyline, I'm afraid. No movie there."

"Am I going to commit suicide now with my own gun? Is that what happened to Mike?"

Annemarie slowly shook her head and made a shushing sound. "You really don't pay much attention, do you? You've already made the movie, but I wonder if you ever really read the script. Our hero killed people by—"

"You mean the villain, don't you?"

"Potato, potahto. It's all about point of view, isn't it? I prefer to think that Leland viewed his mother as the hero."

Annemarie waved the gun then settled her hand with the barrel aimed directly at Teri's face. "But we're getting off topic here. Let's go through it again. Our hero disposes of her enemies by—"

"Hypnotizing others into killing them for her."

A shadow appeared on the ground behind Annemarie. Sure enough, someone else was there.

A familiar figure stepped into view. Tom Tucker, Teri's father.

He walked up beside Annemarie, who handed him the gun. "There she is, Tom. The woman who killed your son."

CHAPTER 55

TOM TOOK THE gun, his face devoid of emotion. His eyes were on Teri, but she knew he saw nothing more than what Annemarie had just pointed out to him. Not his daughter, but the woman who killed his son. The woman who killed Adam. The woman he had never forgiven for the past twenty years.

A lump rose in Teri's throat as tears filled her eyes. "Daddy? It's me. Peggy."

"Her name is Teri now," Annemarie said. "Peggy killed your boy, then abandoned you. She ran away to California. Changed her name. Changed her face. Buried her past, just like she made you bury your son."

Tom raised the gun and aimed it at Teri, just as Annemarie had done.

"What was your boy's name? Adam, was it? Your pride. The boy who would carry on your legacy on your ranch. Who would carry on the Tucker name."

"Daddy, you know what really happened," Teri said. "Don't listen to her. Don't even listen to me. Listen to your heart."

Emotion filled her voice, which came out in a husky whisper, barely audible, yet echoing in the high-roofed barn. Tears streamed down her cheeks, rivulets joining at her chin and dropping to the floor.

"Crocodile tears, Tom," Annemarie said. "She's an actress. She's used to playing on emotions. Playing *with* emotions. Your emotions, Tom. That's all she's doing now. Just more playacting. And all the while your boy is rotting in his grave."

Moving as an automaton, devoid of emotion, devoid of expression, Tom stepped forward, gun still pointed at Teri.

"Listen to your heart, Daddy," Teri said. "You knew, didn't you? You knew all along what really happened."

There was a slight hesitation in Tom's forward progress. A blink, more of a flutter, of the eyelids.

Annemarie spoke in a harsh tone. No longer the soothing hypnotist; she was now the commanding shrew. "You've wanted to do this ever since you buried Adam. This woman hated Adam, the son you loved. She hated the attention you gave him. She knew she could never live up to him in your eyes, so she did the next best thing. She took him away from you."

"Mama knew, Daddy. And I know you knew."

He took another step forward, the gun held at shoulder level. When he stopped, Teri took a step toward him.

Then another step, and another, until she was at arm's length from him. She leaned her head forward, the barrel of the gun making contact in the middle of her forehead. She pressed against it, grinding the barrel into her skin as she dropped the pitchfork, which clattered to the floor, and held her hands at her sides.

"If you hate me that much, then I won't stop you, Daddy."

She looked him squarely in his eyes, staring down the barrel of the gun, her gaze locked onto his. "Go ahead, Daddy. If that's what you want."

His eyelids fluttered again. Then a single tear squeezed over the rim of the bottom lid and spilled onto his cheek. His lips moved, as if he wanted to speak.

"What is it, Daddy?"

"It wasn't your fault," he said. "You had to do it."

"That's right, Daddy. I'm sorry, but that's right."

"Adam raped you?" It came out as a question, but then Tom

repeated it as a simple declarative statement. "Adam raped you. He would have done it again."

He lowered the gun and held it at his side.

"No!" Annemarie screamed. She lunged forward and jerked the gun away from Tom.

In the same instant, Teri picked up the pitchfork and spun to face her. Annemarie swung her gunhand up. Teri plunged forward the pitchfork and ducked to the right.

The gun went off, the bullet zipping harmlessly by Teri's head. But the pitchfork hit its target, driving deep into Annemarie's chest. She opened her mouth, but the only sound that came out was a soft wail, like the mewling of a cat.

Teri pressed forward, leaning into the pitchfork with her entire body. Her face was inches from Annemarie's as she moved her hands up the handle, closer to the fork itself. She stared into Annemarie's black, lifeless eyes. Annemarie bent backward then fell to the ground on her back, almost as if in slow motion, suspended on the metal tines.

As Teri stepped forward, she felt hands on hers. She turned and saw her father standing next to her. He gently pried her fingers loose and gripped the pitchfork himself. He leaned into it, the full weight of his muscular body driving the tines all the way through Annemarie's torso until they met the concrete floor of the barn.

Annemarie gasped, her eyes opened wide. She gurgled. Blood welled up in her mouth then spilled over, running down the side of her cheek to the floor. She coughed. Blood erupted from her mouth then fell back onto her ghostly white face.

Her eyes closed.

And she lay still.

Tom backed away, leaving the pitchfork standing upright in her breastplate. "Go, Baby," he said. "You were never here. I did this."

"No, Daddy." She put her arms around her father and pulled him to her. "This time, we rely on the truth. The whole truth."

EPILOGUE

TERI BRUSHED DOWN Gretel in the corral while Hansel strutted around, watching and waiting for his turn.

"You look good doing that."

She turned and smiled at Chad, who approached, damaged arm in a sling. He was pale, but moving well.

"It feels good," she said. "I never realized how much I missed it until I did it again."

"I thought you'd want to know I got through to the hospital in Los Angeles. Mona's brother is there with her. He said she's out of danger and is gonna be just fine. I told him to tell her she was welcome to come to Texas to recuperate. Who knows, maybe you can teach her to brush down a horse."

Teri laughed. "Fat chance. She'd be too worried about breaking her nails."

"Things aren't looking so good for Doug Bozarth, though. It turns out that, in addition to oil and gas, he was into weapons and drug trafficking in the Middle East. But I think that's going to be the least of his troubles. Bandera County's got him on state charges, and they might even be able to get him for felony murder."

"But I shot those men in the woods."

"One of them was shot twice, and the fatal shot was from a handgun fired into his head. They've got Bozarth's fingerprints on the gun that fired the shot. He's probably going to be looking at the death penalty."

"Couldn't happen to a nicer guy."

She kept brushing, as if the effort, alone, would brush away all memories of what had happened.

"Your folks are here," Chad said.

Teri looked back toward the house, where Mary stood on the back porch. Mary called inside, and Tom exited, a newspaper in his hands.

"How are things with your dad?" Chad asked.

"We're going to get there."

Tom waved the paper as he approached. "You seen this yet, Baby?"

"I don't read the papers anymore," Teri said.

"It's a blockbuster. Biggest box office opening in history."

"That's great, Daddy."

"Phone keeps ringing off the wall back at the house. Lots of people in Hollywood want to talk to Teri Squire."

Teri looked at her dad for a long moment, and then smiled. "I don't know who that is. My name's Peggy Tucker."

Then she turned back to brushing Gretel.

Mike Farris

Acknowledgments

No matter how long you sit alone in a room, staring at a computer, a book is always a collaborative process. Big thanks to my agents, Donna Eastman and Gloria Koehler, for their faith in me. I also want to thank Ken Coffman, Stacey Benson, Chris Benson, and the folks at Stairway Press, for their professionalism and enthusiasm in shepherding this book to its final product. I couldn't have done it without you

www.ingramcontent.com/pod-product-compliance
Lightning Source LLC
Chambersburg PA
CBHW020934260626
47169CB00006B/1717